DEATH AND THE INTERN

Jeremy Hanson-Finger

DEATH AND THE INTERN

Jeremy Hanson-Finger

Invisible Publishing
Halifax & Picton

Library and Archives Canada Cataloguing in Publication

Hanson-Finger, Jeremy, 1987-, author
Death & the intern / Jeremy Hanson-Finger.

Issued in print and electronic formats.
ISBN 978-1-926743-91-2 (softcover).--ISBN 978-1-926743-94-3 (EPUB)

I. Title. II. Title: Death and the intern.

S8615.A575D43 2017 C813'.6 C2017-900453-0
C2017-900454-9

Edited by Leigh Nash
Cover and interior design by Megan Fildes | Typeset in Laurentian
With thanks to type designer Rod McDonald

Printed and bound in Canada

Invisible Publishing | Halifax & Picton
www.invisiblepublishing.com

We acknowledge the support of the Canada Council for the Arts which last year invested $20.1 million in writing and publishing throughout Canada.

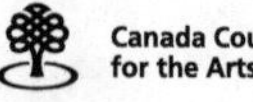

For Dr. Navraj S. Chima, good buddy since ’96

Doctors, as a rule, are the least curious of men. While they are still interns they hear enough secrets to last them a lifetime.

— Raymond Chandler, *The Lady in the Lake*

No, this is not a disentanglement from, but a progressive knotting into...

— Thomas Pynchon, *Gravity's Rainbow*

PROLOGUE

The Delicate Art of Kneecapping – Blue Monday

Janwar will anaesthetize eight patients before he kills one.

This isn't a probability; it will happen on Wednesday. The solution has been planned for a long time, planned before Janwar even applied to the placement at Civic. Janwar doesn't know anything about his role. And he won't until he has played it.

On Tuesday night, a man wearing a hooded sweatshirt holds a pungent dishtowel over Diego Acosta's face while his partner smashes Diego in the knees with a bat. The two men then drag Diego behind an advertisement for MEC-brand dog backpacks, where they rifle through Diego's pockets. They take his wallet and cellphone, although the theft is for show: later that night, the henchmen crush the cellphone and shred the cards from the wallet before they toss all the fragments into the Rideau Canal, not far from where a university student drowned himself a few months ago.

The henchmen do take the cash before they dispose of the wallet, however. Henching doesn't attract the ascetic.

At the emergency room, the doctors say Diego is healthy aside from his fractured kneecaps, which is true, these thugs being professionals in the delicate art of kneecapping, among other body modifications both temporary and permanent. Diego's knee surgery is scheduled for the next day.

Horace Louisseize supervises Janwar during Diego's operation on Wednesday morning. As a medical student intern, Janwar is not allowed to perform anaesthesia unattended, so a senior staff member has to be present.

From the hallway, Janwar hears rubberized wheels squeak and Llewellyn Cadwaladr's singsongy voice saying that a certain half-soaked fuck should watch where he's going.

José Almeida rolls the anaesthesia cart into the OR, freshly filled at the dispensary.

Janwar draws 7 millilitres from a vial labelled "1% solution of lidocaine" into a syringe, enough for Diego's 70 kilograms, followed by the appropriate amounts of fentanyl and propofol. He prepares another syringe of rocuronium and switches on the ventilator.

By then José has already departed to retrieve the materials that the surgeon, Victor Kovacs, and the attending, Karan Gill, need for surgery.

Rasheeda Mohammed is the scrub nurse assigned to the operation. Following Janwar's instructions, she attaches the ECG leads, pulse ox, and BIS, and swabs Diego's arm.

As Rasheeda performs her tasks, Janwar walks Diego through what is going to happen: Janwar will inject a mixture of drugs into Diego's IV feed, and less than a minute after that, Diego will be out cold until the operation is over.

Janwar pats the BIS, a blue machine the size of a shoebox, and points at the display, which at that moment reads "97." He explains that when he administers anaesthesia, Diego's brain activity will slow and that number will drop, and once it drops enough, the surgeon will conduct the operation by peeling back the skin, drilling into the bone, and laying the latticework to brace Diego's patellas as they heal. Janwar will watch the glowing number and adjust the IV drip to keep Diego unconscious, as well as monitor his vitals to make sure everything goes fine.

This is what Janwar says to Diego, and what Janwar believes—that everything will go fine.

Instead, everything goes fine according to the solution, which is not the same as going fine for Janwar, since Janwar does not come out of the solution looking good. And it's definitely not the same as going fine for Diego, who doesn't come out of the solution at all: the permanent removal of Diego is the solution.

Diego doesn't know any more about the solution than Janwar does—although, being the problem, he does possess information concerning the series of events that have led to his forthcoming negation. He doesn't flinch as the IV goes into his vein. Diego thinks the hospital is a safe space. But he is wrong. The hospital is a much less safe space for him than the street.

Rasheeda tapes the IV down. Janwar slides the first syringe into the port in the tubing and depresses the plunger.

Diego's ECG spasms into the twisted party-streamer shape of torsades de pointes. Before any of the staff can intervene, the display flatlines.

Janwar shouts that Diego is in cardiac arrest and orders José to page for a crash cart.

José snatches up the intercom and makes the request, but by the time the cart thunders down the hallway and screeches around the corner, Janwar and Horace and Victor and Karan and Rasheeda and José all know Diego is not coming back.

But right now it's Monday morning. Diego is still asleep in his own apartment. He is a consultant; he has no meetings scheduled. He can sleep in.

And Janwar is about to anaesthetize his first patient.

PART I: THE WINDUP

CHAPTER 1

Grime – Boys from Brazil – Nursing Rebellion – Supplies – The Mixers – Chthonic Breakthroughs – Pimp and Fail – Contingency – Moonboots – Spray Tan – A Simpler Way – Hardball

Monday, July 7

Batman bandana over his hair, scrub mask over his nose and mouth, gloves on. Syringes laid out. Janwar's own pulse and breathing steady. Dr. Carla Welrod, the senior staff anaesthesiologist who showed Janwar around, sits in the corner with her tablet, but Janwar can tell she's paying more attention to him than to the condo interiors she's swiping through.

The operating room, OR II, is pretty much the same as the operating rooms at UBC, where Janwar spent most of his third year of medical school. At UBC everyone in the OR wore green scrubs, but here the staff wear a light blue-purple Carla called "mauve," which Janwar thought until now referred to a much more vibrant colour between magenta and fuchsia. This colour shift is just one of the many changes Janwar must accommodate.

Nothing about this OR is vibrant. Grime has infiltrated the room the way it does all ORs. Only the site of the operation itself needs to be sterile, where the patient's skin peeks out through the hole in the surgical screen. Sanitizing the entire operating room would be impossible; pathogens ride in on the soles of needle-resistant Crocs, dally in the crevices between computer keys, bloom underneath the sink's grout. Plus nobody wants superbugs around, so sanitizing is done only where necessary.

Nurses get divided into two types for the same reason. A scrub nurse wears sterile clothing and can touch only items that have also been sterilized. A circulating nurse, in comparison, does not, and can go anywhere in the room and touch anything.

The OR griminess also stems from the building's age. The Civic's walls have shifted since it was completed in 1924, and its equipment and furniture come from every decade between then and now. Hospitals stop looking brand new very quickly. Surfaces get scratched or rubbed or warped or discoloured, or plain go out of style, like beige computers and wood-finish televisions, both of which Janwar's father still has in his home office.

Unlike Ajay Gupta's Compaq desktop (and, across the room, the Zenith Solid State Chromacolor II, knobless but perma-tuned to cricket), the hospital equipment isn't any less effective because of its age, but patients who watch TV medical dramas are often uncomfortable with the lack of shine on the steel, the cracks in the vinyl, the mottled, yellowed, uneven floors. The occasional fly turning lazy circles.

The nurses have strapped Mrs. Bradford's limbs to the cross-shaped table. She stopped talking about her grandchildren a while ago, when Janwar inserted the IV into her arm.

Now she's waiting with the zen patience of the elderly, her mind blank. If she's filled with a private terror beyond words, Janwar can't tell. She seems at peace, her fingers and lips still, her vitals all within the normal range.

Three lights illuminate her with a perfect white halo. Past the table, the two IV trees cast skeletal shadows against the wall, but the overhead fluorescents wash out their edges.

The shadows are more unsettling for their lack of distinction, or maybe Janwar's already unsettled, this being a new experience for him, in a new city, among strangers, even if he has anaesthetized a number of people back in BC and received glowing reviews from supervising physicians. Most memorably, one of his preceptors wrote in his evaluation, "It's a rare pleasure to see Janwar Gupta intubate a patient," although a masked man shoving a tube down someone's throat isn't a pleasant thing for anyone to see, no matter how efficiently done.

Mrs. Bradford has a multipage chart of drug contraindications and allergies. If Janwar induces anaesthesia using the standard drugs in the standard sequence, she could go into anaphylactic shock. Her throat could swell up and strangle her, shutting off her supply of oxygen. While in an operating room, doctors have ways of preventing anaphylaxis from becoming fatal. But if you can avoid it in the first place, you probably should, is Janwar's thinking in this respect.

The anaesthetic machine and the anaesthesia cart form a V by Mrs. Bradford's head, and Janwar feels comforted by the right angles and cold metal. No matter what he does, the machine's components will perform according to the instructions baked into their circuits.

If he mixes all the drugs to put Mrs. Bradford to sleep together with a serious antihistamine and injects them into the IV at the same time, he will need to inject only one other syringe—the one with the paralytic. That way he can have the breathing tube down Mrs. Bradford's sedated, relaxed, and paralyzed throat as quickly as possible, in case the antihistamine doesn't stop her airway from closing fast enough. He weighs the pros and cons and decides on blending the drugs together.

His technique matters here, and not only because Mrs. Bradford needs to stay alive throughout the operation. Janwar is on his first placement outside of med school, and also his first placement after setting his sights on anaesthesiology, so he has to make a good impression on his colleagues. From here on, every move he makes will impact his career. What Janwar likes most about anaesthesiology is how the goal is to keep the status quo. To maintain homeostasis. As long as the patient's vital signs remain steady and she doesn't wake up during the operation, the anaesthesiologist has done his job.

Sometimes he has to solve drug interaction or allergy problems like Mrs. Bradford's, but they're always problems within certain boundaries. He has all the tools at his disposal to keep someone alive, even if they're not always shiny. The anaesthesia machine is already breathing for them, so the anaesthesiologist can leave the heroics to the surgeons. If a surgeon is a surly detective making great leaps of intuition and following serial killers into catacombs without backup, an anaesthesiologist is good old Constable Gupta patrolling his beat by bicycle and making sure all is as it should be. A boring day for an anaesthesiologist is a good day.

And there's also the money. Anaesthesiologists can monitor several operations at once, meaning they can also bill hours concurrently. This is a trick surgeons can't pull off. Which is why surgeons resent anaesthesiologists, even to the point, on occasion, of manslaughter, even of manslaughter in the operating room, which Janwar read about in a recent news story from Rio de Janeiro. Some boys from Brazil took their professional feud really, really far, and, despite the stabbing happening in the one place you most want to find yourself if you're in a life-threatening condition, the anaesthesiologist was pronounced dead less than five minutes after the fight started, because of two factors in the surgeon's favour: amphetamines, heavy intake of, and knives, dexterity with.

The Civic surgeons have been civil to Janwar so far, but then again, he's not making any money yet, let alone the $500K of a mature anaesthesiologist. He's still paying for the privilege of being here. Plus, he's not bossing them around.

Both the senior staff surgeon, Dr. Victor Kovacs, and the attending, Mildred Zhang, are studiously ignoring Carla, as if her rhythmic tablet swiping is merely the pendulum of a grandfather clock, marking time until they can leave this room and spend their money. In return, Carla hasn't acknowledged their existence either. She looks right through them at Janwar, in between condo floor plans.

Janwar swirls his syringe around to mix the drugs together before inverting it and squeezing out a couple of drops, which fall onto the tiled floor, dosing any microscopic organisms in the area. Fentanyl, ketamine, propofol, and dimetindene—the analgesic, the coinduction agent, the induction agent, and the antihistamine, respectively—will all hit Mrs. Bradford at the same time.

The nurses, Henry Wilshire and José Almeida, scrub and circulating, respectively, take this moment to voice their disagreement with the method Janwar has chosen in order to put his patient to sleep. They are anti-mixing.

Janwar looms over them, but he isn't tall in an imposing way, just tall in an awkward way, with a size 29 waist and a size 34 chest. He straightens his spine and puts his hands in his pockets, in case he starts fidgeting.

Henry leans against the wall as he elaborates on his reasoning re: mixing. His shaved head shines. "This is no place for experimenting." Henry's voice is so deep Janwar can feel it in his own chest.

"Yeah, who do you think you are? Dr. Mengele?" José adds.

Henry's jaw hangs slack for a moment, and then he holds his hand up for a high-five, which José doles out with a crack that echoes throughout OR II like a gunshot.

Janwar doesn't know who Dr. Mengele is, but from the context he can guess that the comparison doesn't make Janwar look good.

"I'll take that into consideration," Janwar says. He smiles, but the nurses aren't buying it.

Mixing induction agents and other drugs in a single syringe is not the traditional approach, but as long as Janwar induces sleep before paralyzing Mrs. Bradford with a separate injection, his technique is still kosher. The nurses must know that, and in this case, Mrs. Bradford's chart of drug contraindications makes mixing the best option.

The nurses don't move to stop Janwar as he aims his rainbow-labelled syringe at the port in the IV tubing connected to Mrs. Bradford's elbow.

Janwar inserts the syringe and depresses the plunger. The milky white solution disappears from the barrel and joins the saline flowing into Mrs. Bradford's median cubital vein.

Henry and José could have restrained him and prevented him from going ahead with his plan if they believed he was making a dangerous mistake, but they let him proceed. Carla doesn't say anything either.

"Now count backwards from sixty," Janwar says.

Mrs. Bradford reaches fifty-three before her voice lurches into a last-call slur. Her vital signs remain steady after thirty seconds, and Janwar can see no signs of swelling—the antihistamine has done its work—so he picks up a second syringe from the anaesthesia cart, this one labelled in red, and administers the paralytic, rocuronium, which his fellow med students at UBC referred to as "the roc." When it takes effect, he snakes an endotracheal tube down Mrs. Bradford's throat to maintain the flow of oxygen to her brain now that all her muscles, including her diaphragm, are immobilized.

Mrs. Bradford's gall bladder needs to be removed via laparoscopic cholecystectomy. She suffered several rounds of biliary colic—gallstones—and taking the whole organ out is the best option. Janwar fires up the anaesthesia machine, which wheezes and sucks and blinks and burbles. He monitors it while over the next hour Victor, with Mildred's assistance, makes four one-centimetre incisions in the square of Mrs. Bradford's abdomen visible through the cutout in the sterile drape. Through the different openings, Victor inserts an insufflator, an irrigation tube, a fibre-optic camera with a light attached, and a hook cautery.

Janwar is proud of himself for fidgeting only a little, interlocking his knuckles from time to time. Mildred also fidgets when her hands aren't busy, and her breathing is fast under her mask. Victor doesn't stop accomplishing tasks long enough to fidget.

Mrs. Bradford remains immobile, the LED lights on the display showing her brain activity is below conscious levels. "First sleep, then paralysis" is one of the cardinal rules of ethical anaesthesia. If Janwar paralyzed a patient before inducing sleep, she would "get stuck in the boogeyman's closet," as Janwar's preceptor Benjamin Rausch put it, awake and aware of everything going on but unable to move, communicate, or breathe. Patients usually survive a trip to the boogeyman's closet unless they have a pre-existing condition—such as a brain aneurysm—that the intense anxiety of the experience could push into the danger zone, causing rupture and almost certainly death.

But even though odds of survival are good, most closet visitors do suffer post-op trauma. On occasion, an important medical reason prompts paralyzing patients without putting them to sleep, but most of the time it happens by mistake. Which is why Janwar labels his syringes so carefully.

Using a scissor-shaped controller, Victor inflates Mrs. Bradford's abdomen with carbon dioxide like a tennis dome. Once he can see what's going on under the dome, he dissects the gallbladder away from the liver, removing it tidily in a little pouch through a hole near Mrs. Bradford's navel.

Victor and Mildred take off their masks when the operation is over. Janwar puts Victor's age around forty-five and Mildred five years younger. The two surgeons depart, and Janwar administers the various drugs needed to return Mrs. Bradford to wakefulness. All proceeds according to plan, until, as Janwar is bringing her back to consciousness, blood rushes out of Mrs. Bradford's nose. She opens her eyes and registers the masked faces, the red slick on the pillowcase.

"You were supposed to operate on my gall bladder." Mrs. Bradford looks more disappointed than anything else. "Why is there blood on my pillowcase?" She licks her upper lip and draws a smear of blood into her mouth. Her eyes widen. "And on my face? Doctor? Did you do the wrong operation?" The mountainous line on the EKG quakes.

Mrs. Bradford is still under the influence of Janwar's anaesthetic cocktail. The nurses are trying not to laugh: a vein throbs in Henry's forehead and José's chest heaves.

Janwar places his hand on the woman's bony shoulder. "Don't worry, Mrs. Bradford. We didn't touch your face.

You had a nosebleed as I was waking you."

He motions to Henry, who applies pressure to the bridge of her nose with his latexed fingers as Janwar injects a dose of a mild sedative into the IV. Henry's scrub sleeve rides up and Janwar can see a large tattoo, but he can't make out the design on the nurse's dark skin. Mrs. Bradford relaxes and smiles at Henry's touch.

"*Zwillinge* clean you up and have you *heraus* of here in no time," Henry says, and now it's José's turn to hold up his hand for a high-five.

"Nicely done," José says.

Carla removes her cap and mask and shakes her platinum-blond hair out of its operating configuration. Her hair is very long, far longer than Janwar often sees on middle-aged women, but it's healthy and, because she's tall, only a few inches shorter than Janwar, it looks good on her.

"Good work, Janwar."

"Thank you, Dr. Welrod."

"Carla."

"Thank you, Carla."

"One thing? Not something you did wrong, but something you should know. At the moment, we're all using lidocaine instead of ketamine as the coinduction agent. There's a bit of a supply problem."

Janwar thanks her. These things happen. With so many orders going through the hospital, sometimes a shipment ends up in the wrong place and takes a while to track down. A hospital is a bureaucracy like any other. And sometimes it's not even the hospital's fault. The market doesn't incentivize producing certain drugs at scale, or there's a problem at a manufacturing facility, or there are regulatory issues.

"Any questions?" Carla is looking straight into his eyes. Hers are battleship grey. Maybe if Janwar were into sexy older ladies his heart rate would have spiked like Mrs. Bradford's, but he isn't. Janwar's dream girls have always been strictly same age level, which means he watched some material in the early days of peer-to-peer file sharing, circa age thirteen, for which he still feels guilty.

He wants to ask if José's and Henry's behaviour was a test. Was there a real nursing rebellion or not? The two men are gone, so he can ask now, but he's blanking on how to phrase it without sounding paranoid. He'll start with a less important question and hope his subconscious grinds out a solution before Carla departs.

"I'm used to scrub pants with ties, not elastic." Janwar tugs at his waistband, which sags under the weight of his Leatherman Raptor paramedic shears, which he carries always, because you never know when you'll need to remove somebody's clothes quickly: Janwar sure wishes it was more often. "How do you get them to stay up with stuff in your pockets?" Janwar asks.

Carla tucks a thumb into the elastic waistband of her scrub pants, revealing a second pair of scrub pants underneath.

"Clever. I can requisition another pair of scrubs?"

"Sure can." Carla looks at her Rolex, which probably cost more than Janwar's Toyota back in Vancouver. "Okay, I've got to go. See you at the next operation."

Janwar is putting away his equipment on the anaesthesia cart when someone taps him on the shoulder. He turns. A white-haired, white-bearded man with blue eyes that are almost too bright to believe is smiling at him. His hand is out for Janwar to shake. Janwar shakes it. This handshake says that they are professional men who respect each other.

"Dr. Llewellyn Cadwaladr. The dean of anaesthesiology." Dr. Cadwaladr speaks with a mellifluous Welsh accent befitting his name.

"Janwar Gupta—"

"The new intern. I've been looking forward to meeting you, boyo."

"This is all very exciting," Janwar says. The man's name is familiar.

"I should tell you, boyo. This is the teaching OR. We scheduled this operation here for a reason." Dr. Cadwaladr gestures at the mirror. "This is a two-way mirror. Students can watch the operation without distracting anyone."

As this is Janwar's first operation at the hospital, he doesn't find it unreasonable that an administrator observed him without his knowledge or consent. Janwar has been observed his whole life by teachers at school and his parents at home. The main reason he does any of the things that make him a human being is the knowledge that someone could be watching him at any time. His brief foray into living alone one unemployed summer, and his apartment's rapid takeover by empty cans of organic chili, as well as his almost instantaneous descent into constant nudity and excessive daytime masturbation, taught him that.

For that reason, his dependence on being watched to know where he ends and the world begins, Janwar isn't going to get upset about it now that he is on a placement with life-and-death-type responsibilities.

And meeting expectations with respect to those responsibilities: that Janwar's first impulse was to mix his induction agents, as well as his sticking with his plan despite the flak from both nurses, impresses Dr. Cadwaladr deeply.

"You're a dab hand, boyo. I knew you for a born Mixer." Dr. Cadwaladr claps Janwar on the shoulder. "Maybe it's too early to say this, but I hope you consider the University of Ottawa when the time comes for you to apply for your residency."

A pinpoint of light roves around behind the mirror and then goes out. An absent-minded student looking for keys, maybe. A door shuts.

"Thank you, sir," Janwar says. He remembers where he knows the name from—Dr. Cadwaladr signed the letter offering him the internship.

Heels click down the checkered hallway flooring.

"We'll have none of that 'sir' business, boyo. Call me Llew."

Janwar says he will, but also that he isn't sure what Llew means by "born Mixer."

"Ah, I botched that. I thought someone would have told you already. We believe that blending drugs in one syringe is the best induction method in all cases. So we call ourselves the Mixers."

"Shoot 'em all and let the patient sort 'em out."

Llew laughs. "There you are, then! Any other questions, boyo?"

"Yeah, if mixing is the position of the department, why are the nurses so negative about it?"

"It's not the whole department who are Mixers. Just a few of us. Some of the others are more traditional. Most of the nurses are as well." He waves them off.

Henry and José weren't only messing with Janwar, then; their animosity toward his mixing was a serious position, even though as nurses they don't get to make those kinds of decisions.

Nurses, especially male nurses, are often jealous of doctors, but most of the time they are happy to leave the decision-making to their higher-paid and more-sleep-deprived colleagues. The rivalry isn't anywhere near as intense as the surgery-anaesthesiology conflict.

"I'm happy to be on the side of experimentation, Llew," Janwar says. One of Janwar's greatest strengths is in understanding how drugs interact, according to all his instructors at UBC. If he has to choose between "always be mixing" and "never be mixing," he'll choose the former.

Janwar wrings an operation's worth of sweat out of his bandana into the metal sink and reties the Batman-print fabric. His hair is thinning at the top, but it started from a level of such luxuriant thickness that the thinning now, at age twenty-five, is still unnoticeable to others. He takes off his glasses, careful to lift the titanium earpieces using the same amount of force with each hand, and wipes his face with the bandana.

The dean lopes toward the OR door, each step causing his upper body to dip by several inches. Janwar almost laughs: Dr. Cadwaladr walks like a sine wave.

"Drop by my office sharpish when you're off-duty, boyo," Llew says. "It's in the department. B309. I'll be here till seven. We'll have coffee and chat about how things work here. I've got a blend that could stop your heart."

Janwar appreciates Llew's comments and fatherly presence more than he wants to let on.

Despite his confidence during the operation, once Victor stitched Mrs. Bradford back up and the nurses wheeled her off, Janwar began to second-guess his judgment in mixing.

Once in a while, Janwar experiences what his therapist, Dr. Marilyn Brank, calls "chthonic breakthroughs." She added the word *chthonic*, meaning "concerning, belonging to, or inhabiting the underworld," to separate them from the "good" kind of breakthroughs, which happen when a patient escapes a matrix of negative thoughts. Chthonic breakthroughs are instead more of a "return of the repressed" thing, Marilyn says.

Janwar's breakthroughs often start with him questioning his judgment in a recent situation, such as whether the sweater he bought fit properly, or whether he jaywalked at a safe time, or whether he performed the appropriate steps when injecting drugs into a real live human being. This mistrust spreads like a black net to encompass the entire universe, leaving Janwar leached of any emotion but fear, stuck in his own boogeyman's closet.

Janwar didn't get all the way to a full chthonic breakthrough this time, and his normal perspective has returned. Llew's praise pulled him out of the closet. Janwar is a talented prospective anaesthesiologist and an all-round charming and likeable person. He is successful at most things he attempts.

Janwar's mother told him, in a context Janwar cannot remember now, that she was glad to see tiny Janwar find some tasks difficult. Take playing basketball: as a point guard for the Glenlyon Norfolk School Grade 4 B-team, he had an embarrassing double-dribble problem. One opposing player memorably celebrated Janwar's fifth double-dribble call in one game by performing the "suck it" gesture in front of the entire gymnasium. Garati, in the stands, had been happy to see the ball taken away from her son and used to score on a breakaway because she was afraid that Janwar was so successful at everything he'd tried by age nine that in the future he'd be unable to cope with failure.

But Janwar had failed at a number of other things in his life no matter how hard he tried, like being in a serious romantic relationship before age twenty, so Janwar figures Garati's fears were unfounded.

Janwar is filling up his mug with fair-trade Colombian in the cafeteria, the Tulip Cafe, when Dr. Fang Jin, the newest resident in the anaesthesiology department, introduces herself.

"It's nice to meet you, too, Fang." The stream of coffee stops with Janwar's mug only two-thirds full and, after a couple of attempts to get the last remaining drops from the container, Janwar moves his cup over to the Ethiopian tap and finishes pouring. "And Llew too. He seems pretty down to earth for an administrator."

"Did you know before he took his admin job with the university, he was a genius anaesthesiologist?"

Janwar didn't know this. The Tulip Cafe, much newer than the rest of the hospital, is decorated in brown and black, with halogen spotlights scattered throughout instead of overhead fluorescents, which makes it feel more like a high-efficiency bistro than an institutional cafeteria. Janwar isn't sure if he finds the pools of darkness comforting or creepy. As he walks past the entrance to the kitchen, he feels the fryer oil in the air glom onto his lungs.

"Lleweyville Slugger, the Sultan of Sedation," Fang says. "He was a fucking baller with GHB before most doctors switched away from it because sedation lasted so long. The staff put up cut-outs of him at Christmas parties because he worked so hard on improving his technique that he'd never leave the hospital. Man deserves his break."

Janwar smiles. Fang smiles back, and one side of her mouth rises higher than the other, but the overall impression Janwar gets is of sincerity, and he feels that they would make good colleagues.

"It's pretty pimp here," Fang says. "You'll like it." She shakes out her bangs.

"Pimp?"

"Oh. You went to University of Alberta, right?"

"UBC. Grew up in Victoria, then moved to Vancouver for school."

"Well, when I was in med school at U of T, anything good was 'pimp' and anything bad was 'fail.' All the young doctors talk like that here, too."

"Maybe it's Ontario slang. At UBC we all said that good things were 'beastly' and bad things were 'rough.' Like, 'Alejandro is beastly at induction.' Or, 'That suture job is fucking rough.' Pardon my language."

Fang laughs. "I don't know where you BC guys get your slang. Sounds like some backwoods shit to me."

"It may be backwoods, but it's grammatically correct."

"Where I was going with all this, before we went off the rails," Fang says, "was that this is a good place to be, and we're glad to have you. I heard about how you fucking crushed it with Mrs. Bradford."

"Thanks." Janwar pauses. "It was—what's the word? Means that it could have been otherwise." He shakes his head. "Whatever. You get the idea. But it went the way it did. I'm glad it worked out."

"You're too humble."

Mrs.Bradford could still have died as a result of Janwar's mixing—even out of the chthonic breakthrough, Janwar is careful to acknowledge that to himself—but she also could have died as a result of following the traditional one-drug-per-injection process. Or she could have died without anybody's interference.

"Anyway. You guys do seem pretty pimp," Janwar says.

"You got it." Fang smiles again and holds up a hand for a high-five. "Civic Hospital Mixers, what's up!"

Something that could have been otherwise is *contingent*, Janwar remembers now. He has to learn so many new medical terms every day that less-critical words and memories drift away like the lingering euphoria after shooting a propofol bolus. He tells friends he can't remember anything before age eighteen, though that's an exaggeration he admits when pushed: he can remember back to about age seven, when he fell into a pond during a school field trip. That's still late for a first memory, as most people he knows can remember back to at least kindergarten, but it's also not quite into Hollywood amnesia territory.

Janwar hopes his memory loss won't get to that point, the fog creeping inexorably forward, swallowing up history tests about the Iroquois and their penchant for causing acute pain to missionaries without anaesthetic; field trips to Science World where he and his classmates got to mix chemicals together to make fun gooey reactions; his first sexual encounter in a school stairwell with Lucy Kaufman, after which she claimed to feel "strangely tranquil"; trombone performances in the pit orchestra for the musicals *Evita* and *Les Misérables* where sometimes he snuck in harmonies that weren't in the sheet music because, with a head full of music theory, they made more sense that way; his Grade 11 citizenship award for being the nicest person out of a class of 150 ("the person you most want to be your neighbour," headmaster Buddy Rainier said about the prize; "a real social butterfly who blends in well in any situation," Head Boy Yu-hao "Howard" Chen said about its being awarded to Janwar); discussions about his future with his parents, Garati and Ajay Gupta, BA (Hons), JD, and BSc, MSc, PhD, respectively—the amnesia maybe even reaching a point one day, far into his career, where he'll go to bed one night and wake up the next and the only thing he can remember from the past is that he is an anaesthesiologist and he has to be at work at 6 a.m....

Janwar anaesthetizes two more patients before the end of the day: Mr. Nakamura and Ms. Burton. Carla sits in the corner with her tablet, constantly swiping left across the screen. Both procedures take place in operating rooms without mirrors, rooms I and III. Carla could report back to Llew, so whether Janwar is being observed in a *sub rosa* manner or not is moot, but now that Janwar knows that such mirrors exist he can't help but look for them.

Mr. Nakamura needs a precancerous tumour removed from his right shoulder blade. He is healthy and has no blood-pressure problems or drug contraindications, so Janwar might not normally have mixed his induction drugs in one syringe. But Llew had welcomed Janwar into the group of Mixers under the impression that drug mixing was in his blood, so now is the time to commit.

Janwar unlocks the anaesthesia cart by launching the cart vendor's app on his tablet, pressing his thumb against the biometric reader to activate it, showing that, yes, he's Janwar Aashish Gupta and he should be allowed to open these drawers. He holds the tablet in front of the sensor on the cart until the door snicks open.

He draws his coinduction agent (lidocaine this time), fentanyl, and propofol into one Syrinx syringe.

Under their cap-and-mask disguises, he notices the

nurses for this operation are different—two women.

"So you're a Mixer," Emanda MacDougall says, her mask puffing out and sucking back into her mouth as she speaks. "I could have guessed."

Janwar nods. He's in operating mode, and he doesn't want to get drawn into a conversation. Plus, he has a knee-jerk reaction to her badge: the purposeful misspelling of the name Amanda suggests she is one of those extraprivileged girls of the kind he met in university who wear their hair in head-top buns and sport sweatpants and suede moon boots year-round. But she seems less aggressive in her anti-mixing attitude than the two male nurses from his first operation.

Janwar depresses the plunger, and the solution flows into Mr. Nakamura's IV.

When Emanda isn't looking, the circulating nurse, Rasheeda Mohammed, makes an egg-beater motion and gives Janwar a thumbs-up. The attending surgeon, Dr. Karan Gill, must have noticed, as Rasheeda is in his line of sight, but Janwar can't read Karan's expression in the shadow of the Sikh man's scrub-cap-covered turban. Karan moves in controlled fits and bursts as he readies himself for the operation, like he's receiving instructions by radio.

Mr. Nakamura's face slackens and his eyes fog over, but his breathing remains steady. His blood pressure is acceptable. Janwar draws a new syringe of the paralytic agent, injects it into the now-unconscious Mr. Nakamura's IV, and then intubates him.

Dr. Gertie Toledo slices into Mr. Nakamura without incident, Karan cauterizing as Gertie cuts. Sizzles periodically emanate from inside Mr. Nakamura, along with the smell of burnt flesh. Gertie removes the tumour while Janwar monitors the vital signs, which beep and flash and squiggle within the normal range.

While Emanda is swabbing Ms. Burton's stomach with antiseptic before the first incision, the skin changes colour, from orange to fish-belly white, and the staff all laugh together—Janwar, Gertie, Karan, Carla, and the nurses, regardless of their induction politics.

"Why would you," Gertie gasps, "spray-tan before an operation?" Under her scrub cap, her hair is damp. She made the last operation look easy, but she's sweating. Karan is sweating, too, under the triple layer of hair, turban, and scrub cap, tributaries running down into his beard. Gertie's laughter goes on longer than Janwar expects, and when she's done she still seems giddy.

Ms. Burton has acute appendicitis, and her operation is even quicker: lidocaine-fentanyl-propofol, rocuronium, a few slices into the right side of the abdomen, and twenty minutes after the start of surgery, the patient is closed up again and her swollen appendix glistens on a tray like a sausage. Karan whips out a cheapo flip phone to check for messages as soon as the operation is over, which strikes Janwar as odd. Who still uses a flip phone?

On his way to the department to meet with Llew, his Crocs squeaking on the black-and-white-checkered tiles, Janwar thinks about how his situation could just as easily have gone in a different direction. If he'd seen Mr. Nakamura before he saw Mrs. Bradford, maybe he wouldn't have mixed his drugs, because the situation didn't require it. And if Llew had been watching that operation, maybe he wouldn't have decided Janwar was his new protege. Janwar disagrees with Llew; he isn't a born mixer. He mixed in that particular operation because it seemed like the best choice. But now he's bound to mixing, unless he wants to piss off the dean of anaesthesiology. And the dean's not looking upon him kindly could have a majorly deleterious effect on Janwar's career, which is still in its incubation period. So a-mixin' he will go.

Light blue trim surrounds all the doorways in the corridor leading to the anaesthesiology department. It clashes with the bright wood of the doors themselves.

Emanda has reached the department before Janwar. She leans against a wall, telling a bulky man with a red face and freckles that she doesn't understand the point of what they're doing.

The man rolls his eyes. "The mighty have spoken."

"But isn't there a simpler way?"

"You're telling me."

Both turn and stare at Janwar as the door swings back, and Emanda pushes past him and out. The man turns the corner.

They are terrible actors, their movements as exaggerated as a marionette's. What Janwar has heard is close to meaningless, however, so they don't have to worry. Something complicated that could have been simpler—that could be pretty much anything in the hospital.

Grey is the primary colour in the anaesthesiology department's common area. Transit-seat material covers the couches. An old TV inside a metal cabinet hangs from chains attached to the ceiling. The kitchenette features a microwave, a double sink, and a yellowed coffee maker. The room smells like burnt bread crumbs, popcorn, and some sort of nut spread. A peeling sign adorns the coffee machine, written in a hand so poor that Janwar can barely decipher it.

He decides in the end that it reads, "There's no rainbow at the end of the pot of coffee. Just you making more coffee."

Sediment has formed at the bottom of the coffee pot. Janwar can imagine why Llew would want his own machine. The TV plays an old detective show on mute: *The Rockford Files*. A Pontiac Firebird is reversed and spun around. A gun is pointed. Words are exchanged. Handcuffs are clapped. A head is pushed down into a squad car.

A hallway extends in a U shape from the kitchen area. Llew's office is at the end of the hall, between the conference room and the frosted-glass door that reads, "Sylvie Dalsgaard, Head of Anaesthesiology," in gold art deco letters. Janwar hasn't met Sylvie yet, but the department head is probably too busy to concern herself with medical student interns. The dean, technically part of the university faculty, does make more sense as the person to get Janwar settled.

Llew's wingtip shoes rest on his desk when Janwar knocks on the door, which is also made of glass, but not frosted like Sylvie's. A fan spins in the centre of the ceiling, a holdover from before the hospital was fully temperature-controlled. Llew gestures for Janwar to enter, but someone jostles Janwar as he is about to open the door.

"So you're Cadwaladr's new blue-eyed boy." The speaker is the bulky man who Janwar saw talking to Emanda. The spray of orange freckles across his cheekbones clashes with his ruddy skin. His name tag bears the label "Dr. Shaughnessy O'Deady."

"The new Mixer..." Shaughnessy peers at Janwar's badge. "Janwar Gupta." His lips twist and he opens his mouth like he is going to keep speaking, but instead he mutters that Slugger isn't always going to be around, and maybe one day he, Shaughnessy, will give Janwar a real push. He jostles Janwar again with his left shoulder, harder this time. "You're not push league, John G."

"Push league? You mean bush league? You know what's bush league? Getting an idiomatic expression wrong," Janwar says. "Also, John G.? Come on, man." But Shaughnessy has already stalked off by the time Janwar gets through the second sentence.

Light burns in through Llew's venetian blinds, casting angled shadows against the wall. The July sun won't go down for another couple of hours.

Llew lowers his feet from his desk. "Don't mind him. He's a Pusher."

A Pusher? Janwar is struggling to keep up with this department jargon. "Well, yeah, he did push me, and he called me John G. He seems like a bit of a bully, but—"

"He's always got his hair off. If he aggravates you again, let me know. You can have a seat."

Janwar folds himself into the chair. "But what—"

"Some of us are going to cop a pint tonight at D'Arcy McGee's. Right by Parliament. Meeting at seven. You can get to know everyone in a proper tribal state of altered consciousness." He leans back in his chair. "You a drinker?"

Janwar nods. "I'll be there."

"Righto. Americano or espresso, is it?" Llew turns on the bean grinder and smiles in apology as it roars to life.

"Americano would be great."

Llew slots the basket into position in the gleaming chrome machine. They both watch the black liquid drip from the nozzle. Llew hands Janwar a cup with crema as perfect as Janwar has ever seen and bangs the basket on the edge of a trash can. Janwar glances out the window. A big dark cloud scuds across the horizon.

In the window's reflection, Janwar sees Shaughnessy O'Deady standing outside the door, gesturing toward Llew's office, pointing Janwar out to a moustached man and a short woman with a ponytail shaped like pineapple leaves. Janwar recognizes her as Aspen Tanaka. She'd visited UBC to talk about anaesthesiology at the Civic.

"Ellis's condo okay by you?" Llew says.

Dr. Flecktarn is on holiday somewhere cold during Janwar's two-week placement, so Janwar has the place to himself. The one-bedroom is minimalist, not unreasonable for a rich person's home, but it feels more sterile than Nordic.

"Great, thanks. I was expecting to have to live in a hotel, so, much appreciated. Student loans."

"We take care of our own by here, boyo."

Janwar points at the hickory baseball bat and worn-in glove leaned up against one wall. "Do you play softball?"

"Hardball. Ain't nothing soft about me, boy," Llew drawls. "Call ourselves the Stitch Hitters." He reaches for the bat and glove, then stops, switching back to his regular melodic tones. "Can you do me a favour? Aim these in the Rubbermaid tub in the closet on your way out? If I put them down any old place, the cleaners play baseball in here." He gestures to a glass trophy with a chip missing and a crack down the centre.

"Sure will," Janwar says.

EXHIBIT A

TRANSCRIPT OF AUDIO RECORDING FOUND ON SUSAN JONESTOWN'S CELLPHONE

SPEAKING: SUSAN JONESTOWN, ALAN TURNER, DENIS ALLEMAND, MARTINA GONZALEZ

Friday, July 4

Hey Siri, take a note. Oh, you're already going. Cool. Cool. Testing. 1-2. Check. Check.

The number Professor Palomino assigned me was six, which matched a pushpin stuck in Applewood Park. Nothing significant, interesting, or new, has ever happened in Alta Vista, let alone in Applewood Park. I've got to head there anyway. Hey Siri, stop—

Alan's a contractor so he's one of the few people I know who drives. I'm walking over to his place because he said it'd be cool if I borrowed his truck.

ALAN TURNER: Hey, Susan. How's grad school going?

SUSAN JONESTOWN: Okay so far. My reporting prof has got this drawing his kids did of him in his office. They might think he's Satan. Ned seems all right to me, though.

AT: That's Satan's thing. Seeming all right.

SJ: Guess so.

AT: Did you just come from class?

SJ: Yeah. Libel and slander.

AT: Learn anything juicy?

SJ: There's such a thing as "the small penis rule" in libel law. The guy who wrote Jurassic Park used it as a defence in 2006.

AT: A defence against what?

SJ: Couldn't tell you. Anyway, I'll have Black Magic back tonight and I'll fill her up for you. Thanks for lending her to me. Oh and say hi to Jess.

AT: I will. How're your parents?

SJ: Dad sunk the boat again trying to get it into his boathouse.

AT: Classic cottage dad move. And your mom?

SJ: All about real estate. She wants me to get into this condo market while it's hot, but unless she's willing to front forty grand...

AT: It's not worth it. I should know—I'm the guy building them.

The park is even less exciting than it looked on Google Maps. Bunch of trees and a safe-looking playground. Plastic play structures. None of the splintery wood I remember.

Could write about the death of risk in playgrounds. But that's nothing new. Play structures have been plastic for years. What quotes am I going to get? Kids saying they miss the danger of wood toys?

Wish I'd bought some coffee before I left the university.

Shit, loose German shepherd charging toward dogwalker and pack. Snarling. Tail straight out.

All dogs wearing backpacks. On trend.

Burly man with grey ponytail and goatee chases shepherd.

DENIS ALLEMAND: King, you fucker, no.

Dogwalker's pack panicks. Dogs attached to woman's belt can't escape.

Shepherd tears through grey dog's pack. Canister falls in grass. Shepherd spits out nylon and lunges. Grey dog falls onto back.

Other dogs yowl.

Dogwalker punches shepherd in ribs.

Dog pauses. Owner tackles, flattens dog.

DA: I'm going to kill you. You fucker.

Am hiding behind fort wall in playground. Don't think they spotted me. If I whisper and keep my mouth close to the mic...check, check, yeah.

Pack made up of wide range of dogs. Two tall black ones, two bulldogs. Some medium-sized ones, unknown breed. Purebred though. Too glossy to be mutts.

Dogwalker inspects grey dog's sides. Seems okay.

DENIS ALLEMAND: Shit, I'm sorry, Martina. Is he all right?

MARTINA GONZALEZ: Who's a good assault victim?

DA: He jerked the leash right out of my hand.

MG: Maybe time to think about a muzzle.

DA: He never does this.

MG: Really? You're going to be one of those people? Want a do-over on that line, Denis?

How do they know each other's names?

Snuck a photo. Five-foot-five woman with pack of suburban purebreds lecturing biker and junkyard dog.

DENIS ALLEMAND: Okay, okay.

MARTINA GONZALEZ: It's not like you can't take it off, if you do want him to bite.

DA: Sure, yeah. Are you going to be cool, King?

King's not going to be cool. Denis cuffs him in the head. King slumps down. Martina looks around.

MG: Here's your wax.

Martina reaches into hole in grey dog's backpack. Tosses canisters in front of Denis and King. Like the one that fell on the grass.

Martina's neon green windbreaker and yoga pants put her anywhere between twenty-five and forty-five.

MARTINA GONZALEZ: We're going now. Come on, guys. And Denis, don't ever let this happen again, or Jacques is going to hear about it.

Going to stand up and approach them now.

MARTINA GONZALEZ: What are you looking at, blondie?

SUSAN JONESTOWN: I'm a journalist. Can I ask you a couple of questions?

That didn't go well. Martina shoved me aside with her dogs. Is now moving diagonally across the park, a fluorescent bishop.

Denis didn't respond. He picked up the containers and stuffed them in his shoulder bag. Now walking off in the other direction from Martina, King slinking behind him. Says "Support Crew 81" on the back of his T-shirt.

Hells Angels are very public about their allegiance. Eight and one, H and A. Not too complicated a code. The "Support Crew" means Denis isn't a true Hells Angel. Just a hanger-on who aspires to angelic status. That's in Ned Palomino's book Whole Hog.

Can't see any high-viz neon green. Waited too long to start following Martina.

Heading east, hoping I see Martina in the distance.

No luck, but the container that fell earlier should still be in the grass. Crossing back over where the altercation took place. There it is. Red Lantern-brand paw wax.

Can feel something loose moving inside it. Might be nothing, but my first thought is "false bottom." And "false bottom," plus "handoff," plus "Hells Angel," could equal "crime."

Opening the tin. The liner has come free from the exterior.

Under the liner there's a plastic bag. And inside the bag—orange pills with "30" stamped into one side and "OC" into the other. 30 mg of OxyContin.

CHAPTER 2

Trans Am – Weird Foam – D'Arcy McGee's – The Damned – Love Games - Fang Spears a Rat – Entry-Level Rape Culture Behaviour

Monday, July 7

Inside the air-conditioned hospital, Janwar could forget that he was in mythical Eastern Canada, where on good days smog shrouds the tops of tall buildings and on bad days it settles in the valley at ear-nose-and-throat level. Ottawa is the land of real seasons, not just the "wet" and "slightly less wet" climate of Vancouver, and the "slightly less wet than Vancouver" climate of Victoria. But out here, even walking north along Bank Street, Janwar has trouble breathing because the air is so hot and thick. Plus the smog.

This is the kind of heat that makes murder rates go up in Port-au-Prince and Miami, and probably also Ottawa.

Trying not to think about the temperature and the way his clothes stick to his skin, Janwar focuses on the street's details. Nestled among the federal-government office towers are corporate coffee shops, muscle-building-supply stores, takeout shawarma joints. Dotting the sidewalks: red fire hydrants with flags sticking out of the top so they don't get buried in snow, bus shelters, grey plastic garbage bins, eight-foot-tall advertising frames.

The advertisements in the frames are all part of the same series, designed in a faux-1950s style and featuring the face of a pudgy and deeply tanned white man. In one ad he wears a Hawaiian shirt and stands on a condo balcony above the slogan "Live the high life. Call Lowell." In another he sports a gingham shirt and overalls, relaxing in a rooftop vegetable garden above the words "Lowell impact living."

Given that the man's skin is even darker than Janwar's, the almost-certainty of skin cancer befalling this Lowell Chilton Corp. poster boy reminds Janwar of the threat of cancer in general. He takes the opportunity to surreptitiously palpate his testes through his pocket and ensure they are lump-free, which they are. His family doctor told him when he was a teenager that it'd be a shame for a young man like him to let testicular cancer get too advanced because he didn't palpate his testes enough.

"Don't worry about that," Janwar said. Dr. Adam Lehman didn't laugh.

On the street corners sit newspaper boxes for publications Janwar doesn't recognize—*Xtra*, *XPress*, *Metro*, *24*—with headlines like "OxyContin: Ontario's New Obsession," "Queer Youth Sex Workers Remain at Risk," and "Bronson St. Condo Development Passes LEED Platinum Environmental Certification." As Janwar waits for the lights to change, he bends down and looks at the article about OxyContin, or at least what he can see of it above the fold, but he doesn't learn much in twenty seconds, except that if there's an OxyContin Obsession and Queer Youth Sex Workers are at Risk, Ottawa's murder rate could be above average.

Janwar visited Ottawa once before as a teenager, in the early spring, when it was still cold. His strongest memory now, not yet pushed aside by drug-interaction statistics, is of visiting the National Gallery in the rain. Specifically, he remembers the thirty-foot-tall spider that stood in front of the building, as if it had crawled up out of the Rideau River after years of narcotized slumber. Upon closer inspection, he saw the spider was made of bronze, and held visible marble eggs in its egg sac. It was named "Maman"—French for "Mother."

"Spiders are helpful and protective, just like my mother," the artist's plaque at the base read.

Janwar's mother, Garati, is also helpful and protective—and not protective just of her only child, because she'd once leapt over a six-foot fence into the neighbours' yard to save a kitten from a mastiff. She's also tall and spindly, like Janwar, especially next to Janwar's fireplug-shaped father, but she probably wouldn't like being compared to a spider.

Inside the gallery, desperate to get away from his parents as they perused pictures of everyday Flemish folks feasting and celebrating and illustrating proverbs (like "Fools get the best cards" and "The herring does not fry here") in the Middle Ages, Janwar wandered through the postmodern art exhibit. Most of it went over his head, but he found himself drawn to an installation called "Trans Am of the Apocalypse," a seventies muscle car spray-bombed matte black, the entire Book of Revelations carved into it with a box cutter.

"Neither repented they of their murders, nor of their sorceries, nor of their fornication, nor of their thefts," the scratches read above the driver-side door handle.

Janwar has almost reached Sparks Street, with its clouds of hookah smoke and kitschy souvenir shops selling Canadiana, when a woman calls his name. He turns. Fang waves from a parking lot, where she stands with a man in his early thirties. The man's black hair juts upward in spikes. It looks hard to the touch, the consistency of uncooked glass noodles. He wears rimless glasses with transparent plastic temples, and at first Janwar thinks the trippy distortion around his eyes means something is wrong with Janwar's own vision, until the lenses catch the reflection of a passing car's lights.

Fang sips from a can-shaped paper bag. "Sometimes these group outings are a little awkward at first, so it's kind of a ritual for us to pound tallboys in the parking lot before we hit the bar. Janwar, this is Peter Wongsarat. He's the Fellow in the department."

"Jolly good," Janwar says.

Peter holds up another paper bag. It has "Liquor Control Board of Ontario" printed on it in green. "You want a drink, Janwar?" His Southern drawl flows from his mouth like a river that's enjoying the inland sun and isn't in much of a hurry to get to the sea.

"Sure, why not." Janwar feels a twinge of guilt about drinking in public, but they aren't operating any vehicles, and it isn't tribal group bonding unless you drink enough to lose control a little. He cracks open the can, and foam pours over the edge of the bag. He has to work tomorrow, but so do they. Placements are as much about networking as practising hard skills. He has to take it easy, try to drink water in between beers, which is always harder to remember than it should be, for Janwar at least.

Peter shrugs. "Guess it got a little shook up in my bag. Well, cheers. To the Mixers."

Janwar shakes the foam out into a puddle of motor oil, and the three clink their paper bags together. "To always pimping," Janwar says. "And never failing."

Fang reaches up and pats his shoulder. "You've almost got it." Her phone buzzes and she angles it away from him and Peter as her fingers fly over the screen. The juxtaposition between Peter's drawl and Fang's big-city yap is disconcerting. Janwar feels like he's switching languages in order to understand them both.

"Next time." Janwar sips and swallows. He peels the bag down enough to see the brand. Pabst Blue Ribbon—Vitamin P. Well, if he's going to power through a beer as fast as possible, it might as well be inoffensive. A dark shape scuttles between two Dumpsters. A groundhog? Ottawa is known for its groundhogs, the way Victoria is known for its rabbits. The shadows are too deep for Janwar to identify it. Regardless, a rodent of unusual size.

"I have to ask, where's that accent from?" Janwar asks.

"N'awlins."

"Bit of a change, weather-wise."

"It's July and I'm still cold. The first year I was here, I had to ask if it'd ever get warm enough for me not to wear a sweater. How do you like Civic so far?" Peter asks.

"It's good. I'm glad you guys are pro-experimentation. And Llew seems like a good dude."

"He's got his quirks."

Fang laughs. "Understatement."

"Like the GHB?" Janwar says.

"That's more than a quirk." Peter grimaces. "It gives me the howlers. I know GHB was used in anaesthesia before it was used in date rape, but the idea of someone being a wizard with GHB scares me, to be frank."

"He talks about it a lot, too," Fang says. "But maybe he just misses being an anaesthesiologist. Misses the action."

Peter winces and raises his paper bag.

Janwar sips his PBR. Whereas Peter is dressed as if he is on clinic duty, Fang is wearing a form-fitting black dress and leopard-print tights. Her voice is even louder than at the hospital, like she's maybe done a line or two of coke. Any dilation of her pupils isn't visible in the dark parking lot.

Janwar has done coke only once, in a medically supervised environment. At UBC Med, a professor had instructed him and his classmates to examine each other's vocal cords. The accepted manner of doing so is to insert a fibre-optic camera up your nose; in order to perform that step, all your nasal secretions have to be dried up, and the way to accomplish that is to administer a 5 per cent solution of medical-grade cocaine. So, on a Thursday morning, Janwar, who had never even smoked cigarettes or cigars or anything, including marijuana, had nasally self-administered enough cocaine to feel a little euphoric and light-headed, at which point his classmate Samson shoved a tiny camera up his nose and down his throat. Janwar felt pretty good for a couple of hours afterward, even considering the nose-camera thing, and if peer-pressured to do more in a similarly safe environment with certified pure cocaine in a controlled dosage, he's concerned he might not say no.

"Come on, slam it." Fang drops her can on the ground. She sniffs.

"Okay there?" Janwar says.

"Just these fucking tulips." She sneezes almost hard enough to lift herself off the ground. Her height is disconcerting; her pointy heels are gothic in the architectural sense, like twin inverted Peace Towers.

"Aren't the tulips done—" Peter says, and Fang shoots him a look. He crunches his can underfoot. "All right. Chug that beer, Janwar."

"Hey, I was going to ask you guys, what's the deal with Shaughn—"

"Bad news. We'll talk after."

Janwar tips the paper bag back and swallows the last of

the lager. It reminds him of the rocky beaches of the West Coast, not because of the taste but because its consistency is similar to the weird foam that sometimes washes up along with the non-venomous jellyfish and giant whips of bull kelp.

D'Arcy McGee's is a standard Irish pub on the inside. Its mahogany surfaces and dim chandeliers keep the tone rich but not gloomy. Llew sits at a window table with Carla and another doctor Janwar hasn't met, an Asian man in his forties, short and powerfully built. Light-coloured craters mar his jawline, probably the aftermath of a war between Accutane and teenage acne. He's chosen not to cover it with a beard, which Janwar feels is a mistake.

Llew waves the three new arrivals over. "Janwar Gupta, this is Dr. Horace Louisseize."

The moonscape jaw nods hello.

"I've ordered us a couple of pitchers," Llew continues. "Put a glass in your hand. First to the mill can grind."

"Oh, I can get—"

Llew waves Janwar's objection away. "I did well this week."

Well at what? Janwar wonders.

Janwar, Fang, and Peter sit.

"What kind of beer did you get?" Fang says.

"Innocent Gun. It's brewed in old whisky barrels in Scotland."

Janwar peers at the pitcher. "Innocent Gun?"

"Aye, boyo."

"Guns don't kill people. People kill people." Janwar jackets a couple of rounds into a finger gun and discharges them into the ceiling.

Llew laughs. "Innis and Gunn. Two blokes."

"Ah." Janwar mimes holstering his revolver. "I guess I just like shootin' too darned much."

"Now, that's why you're an anaesthesiologist, cowboy," Llew says.

Janwar can feel the warmth of the Vitamin P spreading through his body. He feels good, relaxed, but not sleepy. Behind the bar, a busty Teutonic girl pulls pints from a lengthy series of taps. One of them has a devil's tail on it.

Janwar can taste a hint of vanilla, which he finds pleasing.

"Careful, cowboy," Carla says. "It's 6.6 per cent."

Janwar wipes his mouth and clunks his pint glass down. "More 'gun' than 'innocent.'"

"Hey, that makes me wonder," Fang says. "When you were a kid and you played cowboys and Indians with your siblings...uh..."

"I was an only child," Janwar says, "so I just played Indian cowboy by myself."

Turns out Llew was right about the tribal bonding. Janwar feels pretty familial toward everybody, including Horace, who, despite the steady disappearance of liquid in front of him, remains just as ramrod straight, and whose diction remains just as precise, such as when he answers Janwar's question about who Dr. Mengele is with "That Nazi doctor who performed fatal experiments on twins and dwarves and gypsies at Auschwitz."

"I thought he might have been a Nazi with a name like that," Janwar says. "But most of what I know about the Nazis is just their battleships and stuff."

This is true: Janwar was obsessed with warships as a child, to the point where his pacifist parents had worried a little. They soon figured out from the book Janwar always had out from the library, *Jane's Fighting Ships 1943–44*, that it was the machinery that interested him, the specifications, the cannon bores and the dazzle camouflage and the types of propellers, not the actual killing of people.

"*Zwillinge heraus*," Horace continues, in response to Janwar's second question, could be translated to "twins out," which was what Dr. Mengele would say to a room of potential subjects before taking the twins out to be experimented upon. Horace knows this because he did his undergraduate thesis on eugenics.

With little evident concern about the increasingly dark tone of the conversation, Peter tells the group he saw a documentary recently about the persecution of gypsies. A friendly-looking old man talked about how after all the *zwillinge heraus* business was dispensed with, Dr. Mengele used some sort of hand-cranked augur to drill so far into him, starting between his legs, that he thought the doctor was planning to take his heart out, before various other bad things happened that Peter declined to describe. By that time the primal, mythic quality of a person actually *stealing your heart*, more than the stomach-churning violence of the unanaesthetized surgery itself, has drilled an augur into Janwar's own chest, and he can't imagine how much worse any other details could make him feel.

Janwar takes a deep breath. He has a grudging respect for Henry's and José's skill with puns, but now he sees that their joking was far more malevolent than he had initially thought. He means to ask for more details about the two nurses, but the arrival of a group of four stocky men distracts him. They sit at the table to the left of the anaesthesiologists.

"I wasn't a eugenics *major*," Horace says to Fang. "I wrote a paper on eugenics." He turns to Janwar. "I did a BSc in posthumanism. Eugenics is part of the history of posthumanism. I'm not *for* it." The alcohol has finally loosened Horace's monotone into the rise and fall of normal conversation.

The Valkyrie from behind the bar deposits a round of whisky glasses in front of the four men at the next table.

"Come on, leave poor Dr. Louisseize alone." Peter waves his pint glass and Fang jerks backwards to avoid the falling suds. "He's telling the truth. He wouldn't have taken his wife's last name if he was into eugenics."

"Wait," Janwar says, "so the name Louisseize really is related to King Louis the Sixteenth?"

"Meaning his wife's a bit of an..." Peter strums an air banjo. "Inbred," he stage whispers.

Horace snorts and turns to Carla and Llew.

"But that's not how names work!" Janwar whispers to Fang. She shrugs.

The men at the other table are all looking right at Janwar, or, at least, right at the group of doctors. Their jackets fit well; they are expensive, fashionable leather jackets, but the men all radiate the aura of blue-collar menace Janwar has felt as a non-white when visiting smaller communities in British Columbia's Interior.

One of the men waves. He speaks in a heavy Québécois accent. "Horace!"

Horace looks over at him. "One of my patients," he says to the group. "How's your recovery going, Jacques?"

Jacques shrugs. "Horace, will you join me at the bar for the next one?"

Horace nods. "I will. Thank you."

Jacques heads toward the taps as his three friends finish their drinks and go outside. He takes a seat at the counter by the tap with the devil's tail on it.

"Maudite, *s'il vous plaît*, Beatrice."

The bartender pulls the tail down and darkness hisses out.

All the other anaesthesiologists' cellphones buzz at once, but by this point in the evening, Janwar finds it interesting more in a ballet-performance sort of way than anything else, and he lets his mind wander.

Midnight approaches. Peter and Fang are the only two anaesthesiologists left at the bar besides Janwar. Jacques spoke with Horace, then departed, leaving half his drink on the counter. He'd unzipped his leather jacket to reveal a T-shirt that read "1%." The other men never came back in. Not long after, Llew left and Horace went home to his wife, Marguerite—a relationship that wasn't at its healthiest these days, Fang said, which made her feel bad that they had razzed Horace about his name change.

"What happened?" Janwar asks. Out of the corner of his eye he can see Peter talking to a woman in her mid-forties wearing a suit.

"It's not juicy. He didn't cheat on her or anything, although I guess his being so close to his friend, what's her name, bothered Grete a bit. But I think the issue is just kids."

"Hm," Janwar says. Based on his romantic experience so far, he can't even imagine a relationship getting to the point where kids would be the issue.

Carla Welrod and her partner, Anastasia, have already committed to doing the kids thing, Fang continues. They're going the adoption route, waiting for more of the endless paperwork to go through.

"Anastasia and anaesthesia," Janwar says. "There's a joke there but I'm a little too hammered to make it happen."

Fang rolls her eyes. "Probably for the best."

"You're not into jokes?"

"I'm into jokes. Puns aren't jokes."

Janwar runs his finger around his empty glass. "Now that you have hurt me so deeply...can I get you anything?"

"I'm fine for now," Fang says. "Going to the ladies' room."

Janwar notices a tall girl with short blond hair sitting at the bar wearing black leggings and shiny black cowboy boots that outline her calves. Janwar likes girls in boots. Insofar as an article of clothing gets him going, it is leather boots paired with tight jeans or leggings. Maybe, subconsciously, he wishes he were a horse. He hasn't had the courage to tell Dr. Brank that yet.

As Janwar reaches the counter, the girl's fingers dance over a piece of loose-knit green cloth, a scarf or a big sock. She turns when he puts his glass down on the bar.

She has a large nose, but as her head finishes its rotation he realizes she isn't pretty in spite of the nose, but because of it. It balances her angular features like the keel of a ship, and she is a knockout. She knows she has a big nose; she's drawing attention to it with a ring. Nobody who is ashamed of their nose would put something shiny in it. Janwar respects that move. His own nose, which he inherited from his paternal grandfather, is also prodigious, but few people ever notice.

Janwar isn't bad-looking. He just doesn't have the kind of cruelly attractive face that draws women to him like flies to a glass of liquor. In fact, the only people who have consistently found his handsomeness noteworthy are the parents of his high school classmates, specifically, their fathers. And even then he figures those dads combined his generally adult level of competence in most things with his middle-of-the-road teenage face and six-foot frame in some fantasy dad calculus that had little bearing on the sexual desires of teenage girls.

"That Janwar must score like a bandit," Mr. Balakian said once to his very attractive daughter Tabitha. She passed that comment on to Janwar in chemistry class in an "Isn't that funny" sort of way, unaware of how painful it was for Janwar to have a beautiful girl tell him her dad thought he had lots of sex, when he really, really didn't—and she knew that, and he knew she knew that.

The girl's glass is empty except for a thin layer of yellow-brown and an orange wedge. She's still looking at him. She's interested in what he has to offer, which at the moment is another drink.

"Hi, my name's Janwar. Can I get your next one?" Janwar isn't slurring too much, but enough to sound a bit more relaxed than he does when chatting up a lady sober.

"Susan. Sure, another old-fashioned."

"Sounds good." Janwar turns to the man behind the bar. Susan's drinking a cocktail so he feels like he has to as well. "One mojito and one old-fashioned."

The bartender's brass moustache bobs with his head.

"What are you knitting there?" Janwar asks.

"A scarf." She holds it up. "Do you knit?"

"No, but I also work with needles."

Susan arches an eyebrow.

"I'm an anaesthesiologist."

"So you put people to sleep."

"Only at work. What do you do? Or is knitting your day job as well?"

"I'm a barista at Lazarus Coffee while I'm working on my master's."

"Which one? Not the one in the Civic Hospital?"

"No, the one in Westboro." Susan kicks her foot against the bar.

Janwar glances down. "Damn, those are shiny. I can actually see myself in your boots."

"Not sure you'd fit," Susan says.

Janwar blushes.

There's no actual sexual context here, Janwar's pretty sure; he made a dumb comment about her well-polished shoes and she said his feet were big, but—

The bartender brings two glasses over.

Janwar sips at his mojito. The cool radiates from the glass. Soon his face will return to normal, and, anyway, it's pretty dark in here.

An Inuit man in an army uniform with lots of gold braid sits at the bar next to Janwar. Susan startles but he takes no notice of her.

"Can I pay for my soda and lime?" the man says. "Cheers." He slides a ten across the bar.

Susan turns back to Janwar and uncrosses and crosses her legs. Leather slides across other leather. "Are you an anaesthesiologist at the Civic?"

"Yeah."

Fang intrudes on Janwar's peripheral vision and Janwar hopes she can appraise the situation. She holds up her hand. Five minutes. Janwar doesn't want to ditch her, she's his new friend, but Susan could be a new more-than-friend, and he has to at least try to get her number. In this new city he's a new, more confident man.

Susan leans closer, and Janwar can feel her breath on his face. "That's exciting. Are you a Pusher or a Mixer?"

Susan's skin smells good, like sport sunscreen. Janwar adjusts his lean against the bar to pin himself against it. He does often have a problem with girls understanding that he's interested in them in a more-than-friendly way, but to openly display his physical arousal might be a little excessive, or gratuitous, as his mother described movies that were too sexy for young Janwar. "A Mixer. Wait, what is a Pusher? No one will tell—"

Susan looks at her watch. Its dial glows faintly. "I've got to get going, Janwar. Do you have a pen?" Her nose ring sparks golden as she raises her glass. She finishes the rest of her old-fashioned in one gulp.

Janwar fishes in his pocket and passes her his space pen, which can write upside-down and underwater and won't fade from whatever it is Susan chooses to write on.

Susan's left hand darts toward Janwar's waist, and his breath catches for a second, but she's going for his hand. She rotates his wrist, lays it on the counter, and writes out a ten-digit number in block capitals, right below his knuckles. Then, with a sly smile over her shoulder, she's gone, her smell and body heat with her.

The air outside the bar is still much more liquid than Janwar would like. He breathes it in as he waits for Fang to use the bathroom again. He imagines perfect spheres of water forming inside his lungs like they do on the aluminum skin of a chilled beer can. Thinking about the outside of a beer can makes him think about the inside of a beer can, and that second thought makes him queasy. The hard alcohol on top of all that beer was a mistake. The iron statue of bear-plus-salmon across from the bar's entrance makes Janwar think of home, until loud voices distract him.

Two men in polo shirts with chests like inverted triangles stare each other down and ready their fists. A third man with an even wider inverted-triangle chest pulls them apart.

"She asked me what I thought of her," the first man says.

"She said to be honest."

"Janwar." Fang has appeared at his shoulder. She has a bit of a Neil-Young-in-*The-Last-Waltz* thing going on with one nostril. It's very evident, even in the darkness, since her light brown skin contrasts better with the white powder than Neil's ghostly face did in the film Janwar's father made him watch over and over as a child. Janwar points at his own nose, and she rubs hers.

"Thanks." Janwar is too drunk to form any sort of judgment about Fang's obvious drug use. It's an element of his environment, like the inverted-triangle men, the darkness, the moisture, the heat, and the Celtic music leaking from the pub.

"Where's Peter?"

"Probably with a girl."

Although Janwar had seen Peter talking to a young woman earlier, he's a big believer in not leaving people behind, and he asks if Fang can text Peter.

"Sure," she says.

Her phone pings back a few seconds later. She holds up the screen: *Go home. I'm with a girl.*

Fang takes a step forward and Janwar follows her. The sticky smell of marijuana wafts by from a group of girls with blond dreadlocks going the other way.

Fang totters on the cobblestones of Sparks Street. Janwar grabs her arm to steady her, but she shakes his hand off, saying she is fine.

They walk in silence for a minute. A long black car with diplomatic plates whirs past.

"Sorry I freaked when you touched me," Fang says. "It's been a bit of a rough few weeks. I've been on a fail streak in the pool."

"What pool?"

"Come on, cowboy, keep up. The gambling pool. The intensive care docs run it. They send out people's patient numbers as they're admitted and you choose one over the course of the week. And then you see who goes from the ICU to the ECU."

"ECU?"

"Eternal care unit."

That takes Janwar a second to process. "Morgue." The left corner of his mouth twitches. He can feel it happening, but he can't make it stop. "You make money when someone dies?"

Fang nods. "Yeah, it's a dead pool."

"That's horrifying."

"It's not like we're killing anyone. It's just a way of picking numbers."

The streets are quiet as Janwar's and Fang's shadows stretch and snap between the lampposts. An unmarked police cruiser with its window-mounted lights flashing roars by in the opposite direction and squeals around the corner onto Albert Street, tire residue melting onto the hot asphalt.

Fang halts and screams. She's looking down at her feet. Janwar follows her gaze. She's speared a rat with her stiletto. There's no blood, so Janwar assumes it was already dead. Fang shakes her foot in the air, attempting to dislodge the furry mass.

"Put your foot back down." Janwar steps down hard on the rat with his Oxford, flattening it even more. "Now pull it out."

During the walk south to Somerset, Janwar having promised to walk Fang home—and just walk her home, they are colleagues, she has made sure to stress this fact—Janwar starts to babble. He trusts Fang, somehow. Perhaps the business with the dead rat has brought them closer together, a shared encounter with the presence of death—tiny death, maybe, but death all the same.

Janwar tells Fang that the girl she saw him talking to at the bar seemed into him. But that isn't as uncomplicated as it sounds.

Here's the deal, he says. He presents himself to women exactly as he is: a friendly, charming, tall, and fairly good-looking Indian-Canadian anaesthesiologist-in-training. The problem is that he is so friendly and charming that nobody ever wants to shoot him down.

For the most part, he has a bit of a cult-of-personality problem, where people he has only recently met, guys and girls, love him right away, far more than seems reasonable. In the case of girls, their signs of interest in him as a charming, friendly person are very difficult to distinguish from signs of interest in him as a sexual being.

Sure, he's dated, his maximum relationship length being about six months, after which his then-girlfriend, Lise, had asked him to choose between medical school and her. Janwar had come out of the womb "checking dilation," as his mother joked to her friends often enough that it made Janwar both uncomfortable and angry, so leaving UBC Med wasn't an option, and their relationship flatlined.

Anyway, Janwar, after each prospect who isn't interested in what Brown can do for them, package-wise, and instead wants very badly to be his friend, starts re-evaluating his situation and gets into a weird mental place where he thinks that being himself—i.e., friendly and charming and someone everyone wants to be friends with—is underhanded and creepy, because behaviour that from other men would seem to indicate sincere romantic interest, which is what he, Janwar, is going for, from him seems to be only further evidence of his being friendly and charming and someone everyone wants to be friends with, and when he says, "Hey, I think you're really lovely, let's hang out again soon," and his prospect says, "Yeah, that sounds great," and he says, "Can I have your number?" and she rattles it off to him and gives him a big hug, pauses, and hugs him again and then smiles shyly and turns on her heel and leaves, that's about as sincere as you can get, and when he texts his prospect the next night and she says, "I'm flattered you want to go on a date, but I'm not interested in you like that," the only honourable way to proceed is to be exactly that which he doesn't want to be—i.e., a creep—solely so he can make situations less ambiguous, but he can't do it, can't actually act like a creep, is too aware of how invading someone's personal space is entry-level rape culture behaviour, like, Janwar is superconscious when walking at night not to get stuck walking behind women walking alone, to the point of jogging out into the street to pass them so they don't think he is following them, because he's not, to the point where once a Starbucks barista told him that she recognized him because the previous night he'd walked past her faster than anyone had ever walked past her before, and, like, once he was taking care of a friend's beagle for a long weekend and he couldn't really love the dog as much no matter how much the dog loved him once he learned that it had tried for years to sexually assault the owner's female cat, or, like, does Fang know that famous picture of the sailor kissing the girl in Times Square when he comes back from fighting in the Pacific, and how that woman was a stranger and didn't consent in any way to being kissed and said in an interview many years afterwards words like *forcibly restrained* and *scared* and *loss of control*, all things Janwar didn't want women to have to feel, unless they wanted to (S&M isn't his thing, but he understands that some people are into it, and that people in that community are generally very safe and respectful of boundaries because they use safe words, and outside of that safe and respectful community, who knows what kind of creep show you'd get involved with and whether they'd respect your saying no), and anyway, where this is going is that even though Susan has given him her number, Janwar doesn't know what her actual feelings are, with respect to—

Fang holds up her hand and Janwar sputters to a halt. "Stop worrying. You're an anaesthesiologist. If it's keeping you up at night, you know what to do." She lets herself into her building, then turns to face Janwar and stops the door before it closes. "Also, what's creepy is persistence. Showing you're interested once is flattering. It's when you don't stop that you're a creeper." The door closes.

Janwar watches her totter up to the elevator and stop to check her phone. He turns away and hails a cab. He heard there'd been an uptick in muggings in Ottawa recently, but he can't remember who told him. He's glad to see that the driver is Indian, though the driver doesn't seem to care one way or another about Janwar's ethnicity and continues muttering into his headset in Hindi—a language Janwar does not, in fact, speak, as he scans the empty road ahead of them.

EXHIBIT B

TRANSCRIPT OF AUDIO RECORDING FOUND ON SUSAN JONESTOWN'S CELLPHONE

SPEAKING: SUSAN JONESTOWN

Friday, July 4

With the crackdown on Oxy, drug traffickers are having to get extra creative. Dog walkers make perfect drug mules. They even have their own mules: canine pack ponies, each with its own trendy backpack. Can see the headline in the *Ottawa Sun*: WHO SNIFFS THE SNIFFERS.

So what's the story here?

I should go straight to the police. But what if it's bigger than one dog walker?

70 OTTAWA DOG WALKERS INVOLVED IN DRUG SMUGGLING NETWORK. GOVERNMENT DENIES KNOWLEDGE.

May be getting a little ahead of myself.

Martina's got to come back for the container once she figures it's gone. Two choices: take it with me, or wait for Martina to come back and follow her.

Got a clip of Martina picking up the container. Now she's heading toward my truck. And getting into the blue station wagon right in front of it. Let's roll.

Followed Martina as she dropped off dogs around the neighbourhood. I put pins in a Google map. Two dogs are still in the car as we pull into the Ottawa Civic Hospital's lot. Big but thin. Dobermans or greyhounds. Haven't been here, in the hospital, since I was in high school, I guess. When Alan ate too many mushrooms and thought he was going to die.

Wherever she's taking these dogs must be public. They don't let dogs into surgery. If they do, I don't want to know about it. Surgeons use pig parts, don't they?

Shadowed Martina into the psych ward. These are *therapy dogs.* She's handing the leads over to a red-haired man in periwinkle scrubs. He's rubbing their nylon-covered sides. Their packs are empty.

CHAPTER 3

Pillows of Salt – Bombay Calculus – The Abyss – Green Light – The Ugly – It Is Okay – Death Valley 7/9

Tuesday, July 8

Janwar wakes up before dawn on Tuesday morning with his glasses folded on the night table next to him and his clothes piled on the floor next to the bed. The last memory he has of the night before is getting into a cab, but he remembers that with great clarity, down to the fact that the radio was tuned to CHEV 95.3, Ottawa's Best Country. He doesn't remember the cab ride, though, getting into Dr. Flecktarn's apartment, or taking his clothes off, but he seems to have managed all three tasks with a reasonable amount of dexterity.

He has a tune in his head that he realizes quickly thanks to his Anglican school education, follows the melody of the chorus to "Battle Hymn of the Republic." Multi-ethnic voices singing not the normal lyrics about glory and things marching on, but only eleven unique words:

Civic Mixers, we'll induce ya!
Civic Mixers, we'll induce ya!
Civic Mixers, we'll induce ya!
Cause Mama said knock you out.

Janwar thinks about shaking his head and then decides against it. He has the beginnings of a wicked hangover. He might still be drunk. Near the pillow, a couple of spots of blood darken the bottom sheet. The fingers on his right hand sting. He inspects them, notes the raw line on the inside knuckle of his index finger and the patches of rough, dead skin on the outsides of several knuckles. His left hand is in a bit better shape, but it feels tight and sore as well, like all he'd have to do is brush it against the edge of a table for the skin to break. This is the most dehydrated he's ever been from drinking. Or maybe he just isn't used to air conditioning, which he never lived with in BC. Janwar rubs his lips and feels dead skin slough off there too. He has to be at the hospital in forty-five minutes. He made a mistake, alcohol-wise, and now he has to deal with the consequences. Janwar's almost a doctor. A little dehydration is nothing to a doctor, so it's almost nothing to an almost-doctor.

He pads off to the bathroom for extra-strength ibuprofen, a Band-Aid for his one knuckle, and hand lotion. Then it's the kitchen for a bottle of off-brand sports drink, which he at least had the foresight to purchase after work, if not the presence of mind to drink last night. The corner store had nothing but fruit-punch flavour, which is Janwar's least favourite, but he toughs it out, chasing it with a glass of water to get rid of the cherry-medicine taste.

Coffee is the next step. Can of ground coffee from cupboard; mug bearing logo for Lowell Chilton Real Estate from different cupboard. Janwar roots around in Dr. Flecktarn's almost-empty shelving for a new filter for the drip coffee maker before remembering he used the only remaining one in the package yesterday morning before his first shift. The situation is dire. There's no instant. There's no French press. There isn't even paper towel to make his own filter. Toilet paper will not work. He's not drunk enough to try that.

He might not make it out of the house without coffee. He might not even make it into the shower without coffee. Dr. Flecktarn's bed, despite the salt stains on the pillows from a night's worth of beer sweat, is more inviting than anything in the world right now. He can't look back.

The garbage can held a fresh bag yesterday when he threw out the filter. He opens the lid on the can, and it is as he remembers: the filter and grounds are the only contents of a bag that still smells like plastic. Could be worse. Nobody is around to see him. He shakes as many of the grounds as he can off into the bag and runs cold water over the filter before placing it back in the coffee maker.

The coffee, sports drink, ibuprofen, and dry toast work their magic and Janwar is able to stand up straight by the time he leaves the shower, able to interact with the bus driver in spoken English by the time he gets on the bus, and able to perform anaesthesia on a patient by the time his first operation is scheduled at 9 a.m.

Over the course of the morning he caffeinates, he mixes, he induces, he paralyzes, he intubates, he monitors, he repeats. Different developing regions of the world blend their aromas in his work mug. (He has left his favourite, the "Induce like a Motherfucker" one, with the text hand-lettered like a sixties concert poster into a syringe shape, at his parents' house in Victoria—hidden away in his night table since his parents wouldn't approve of the language.) Clear liquids go into veins, eyes roll back, oxygen hisses through tubes, knives carve into abdomens and legs and chests and arms, and unhealthy bits of people come out and are deposited on trays. Computer displays beep and blink and warble but stay more or less steady. Nobody dies or, at least, nobody dies while Janwar is monitoring them. He isn't sure what happens to them afterwards, but they are healthy when they leave his care. Constable Gupta is keeping the peace. For now.

Janwar and Fang both get out of their respective operations at the same time. Karan gives Fang the evil eye as she passes him.

"Asshat," Fang mutters.

"What was that for?" Janwar asks.

"Oh, just the usual surgeon-anaesthesiologist conflict. All about that scrill. I mean, I don't make that much yet, but I'm gonna pass him in turbo mode. Surgery is fail."

For lunch in the Tulip Cafe Janwar chooses Bavarian lentil soup, a tuna salad sandwich with flecks of green onions, and a slice of cantaloupe. Fang and Janwar sit at a two-person table, surrounded by so many other staff wearing light mauve scrubs that an outside observer might mistake the cafe for being full of tulips. Janwar's own scrub pants are riding in the sweet spot, his paramedic shears not dragging the waist down, and in the air-conditioned chill of the hospital, the extra layer of fabric is welcome.

"Hey, Fang." Janwar lays down his sandwich. "I have a question for you."

"Shoot away, Cowboy."

Janwar is the least Wild West of anyone he knows, except that sometimes he wears double denim, and while he's seen others chastised for doing so, nobody thinks it's a problem when he does it—but as nicknames go, Cowboy isn't bad. He'll roll with it, or gallop with it, or canter, or whatever it is that horses do.

"I know when you used to get someone's number, they expected you to call."

"Yes."

"But now they expect you to text."

"Yes."

"And it's kind of weird and creepy to call, even though it

wouldn't have been, say, five years ago."

"Yes. That sounds right to me. Calling is fail. I don't remember the last time I had a phone call with someone who wasn't a bestie or family. Usually it's all '9 p.m.—new text message from unknown number: hey babysex dis is Mitch good to meet you last night you are cute wanna hang tonight,' with no punctuation and letters and numbers instead of words, and then after a while it's like '1 a.m.—new text message from Mitch: hey sweetflanks I want you come over.' And 'sweetflanks' would be spelled with an X."

"And you like that? Also, do you only date historical re-enactors with flip phones? Nobody uses textspeak anymore because of autocorrect. It's harder to misspell things than it is to spell them correctly." Janwar picks at his sandwich.

Fang sighs. "That's just how it is. It's not a matter of liking it. It's the register of our times. Once I was seeing an emergency room paediatrician—"

"Aren't you a little too old to—"

"You don't stop with the jokes, do you. What was your question?"

"I guess it's not so much a question, more just talking something out. See, I'd prefer to call this girl—"

"The one from last night?"

"Yeah. It seems more honourable. But it's not, because I don't want to interrupt her, she might not be prepared, and so on. And"—he looks at his watch—"enough time has probably gone by. I mean, it's alien to me to wait. Not so much that there's anything wrong with waiting, but like if I strategize at all, if anything about romance is strategized, I go down this hyper-rational scientific path and I lose track of what I actually feel—"

"Just text your tall pretty white girl now, Janwar."

Is that jealousy? Fang isn't interested in what Brown can do for her, it seems, but maybe her testy expression is a symptom of wider-ranging racial jealousy. Like, even if she thinks she's pretty herself, and she is, she's been out-pickupped by tall blondes one too many times and has an inferiority complex about it.

A few tables away, Janwar spots Shaughnessy and Aspen. They're deep in conversation, but turned toward him and Fang, instead of across from each other like normal people. "Cheating," it's called in theatre, Janwar remembers from his role in the pit orchestra in *Evita*. Janwar feels a chill beyond the air conditioning. He looks at his hands. Still chapped and now that he's thinking about them, itchy.

"If you're going to worry so much about this bitch," Fang is saying, "you should just text her now. Like, she might think you're anxious if you text too early, but since you are anxious, you could get boned by your anxiety if you wait too long."

"Forgive me for asking this, Fang, but do you have the same kind of anxiety? Since you nailed it—that's exactly the way I think sometimes."

Janwar chances another look over at Shaughnessy and Aspen. They've stopped speaking. Aspen has her cellphone out. She's holding it with the camera, facing Janwar. Neither she nor Shaughnessy flinches or even seems to register Janwar looking right at them.

"Janwar," Fang says. "I am an Asian doctor and my parents are Asian doctors. That's all the environmental factors you need. I've got mad OCD."

"Fair enough." Janwar lifts his sandwich and puts it back down. "That makes two of us. Substitute South Asian for

Asian and one lawyer and one non-practising roboticist for two doctors."

"Non-practising roboticist sounds like a religious choice."

"I don't actually know what he does now. When I was a kid, he used to work in the lab at the University of Victoria designing prosthetics for people who'd had their legs blown off during peacekeeping missions and stuff like that. But now he just wears sweatpants and watches CNN using a TV tuner card on this ancient desktop computer that he's been upgrading since 1999. Sometimes he goes to India to visit his family. My friends joked he was a spy. Secret Agent Ajay Gupta." His sandwich tastes like old air. Janwar pushes his plate away. "Oh man, the worst joke about my dad, though."

As soon as he starts, Janwar knows that Fang doesn't want him to continue. She's already reaching for her phone, but it's too late. The stories-that-suck-and-go-nowhere train is already pulling out of the station.

"Or like, not so much joke as...in social studies class in, like, Grade 9 we read an article about a primitive adding machine from ancient South Asia. The article was called 'Bombay Calculus' and my friend Nick whispered, 'Naw, Bombay Calculus is Ajay over Garati equals Janwar,' and I just about choked to death, and we got kicked out of class."

"Mm," Fang says.

"And then when I got older, I realized maybe they were a little more experimental than that, being, you know, from the land of the Kama Sutra, and the equation could instead be 'Ajay over or under or added to the end of Garati equals Janwar.'"

As Janwar suspected, Fang ignores this part of the story as well and finishes whatever she is doing on her phone, like texting Mitch back about how she can't "come over now" because she's busy at work, being a doctor and shit. She looks up. "Anyway, at least your dad was at home."

"He wasn't exactly present. He came out of his office after school to ask how I did on tests, but only as compared to my friends."

Shaughnessy pushes his chair back and walks toward Janwar and Fang. He mock-stumbles as he passes their table and sends Janwar's tray flying into the aisle. A table of priests look unimpressed.

"What the fuck, man?" Janwar says. "What did I ever do to you?" But Shaughnessy is already past them. "What did I ever do to him?"

"Couldn't tell you," Fang says. "I'll go get some more napkins."

When they've finished disposing of the sodden napkins and food remnants, Aspen is still sitting at the other table, with her ponytail spiky and her phone out. Janwar can't tell if she's close enough to be recording his and Fang's conversation over the cafeteria: the rattling of dishes, the conversations in two different languages—medical and not.

"Janwar. Quit stalling. Text that bitch. It's a first date. It's not like you got her pregnant. You're stressing way too hard."

He pulls his phone from his pocket.

Hey babysex, dis is Janwar from last nite.

Janwar shows the screen to Fang. She laughs.

"But seriously." He returns to keying in the message. *Hey, this is Janwar the anaesthesiologist. We met last night. Want to grab a drink this week?*

"I get wanting to drop that you're an anaesthesiologist, and I didn't hear you two talking, but don't you think 'doctor' is enough?"

"No, she perked up when I said anaesthesiologist. That's my in, I think."

"Okay, then ship it."

Janwar presses send.

Fang has gone off to her next operation. In the hallway someone taps Janwar on the shoulder. He turns to face pineapple foliage. Aspen Tanaka again.

"So, Gupta, you gonna join the dead pool?"

"No, I'm only here for two weeks."

"Everyone's part of the dead pool, Pusher or Mixer, permanent staff or garbage-person intern. And don't give me any sanctimonious bullshit."

"Pusher? Nobody will tell me what the fuck exactly a Pusher—"

"Us. We're the Pushers. Me, Tariq, Shaun, Sylvie. One drug per injection. Fo' evah."

"Sylvie?"

"Sylvie Daalsgard. The head of the department."

"Why wouldn't any of the Mixers just tell me that?"

"They didn't want you being lured by our fruits." She sways her hips mock-seductively, or maybe just seductively, or maybe just mockingly. "They want you to stay dumb."

"Forget it. I'm on the side of experimentation. And the side of…not gambling on dead patients."

"Aw, don't be a pussy. Be a fucking man. Face the abyss!"

Janwar breathes out through his nose, flaring his prodigious nostrils.

"Mew!" Aspen says. "Mew! Mew! Mew! Mew!" She places a finger in front of her crotch and mimes an erection shrinking.

"Oh, fuck off." Janwar walks away.

Janwar can see the text-message light blinking on his phone from across OR III. The light turns green when he receives a text message. It also turns green when he uploads a reminder to himself, but since he is over here and the phone is over there, and he is busy prepping Mr. Félipe Gagnon for surgery, it's probably a text message. He leaves his phone on silent during the day, but the light still blinks. If he thought about it, maybe today he would have put his phone face down so he couldn't see the notification light, so the possibility of Susan didn't interrupt his concentration.

But his concentration is already interrupted: he's really starting to worry about his hands. No matter what he's done—and he's practically a doctor, so he's done a lot—they still feel tight and sore, and the ellipse of raw skin on the inside of his right index finger has grown. He wears latex gloves in the OR anyway, so there isn't any danger to anyone else, but it's going to be hard for his hands to heal. The Band-Aids keep slipping off because of the moisture inside his gloves, and he can't work without bending his fingers.

"Hold this for a second," he says to Rasheeda. He scrambles across the room to check the message.

"Doctor, did you just put something pink into that IV?" the patient says. His field of view includes the tubing but not the tree/bag combo, which is located behind him.

Janwar looks up, two steps away from his phone. "No, I—oh, fuck." Blood is backing up the IV into the bag of saline solution. Crimson threads dissolve into blooms of pink. "Rasheeda, clamp that shit down."

Horace is watching him over his tablet. Janwar feels blood rising to the surface capillaries in his cheeks, but the staff anaesthesiologist stays seated.

Rasheeda snaps to attention. "Got you covered, boss."

This would have happened whether he'd moved to check his phone or not, but it's embarrassing that Mr. Gagnon has pointed it out. No harm done, but Janwar still feels a twisting pain in his stomach. Horace's face is impassive.

"Okay, under control."

Janwar changes the bag. Maybe Mr. Gagnon won't remember this happened. He could ensure that Mr. Gagnon wouldn't remember...he is an anaesthesiologist... but the nurse has seen too, and he can't very well GHB the shit out of the nurse. And Horace. That's a dangerous path. Maybe Llew could have done it in the seventies... Janwar shakes himself.

This is the anxiety talking. An incident has occurred that wasn't anyone's fault. He could have been distracted or not distracted and the end would be the same—no, that isn't a good way to think. He will be less distracted in the future. His fingers are wet and he checks his translucent gloves several times to make sure it's just sweat and not blood.

The surgeons this time are Victor and Mildred. Mildred makes clicking noises with her mouth as she works and at one point Janwar notices a tent in Victor's pants, a totally situation-inappropriate erection that takes a long time to subside. Janwar's not watching it per se; it just keeps intruding into the edges of his vision. Seated, as he is, right at waist level. Janwar's starting to think these two are using a little more than caffeine to stay awake. Maybe dexedrine. Some kind of 'drine at least. That'd account for Victor's frequent and prolonged tumescences and Mildred's phonic spasms. But they're doing their jobs okay, seems like. The military use dexedrine as "go pills" so pilots can fly long enough to get in and out of combat zones at full awareness; maybe having greater surgery endurance is worth the side effects if it saves more lives.

Every time he looks across the room to refocus his eyes from the red dots of the vital-signs console, the green dot of the phone's LED winks at him.

When Janwar is finished with the operation he unlocks his phone.

1:00 pm—New message from Susan: Hey Big Cat, good to meet you too! Hope you don't mind that I call you "Big Cat." I just thought of it, cause Janwar sounds kinda like Jaguar ;)

1:01 pm—New message from Susan: And I do want to go for a drink with you! There's a concert Thursday night, the Trillaphonics at Babylon. They're great live. It won't put you to sleep! Want to be my date?

Janwar can feel a movement in his scrub pants. He surreptitiously puts a hand in his pocket to keep it from forming a tent like Victor's.

It's now two. A reasonable time to respond.

Janwar types out *I can't wait to get my claws into you*, then deletes it. Care must be taken while drafting to avoid embarrassment caused by premature release. *Big Cat wants your little pussy*. Ugh. Who is he? That's the perviest thing he's ever even thought to say. He deletes the text again. *That sounds great! And the nickname is perfect, cause my initials are JAG.* Should he risk a smiley face? Would it make him seem unmanly? Or just charming? She's already used one. He decides to risk it. *:)* Send.

Everything is okay because he has a date with a pretty girl. He hasn't just about killed a man, no matter how he feels. He made a minor mistake, one he would be careful not to make again. "Love games, Janwar. Love games have no place at work, boyo," he can imagine Llew saying, his penetrating eyes dulled to cobalt.

Unless Susan doesn't respond. This has been known to happen to Janwar. He loves women, he really does, but sometimes they can be capricious. No, Susan will respond. She came up with a nickname for him and she explicitly said "date." Anything that might involve dancing would be a good venue for him. People have told Janwar he is an excellent, if non-traditional dancer. The notification light flashes.

2:10 pm—New message from Susan: Okay see you there at 10:30 :)

The rest of the day passes into night without incident, except for the brief moment of panic Janwar experiences when, about a minute after putting a serving of dry spaghetti in a pot of boiling water and retiring to the living room to await the beeping of the timer, light flashes in his periphery. He twists in his seat to find that the pasta resting against the rim of the pot has burst into flames that lick at the range hood. He grabs the pot and drops it in the sink and turns on the tap.

Once his heart rate has returned to normal and the steam has dissipated, he dumps the mix of whole-wheat ashes and barely cooked noodles into the garbage, destroying the coffee filter once and for all, and orders a pizza from the wood-fired-oven place down the street.

Janwar is just sitting down to eat when the phone rings. Ajay. Even 5,000 kilometres away, he's still watching Janwar.

"Hey, hey, Janwar!" Ajay yells. "Where were you last night? Why weren't you picking up your phone? What have you been up to? Huh?"

When Ajay calls Janwar, he often uses this exaggerated tone. He doesn't yell because he's angry; Janwar thinks of it as a "trying to be funny and form a bond while still asserting dominance" approach.

"Hi, Dad." Janwar closes his eyes and watches red spiders drift across his vision. "I was out for dinner with my co-workers from the anaesthesiology department."

"Oh, your co-workers, huh? Your lady co-workers? Your nice Hindu lady co-workers?"

"Some are ladies. Some are gentlemen. None's Indian. One's Welsh, one's Thai, one's Chinese, one's Korean, and one's whatever the name Welrod comes from. English, maybe, or Irish? They're all nice though. I managed to induce and intubate a patient with a massive number of drug contraindications using a new method yesterday, and my supervisor was very impressed."

"You didn't come on video chat at all."

"I don't leave video chat on. I thought we agreed that this week I'd call you and then we'd both go on video chat."

"I waited online for you for one-point-five days. It is okay that you did not want to talk to me."

"I'm sorry we had a misunderstanding. I was just busy, okay? I did want to talk to you, but I was busy."

"Sure," Ajay says. "Okay."

Janwar imagines Ajay waving him off. "What's new with the family?"

"Your grandfather fell and broke his hip at the India-Pakistan cricket match."

"Oh no."

"Pakistan won."

Janwar shrugs to show that's okay, his grandfather is more important, then remembers he's on the phone. "Is Grandpa okay?"

"He's fine. But you should go to Mumbai to visit our family."

Janwar says he'll go once he is done medical school, which is only a year away, and Ajay doesn't say anything in response, which Janwar takes as begrudging acceptance. "Anyway, how was your week, Dad?"

"Your mother had her lawyer friends over for dinner. I did yardwork."

"During the dinner?"

"Before. Here, I'll put your mother on."

Janwar holds the phone away from his ear so he isn't deafened by the squeak of his father's office chair and the digital distortion of Ajay's shouting to Garati without covering the mouthpiece.

"Hello, son," his mother says.

Janwar returns the phone to his ear. "Hi, Mom."

"Your father said you don't have any nice Hindu lady co-workers."

"How—?"

"He wrote me a note while he was talking to you."

"What other notes did he write?"

"Supervisor impressed."

"Any others?"

"That's it."

"Okay."

"So, your supervisor is impressed?"

Janwar holds the phone at arm's length, shakes it exactly as you aren't supposed to do with a baby, and screams silently. His head hurts even more now, and he returns the phone to his ear.

"That's right," he says in a calm and measured tone.

Janwar manages to extricate himself from the cross-examination after only fifteen minutes. He curls up on the couch with a blanket and flips through the TV-guide station on Dr. Flecktarn's absurdly large television. After a brief dalliance with a CBC News story about the Canadian Rangers, during which Janwar learns they are charged with defending Canada's arctic, and are being issued new weapons for the first time since 1941, he settles on a channel showing a Western movie marathon.

"My mistake. Four coffins," Clint Eastwood says.

The next morning, Janwar kills Diego Acosta.

EXHIBIT C

TRANSCRIPT OF AUDIO RECORDING FOUND ON SUSAN JONESTOWN'S CELLPHONE

SPEAKING: SUSAN JONESTOWN, JEAN-MARIE DUFOIS, TERRY SMOLENSKI

Friday, July 4

Couldn't follow Martina or the man in the periwinkle scrubs without them noticing me. Might as well talk to the receptionist: baby-faced long-haired man in his twenties, blond neckbeard.

SUSAN JONESTOWN: Hi, I'm just curious. I saw those dogs coming in here. How does one go about becoming part of the therapy dog program?

JEAN-MARIE DUFOIS: First off, you have to be a dog.

SJ: Cut it out. You know what I mean. It's volunteer-based though?

JD: Right. We offer a weekend course for you and your dog. It costs $360. If your dog is selected, you drop it off in the morning a couple of days a week and pick it up after work.

SJ: So the owner has to pay for the course? Does the hospital at least take care of walking the dog during the day?

JD: No, we're cash strapped enough as it is. You need to hire a dog walker, like Martina, who you just saw with those greyhounds.

SJ: That seems sort of unfair.

JD: Most people take part because they want to help the infirm, not because they want free dog-sitting. And they'd probably have a dog walker anyway. The dog walker would just have to pick the dog up at the hospital instead of home. Do you even own a dog?

The dogs' owners will probably start getting home by five to take their dogs out.

Going to stop by my house and pick up my running gear for disguise purposes.

Reviewed the Google Maps pins from following Marina around as she dropped off the dogs. 1393 Kilborn Avenue looks good for a stakeout. Kilborn is wide and busy enough that a parked truck won't stand out too much.

5:31: a fifty-ish man just came out of the house, two bulldogs in tow. They're turning the corner onto Crocus Avenue.

SUSAN JONESTOWN: Nice dogs. How old are they?

TERRY SMOLENSKI: Jasper's five and Nelly's seven.

SJ: I'm Susan. I'm a journalism student working on a story about dog walkers.

TS: Sure, nice to meet you, Susan. I'm Terry. Terry Smolenski.

SJ: What do you do with your dogs while you're at work, Terry? I mean, do you have a dog walker?

TS: Yeah, I do. Her name's Martina. Maybe you've seen the posters around. "Too busy to walk your Golden Retrieva? Call Martina." And, what's the other one...

SJ: Wow.

TS: I'm a sucker for the dad jokes. Being a dad. I guess she knows her market. And Jasper and Nelly love her. She just seems to really get dogs.

SJ: One more question.

TS: Shoot.

SJ: My neighbour uses this paw wax on her dog's paws to protect them from the hot concrete. I'd never heard of that before. Is it common?

TS: Martina actually sold me on it. Shake a paw, Jasper. It was

designed for snow and ice, but it's good in the summer too.
SJ: Did Martina give you samples?
TS: Yeah, that's right. I think she said she's got a connection with the manufacturer.
SJ: Interesting. Thanks. All right, enjoy the rest of your walk.

There's one, a Martina poster. Martina Gonzalez, 613-255-7440, 168 Rachel Street.

PART II: EYE ON THE BALL

CHAPTER 4

Lifeguards – Spaghetti Western – Experimental Farm – The Homicide Detective's Shower – Wild Turkey

Wednesday, July 9

After Victor pronounces Diego dead, José covers the body with a drape, leaving all the tubes and lines in place. The trauma providers wheel away the crash cart, which features a bumper sticker that reads, "Trauma providers are the lifeguards for the shallow end of the gene pool." This slogan has some pretty problematic socio-economic implications, Janwar feels. That said, anybody not employed by the hospital who saw that sticker would have more pressing concerns than parsing text on medical equipment.

Except Janwar is in a pretty traumatic situation right now and he's fixating on a detail like that. Janwar's emotions have been turned off. He can take in sensory inputs, like the acrid smell of bowels voided on death, and produce actions, like turning away from the corpse, but in between the input and the output is nothing but circuits, empty of feeling.

Horace's voice is as level as Diego's ECG's last pattern. "Rasheeda, please lock the drawers. We need to ensure all the vials stay exactly as they are now, in case someone needs to take a look during the investigation."

Behind Janwar, the drawers snap shut and lock. This auditory stimulus prompts Janwar's vocal cords and mouth to speak the word "What" followed by the word "now."

Stimulus: Horace says, "We'll have to wait here for Brett Rutan from the perioperative board. He'll ask a few preliminary questions."

Response: Janwar says, "Has this happened to you before?"

"Yes." Horace strips off his gloves. "Remember, Brett is an *internal* auditor. He's here to protect us. Tell him the truth."

Janwar nods.

"Oh, and don't let the surgeons mess with you."

"I won't," Janwar says, although he'd probably let anyone do anything to him at this point.

Janwar turns away from Horace and Rasheeda and peels off his own gloves. He's becoming aware of his body again. His skin is itchier than he could have ever imagined. He flexes his dry fingers and he feels the skin break, sees and even smells the little dots of blood well up. He washes his hands in the sink, turning the tap warmer and warmer, until stinging pain replaces irritation. The pain disappears with an almost orgasmic feeling of pleasure. He turns the tap off and his blood starts the slow process of flowing back away from the surface of his skin. The itching is gone, temporarily, though he knows it will be back. The bleeding from his cracked fingers has stopped. The cracks are elliptical like the footholds lumberjacks cut into trees with their axes during tree-climbing competitions, such as the one Janwar once witnessed on a school field trip to Campbell River. He hides his hands in his pockets.

A young man in a black robe crashes through the doors.

"Too late, Padre," José says.

"Again! I'm so behind."

"Father. A man just died," Rasheeda says. "You of all people should understand respect."

"Who cares! The final accounting is coming!" The priest runs out. The doors swing behind him.

He's replaced by two porters, who wheel Diego, or the thing under the sheet that used to be Diego, out of the room so the medical examiner can autopsy him. Janwar sits down to wait.

"If I had a dollar for every time an anaesthesiologist killed one of my patients..." Victor is saying to Karan, but he trails off.

"How many dollars would you have?" Janwar asks.

Victor is very interested in his own shoes.

Janwar can't get another word out of either surgeon, even when his unconscious joke generator, which continues to operate under traumatic circumstances, prompts them with "A fistful?"

Brett Rutan wears a dark suit and pointy shoes with pewter angels on the buckles. They are the kind of shoes a spaghetti-western villain would wear while tying damsels to the tracks. He invites the group to follow him to the lobby outside his office, where they wait for him to meet with them one by one. José, then Rasheeda, then Horace, then the surgeons, coming to Janwar last.

The time before Brett reaches Janwar passes very slowly, or very quickly, Janwar's not sure which. He can't remember thinking anything at all. When Brett calls him in, he has an issue of *Stitches* in his hands, but he doesn't even remember the jokes.

"What medications did you administer to the patient?" Brett asks.

Janwar tells him the drugs and the amounts, which Brett transcribes on his tablet.

"And how are you feeling?"

Janwar's emotions kick back in with the unpleasant wobble of an old air compressor turning over. Guilt, sadness, guilt, sadness, guilt-sadness-guilt-sadness-guilt-sadness-guilt—

He can't help but be honest and forthcoming when a professional asks: Dr. Brank has coached, or conditioned, him well, and he begins his play-by-play for Brett, looking away into the middle distance every time he pauses.

"I'd say, not anxiety about whether I could have done anything differently"—Janwar is careful not to use the word *guilt*—"but, like, crushing sadness now, like my eyes are way back in deep tunnels in my face and I can't blink and because of that my eyes are watering. And I feel like my voice is shaking as I'm talking to you."

"It's not."

"I guess it's that everything else is shaking and my voice is staying the same. I have this tightness high in my chest. And what feels like a leather belt around my head, looped around a wooden dowel that someone's twisting around and around and around, and there's a throb each rotation of the dowel as the belt tightens... I mean, this guy was a living person who seemed healthy up until a few minutes ago. Diego came in here because he was mugged and now he's leaving in a bag. Maybe he was a father, maybe a husband. His family didn't get to say goodbye. I didn't when my grandmother died; my parents thought I was too young and wanted me to remember her when she was healthy, and I've always resented them for that. Maybe someone in Diego's family will make the same decision and there'll be this like secondary trauma—" The tunnel-digging machines pushing his eyeballs through his grey matter until they touch his amygdala, the fear centre of his brain, triggering a rush of panic.

"That all sounds like a pretty normal reaction," Brett says.

Brett's measured tone forestalls Janwar's nascent cthonic breakthrough. His eyeballs inch back into the sadness zone, and although the leather belt remains around his head, at least the tightening has stopped.

"This might sound callous, but it does get easier each time." Brett taps his iPad with his gold stylus. "Mr. Acosta didn't list any emergency contacts in his intake paperwork, so he might not have any dependents. He's from Argentina, and he was a consultant, a building engineer. If that matters. It's still awful that he died, but maybe he's the only person affected by his death. Besides all of us, of course. Speaking of which, if you need someone to talk to, go up to the psychotherapy department and I'm sure you can bump someone else off the list."

He looks at Janwar's stricken face. "Oh, poor choice of words. No harm intended."

"It's okay. After all this, I wouldn't want to prevent someone else from getting psychiatric care they'd already booked."

Brett reaches up and claps Janwar on the shoulder. "Put yourself first, kid. I doubt whoever you're replacing would have the same immediate responsibility you do. You're going to have to go back to work and do all the same things you've been doing, knowing that every time there's the possibility that this could happen."

"I appreciate that," Janwar says, but at the word *responsibility*, his stomach twists around his spine like the serpent around the Rod of Asclepius. He'll call Dr. Brank later, probably. Right now he wants to be alone and in a cocoon. He twitches violently and Brett removes his hand.

"All right. Thank you, Dr.—Mr. Gupta. I have your phone number here. I'll be in touch if I have any further questions, or if the medical examiner does."

Janwar paces along the hallway with Brett's self-correction from Dr. to Mr. echoing in his head, a correction that he hopes doesn't reflect his future.

If he's at fault, this could be it for Janwar Gupta's dreams of being a doctor. What else could he do? Anything else he's qualified for also involves medicine, and he'd always be the med student who fucked up and killed a man.

Without anyone around to hold himself together and stay verbal for, Janwar's anxiety displaces his grief. Now all of his thoughts are focused on his role in Diego's death. There is nothing more important in the world than determining his level of responsibility. The hallway dissolves into a blur.

Diego suffered cardiac failure forty-five seconds after the injection. Many different causes could have led to his demise. Janwar weighs each in turn and compares it to the symptoms. The most likely is cardiotoxicity—an overdose. The word *negligence* swims up through Janwar's brain. So does the word *mislabeled*, but *negligence* is more arresting.

"Janwar Gupta to room B309 in two hours." The mention of Janwar's name over the intercom halts his line of thinking.

"Janwar Gupta to room B309 in two hours."

B309 is Llew's office. Janwar's hyperventilating. He takes a slow, measured breath, and then another. He's stopped walking. He can't focus on two things at once.

On autopilot, his head full of toxicity statistics, Janwar changes out of his scrubs into a T-shirt and shorts and leaves the hospital by the main entrance, avoiding eye contact with the people in the lineup for Lazarus Coffee.

The temperature outside is warm again to the point of cruelty, which makes him feel even more suffocated. Air molecules hang in the sky like tiny helicopters, which makes him think of *M*A*S*H*, which makes him think of the theme song from *M*A*S*H*, "Suicide Is Painless." The statistics have ceased to have meaning. Now they're circling around and around, faster and faster, until they're a thick fog blocking out other thoughts.

Across from the hospital lies the Central Experimental Farm. Janwar isn't sure what goes on there. He can't help but imagine hybridized farm animals roaming the grassy hills of the grounds, which stretch all the way to the Ottawa River and Carleton University, body parts mixed up across species, order, even kingdom... By the time Janwar passes an old man reading a newspaper on a park bench close to Dow's Lake, the fog has begun to dissipate. His ability to spend twenty minutes doing nothing but putting one foot in front of the other and looking very intently at the grass and trees means that he's in shock, and he's going to feel a lot worse very soon. "Suicide Is Painless" still stuck in his head: B, A-B, A, B, A... Janwar's hands are shaking and he feels a chill ripple across his shoulders. A honk makes him spin around, his heart pounding. A four-by-four National Capital Commission truck rolls along the path, its headlights boring into his shoulders. Janwar steps aside. The orange-clad workmen in the cab peer at him as they pass, and Janwar flinches.

B, A-B, A, B, A... He shouldn't be in public. He should be somewhere quiet, controlled, indoor. He turns, walks back past the old man sitting on the bench, then decides he should continue with his original plan, turns, passes the old man again, then halts. The idea that he has already passed the old man twice in such a short time makes it impossible for him to change directions yet again, even though he knows the old man doesn't care and isn't judging him.

He commits to his current direction, to looking again at the varied deciduous trees, the beech and the maple and the others he can't identify immediately. They are not signifiers of summer or childhood or new life but the gnarled backdrop of grim fairy tales.

When he reaches the lake, the murky smell of the decaying wood docks is putrid. Squadrons of seagulls wing overhead. People with fishing rods cast into the water, but what sort of fish would live in a manufactured canal? Sinister, sleazy fish that leave a wake of iridescent oils behind them...

Janwar walks faster; maybe endorphins will help keep him from panicking further. Then he remembers Susan. He thinks about Susan, about her nose, about her leggings, and her boots. His hands start itching again. He takes a deep breath. He might or might not have killed a man—No, he definitely killed a man, but it might or might not have been his fault. But either way, he will see Susan on Friday. That's not as appealing as it was yesterday. It adds another level of panic. How will he be functional enough to talk to her by then? How will he be functional enough to talk to anyone ever? Will everything he thinks of remind him of Diego? How could it not? Everything relates to death. B, A-B, A, B, A...A, B, A-B, A, B-A... Take these bushes, for example. Manicured plants grow in mulch made from ground-up bones. He turns back toward the hospital. The old man is gone, Janwar imagining the old man's angular features through the black material of Diego's body bag.

Back in the locker room, Janwar can't face the number of steps involved in cleaning his body and hair, drying, and redressing, so he swipes Tropical Surge deodorant under his arms. It's a compromise solution he remembers as a homicide detective's shower from its prevalence in a certain kind of TV show. He also changes his Band-Aid. At this rate he is going to need a new box soon.

Llew puts his tablet down. "Have a seat, Janwar. You want a drink, is it?" He opens his drawer and displays a bottle of Penderyn: Welsh whisky.

"No thanks." Janwar's reptile stomach is not in a position to consume anything.

"Time was when a bloke offered another man a whisky chaser alongside hard news, the other bloke would be grateful."

"I'd rather you give me the hard news."

Llew shrugs. "Your loss. I'm not trying to have you." He closes his drawer. "I already put myself out by handling this instead of involving Sylvie. And mind you, I don't like being beholden."

Janwar sits in the black leather visitor's chair. The fan spins overhead, tilting a little on its axis with each rotation. It makes Janwar feel like his body is rotating around his stomach. He closes his eyes for a second, but it makes the feeling worse.

Llew's wingtips are flat on the floor this time. The chair sticks to Janwar's back.

"Let's skip the back-and-fore," Llew says. "Diego died from an overdose of lidocaine." He hands Janwar a copy of the examiner's report. "The level in his blood is still higher than it would have been if you'd given him a normal dosage for his weight. That would be 7 ml of the 1 per cent solution."

Janwar slides his dry tongue over his teeth and forces his mouth open. "Which is what I dosed him with." He hands the examiner's report back.

"Don't say stories, boyo." He blows out through his nose. "You proper weren't mingy with it."

Llew shuffles the papers on his desk and holds out another printout signed by the legal counsel and Brett Rutan—an itemized list of the contents of the drawers of the anaesthesia cart. Janwar scans down the list.

Lidocaine 1%, 50 mL vial: unopened.

Lidocaine 10%, 50 mL vial: approx 43 mL remaining.

Janwar's stomach lets go of his spine all at once. The normal dose of lidocaine is 1 milligram per kilogram of body weight. A vial of 1 per cent solution has 10 milligrams of lidocaine per millilitre. Seven millilitres of 1 per cent solution is 70 milligrams. Seven millilitres of a 10 per cent solution would be 700 milligrams, enough to be fatal within forty-five to ninety seconds.

"One more," Llew says. A printout signed by the pharmacist from the dispensary, showing that the vials they placed in the cart made up the standard package of anaesthesiology drugs, including two vials of lidocaine, one 1 per cent and one 10 per cent, both 50 millilitres. Llew places the papers in an accordion file and locks his drawer. "Really speaking, it's a proper poor lookout for you."

Janwar doesn't say anything.

"Keeping your mouth shut is a good idea. You haven't apologized or said anything to show you're responsible, is it?"

Janwar hasn't. He shakes his head.

"Don't. There'll be no end of trouble if you do. Brett might hunt you down again in a minute, but I don't expect there'll be anything he needs to clarify."

Janwar nods. He's still afraid his voice will start to vibrate along with the rest of him if he says anything.

Llew's talking again, staring into Janwar with his burning blue eyes. "But here's the good news. Although you messed up, and you're always going to know it and I'm always going to know it, and José and Rasheeda and Horace and Victor and Karan are always going to know it, and the administrators of your university program are always going to know it, somehow the God of Anaesthesiology up there in his white scrubs is smiling on all of us, and nobody has any reason to palaver over the situation. Since Horace was the supervising physician, he's going to get a good lamping for not noticing you took the wrong vial. But it'll blow over soon enough. Your university's malpractice insurance and Horace's will cover whatever rises. But mind out, you botched it, not Horace. A supervising physician can only do so much, and everyone's going to side with him. Protect our own by here, we do."

"What about—" Janwar starts to say, his voice remaining thankfully level.

"What happens with your program is between you and them. But mind out, I'm the one filing the paperwork. Keeping me happy is in your interest, boyo. You did something radically wrong, and it'll stay with you for the rest of your life. It might get you booted out of medical school, no matter what I say to UBC, but at least it's not going to add to your student debt. And before you ask, I'm not going to let you drop the placement. Keep on what you raised. Now go home, boyo, put yourself straight, and show up in the morning ready to work." He picks up his tablet. Condo towers are laid out across the screen like giant scalpels.

Janwar's brain accelerates out of control as soon as he is inside Dr. Flecktarn's apartment. Today's thunderstorm batters the windows with IV-bag-sized raindrops. He sits at the kitchen table with his head down on the glass. His stomach has turned inside out. He can feel its acidic contents dissolving his organs. He feels bad, as in "is experiencing negative emotions and associated physical symptoms," and also feels bad, as in "has been an objectively bad person and is accurate in his analysis of himself as such."

He drew the correct amounts. He wasn't distracted. The spectre of blood backing up Mr. Gagnon's IV slides in front of his eyes and he swats it away. There are three options.

One: Janwar remembers wrong. He expected the label to say 1% solution, and so he saw it that way and drew from the wrong vial, the one labelled 10%.

Two: The vial he drew from was labelled 1% but contained a higher percentage of the drug than it should have. He can't think of how the switch could have happened between the cart leaving the dispensary, which is right around the corner from the OR, and when Janwar unlocked the cart, but that doesn't mean it didn't happen. But then the bottles, or labels, would also have to have been switched back before the compliance officer saw them. That part would have been easy: during the chaos of Diego's last seconds, anything could have happened without Janwar noticing.

Three: The examination results have been falsified, which means that the perioperative board rep and the examiner involved in the autopsy are lying, and probably even more conspirators besides.

Occam's razor suggests that the simplest explanation is probably the correct one. But Janwar is fastidious about labels. If he isn't at fault, who is? Guilt is one thing to process, but conspiracy is completely different. Janwar's rationalizing of the situation can't handle the introduction of this new variable, and he explodes into a full-on chthonic breakthrough.

He doesn't think anything for a while until a white nebula with yellow edges floats across his vision. He adjusts the position of his head on his folded arms to reduce ocular pressure. The nebula collapses into darkness again.

Janwar wants not so much to go to sleep as to switch off. Does that count as suicidal ideation? Will he hurt himself? Should he call a crisis line? Or an ambulance? His head is under immense pressure and the squeal of his nervous system blocks out all thoughts and outside noise.

He lifts his head and opens his eyes. His phone is in reach. He could look up a crisis line. Or he could call Dr. Brank, since it's now only 4 p.m. in BC. But he feels a visceral revulsion at the idea: he is confronting a serious external problem and to approach it as a cognitive behavioural exercise, as he knows his therapist would want him to, will not help him. This isn't a panic attack about whether a size 36 shirt is too baggy for his IV-tree frame. Best case, he killed a man by accident; worst case, he's fully responsible for killing a man. He has no way of knowing which is true right now. The street lights flicker on. The City of Ottawa is testing new street lamps in his neighbourhood, so the pools of light are all different sizes and colours, one more thing that should be neatly ordered but is instead out of control. Nothing will happen to clear up his questions until morning at the earliest.

He could call his parents, but he can imagine Ajay's response: "No, my son wouldn't kill a man." Which would mean that either Janwar hasn't killed a man or he isn't

Ajay's son. And Garati's hyper-rational past-precedents-based approach: "Exercise will make you feel better. You may not feel like it will now, but you know that it's helped in the past. Why don't you go for a run?" Or maybe she'd look at it from a legal perspective—although she's a corporate lawyer for the BC Ferries Corporation, not a criminal lawyer—grilling him in order to determine exactly what his culpability might be, whether there'd be a case for the prosecution. Thinking about his parents and how they'd feel if he has fucked up his entire career adds yet another variable to the equation.

And if he called a crisis line, would he be able to talk about this to a complete stranger? Janwar's thoughts are spinning faster than he can sort them into coherent streams. He decides to masturbate, and then realizes that he already is, and has been doing so for quite some time now. His hand is down past the elastic waist of his scrubs, though there isn't a sexual thought in his head—and furthermore, he realizes that for a much longer time, though intermittently, and not 100 per cent of the time, he has been masturbating when he is stressed out and unhappy, not when he is horny, which has to be setting up some pretty awful Pavlovian connections in his brain that might be a problem the next time he is able to sleep with a lady. Which might be Friday.

The low point of stress-masturbating took place several years before, after he'd misjudged a run-up while cliff-jumping at Thetis Lake with friends and missed hitting an outcropping of submerged rocks by no more than four feet. At work the next day, he was so stuck in an obsessive loop about it that masturbating in the bathroom of the Canadian National Institute for the Blind seemed like the only way he could hard-reset himself, and when he followed through, using institutional pink lemon-scented soap as a lubricant, he didn't even feel ashamed.

Janwar closes his eyes again and leans back, trying to think of sexy images, of removing high boots and black tights from attractive women he has known, but then the bootless, tightless legs are waving to him from the water thirty feet below and he is standing at the cliff's edge, taking myriad different run-ups. He is hitting the granite, his body crumpling, bone fragments spraying out like dust. His friends are dragging him back to shore, and he can't feel anything. He is in a wheelchair, paralyzed, unable to move his arms or legs, unable to move his mouth, unable to breathe, until the next lightning flash outside burns through his eyelids.

He withdraws his hand from his pants and stands up. Janwar's normally a spiced-rum drinker, but the only hard alcohol on the shelf is Wild Turkey. He pours himself a glass and swallows all of it, coughs, leaves the tumbler in the sink, and moves toward the bathroom. He reconsiders and takes the bottle with him.

He removes his clothes and steps into the shower with the bottle in one hand, sinking down onto the nonslip floor, crunching his knees up so he can fit. B, A-B, A, B, A...

EXHIBIT D

TRANSCRIPT OF AUDIO RECORDING FOUND ON SUSAN JONESTOWN'S CELLPHONE

SPEAKING: SUSAN JONESTOWN

Saturday, July 5

Called my manager at Lazarus Coffee. Asked if I could pick up a couple of shifts at the hospital location, the stand-up counter by the entrance. That'd give me cover for wandering around the Civic. She needs someone this afternoon, which is perfect.

Logged into the news archive through the Carleton Library site and am looking up articles about Civic Hospital. Just me and my whisky and my school's database subscriptions. And it's 9 a.m. so whisky is off limits for a while. I'm going to make some coffee. It's the next best thing.

Out of milk.

The Ottawa Civic Hospital, like Carleton, seems to show up in the news only in stories about bad things happening to women.

There was even a female anaesthesiologist who had assaulted her patients, a Dr. Venolia Parker. There's a CBC article about her, "Ottawa Doctor Faces Sexual Abuse Discipline."

Apparently Dr. Parker testified before the Ontario College of Physicians and Surgeons that she went into a fugue state during the incidents and had no understanding of what she was doing. She felt dizzy and the next thing she knew, her mouth was on the complainant's nipple. She testified she was having a rough time, was thinking about killing herself almost constantly, was diagnosed with OCD, and had some family issues with her husband and children. And she'd been abusing OxyContin for several years.

The article also includes her psychiatrist's take on the situation. She's identified only as Dr. B and no longer lives in Ottawa.

"'Her actions did not stem from a place of sexual desire. Instead, she was regressing to infancy whenever she had a chthonic breakthrough, looking for the sense of security she had experienced while being breastfed, which her mother had allowed her to do up until age three,' Dr. B said."

The assaults happened twelve times, Dr. Parker either placing her mouth on a patient's nipple or resting her cheek against a patient's breast. As a result of Dr. B's spirited Freudian psychology and the fact that there was no penetration, the woman got off easy. She was banned from anaesthesiology because the ability to sedate people, combined with the privacy of the surgical screen, could be too much of a temptation. She was allowed to see male patients only and even had to wear a tag that said as much when she was on duty at the clinic. But she ended up getting transferred to an administrative capacity elsewhere in the hospital.

I've got a subject to interview.

CHAPTER 5

Infinite Gain – Records – The Blade – Rio Mapocho – Minsky's Diner – Reasonable and Productive – Standard Parts Missing – The Wrong Thing to Say

Thursday, July 10

Thursday morning, in the light of day, Janwar feels like a human being again—a human being with a headache; a human being who might or might not still be responsible for the death of another human being; a human being who might fail out of medical school; a human being beset by lingering dream images of Brett Rutan, the perioperative board representative, tying him to the O-train tracks with plastic tubing and then departing as soon as the red-snouted LRV appeared in the distance, dinging its bell like a demented carnival ride—but a human being nonetheless. One who could take things, if not one day at a time, at least one minute at a time. Dr. Flecktarn's bourbon is almost depleted. Flies buzz around the bottle. Janwar has been listening to country music, because when he turned the radio on to introduce the outside world, the dial was tuned to CHEV, not his usual CBC, the singer lamenting his proximity to the tomb. But now Janwar has to get to the hospital, and, for the moment, that thought takes precedence over everything else. He even leaves the flies alone.

Outside, all of last night's rain has already evaporated, but he can feel it lingering in the atmosphere. Once Janwar catches the number 7 bus, which puts him in a controlled environment that is quiet and air-conditioned, he can relax enough to see the situation with a little distance.

It reminds him of Pascal's wager, which goes like this: You don't know whether or not God exists. You can either live as if He does or live as if He doesn't. And you won't find out until you die.

If you believe in Him and He doesn't exist, you occupy yourself with prayer for part of the time you're alive, which is a finite loss. You lose the time you spend praying. If He does exist, you get rewarded in the afterlife—an infinite gain.

If you don't believe in Him and He doesn't exist, you haven't wasted any time praying, so you experience a finite gain. If you don't believe in Him and He does exist, you experience infinite loss in the afterlife, possibly involving fire and brimstone for all eternity.

So, if you believe in God, you end up with either a finite loss or an infinite gain. And if you don't believe in God, you end up with either a finite gain or an infinite loss.

If that's Pascal's wager, this is Gupta's wager: he is responsible for Diego's death or he isn't. He has two possible courses of action.

First, he can believe he is responsible for Diego's death, as he's been told. Guilty until proven innocent. In that case, there's nothing he can do. He'll have to go through the remainder of his placement as if the death hasn't happened, which he isn't sure he has the confidence to do. He'll be forever second-guessing himself. Whether or not he gets kicked out of medical school, or fails this part of the program, he'll always be the medical student intern who killed a patient in his first week, which is about as bad as it can get. So: finite gain (not wasting time if he's guilty) versus infinite loss (not having the ability to clear his name, destroying his future).

Second, he can believe he isn't responsible for Diego's death, in which case he can at worst occupy himself with an investigation, even if it leads nowhere, and at best prove his innocence. He can't feel any worse than he felt yesterday. So: finite loss (having to deal with responsibility again) versus infinite gain (completely clearing his name and continuing his life as if nothing has happened).

Janwar decides he is going to believe in God: the God of Detectives.

Janwar has to come up with a plan. Detectives always have plans—which men to bully, which women to cajole—even if they end up getting knocked out a lot, the backs of their heads growing pulpier and pulpier throughout the case. He still can't think of how the vials could have been switched between the dispensary—which, given its collection of controlled substances, is the most audit-friendly room in the hospital, with constant video surveillance, individual pass codes for pharmacists, and log files tracking all operations—and the operating room. He'll leave that alone for now and try to figure out the who and why...and try to do so without letting any of the anaesthesiologists know he's playing detective.

If someone caused Diego's death on purpose, could they have been involved in other OR deaths? Is someone getting their rocks off by allowing med students to kill patients? He'll visit the records department and ask the librarian to gather a list of all the OR deaths in the last five years. Even if he can't get Victor or Karan to talk, maybe he can find out how many times an anaesthesiologist has killed one of

Victor's patients. But what if one of the other surgeons was involved in Diego's death? The two in Diego's operation appeared to be passive observers. But how intense was the surgeon-anaesthesiologist rivalry here? Brazil-level? Would the surgeons somehow cause the death of a patient just to fuck with the anaesthesiologists? Is that what Horace was alluding to with his warning to watch out for the surgeons? This is a lower-probability scenario, Janwar figures, but when he looks at the OR death records he'll check if any surgeons or anaesthesiologists pop up more than once.

He checks his watch. He has half an hour before his first operation and he's dreading surrounding himself with the same environment in which Diego died. He mops his brow with his Batman do-rag.

Dr. Brank would not approve of this "being a detective" plan. She'd say the idea of a setup is a manifestation of anxiety related to Janwar's issues with failure. That even thinking about other explanations is deeply unhealthy, that he has to move on, to accept his mistake, and not attempt to fight crime.

But, this strategy assumes that every time he worries that he's made a mistake, he has.

A big rift lies between mistakes that might have had negative consequences—misjudging cliff-jumping, driving too fast in the rain and feeling the car hydroplane for a split second, leaning over a gas barbecue while lighting it—and mistakes that have life-changing negative consequences, like this one.

Finding out the truth is more important than Janwar's own mental health. Dr. Brank would say nothing is more important than his mental health, that the problem is not the situation itself, but how he's thinking about the situation. She might be right. His anxiety has often made him think that determining responsibility is more important than his mental health. But a high percentage of false positives doesn't discount the possibility of a true positive.

So, fuck Dr. Brank. Janwar pushes the down button for the elevator.

He shares the elevator with a man in a wheelchair who, seeing Janwar's scrubs with the blue Ottawa Civic Hospital logo, complains that the last time he was in the hospital, they ran out of beds after his operation and stuck him in a supply room with an IV drip and left him there overnight. When the doors open in the basement, a cart heaped with garbage bags sits unattended, blocking the exit. Janwar shoulders it out of the way so the man, whose confidence in the Civic Hospital hasn't improved, judging by the pulsating vein on the side of his head, can disembark.

The entrance to the records room is clean and modern. The radio jabbers quietly. Despite the lack of windows, the plants in the corner are thriving. The chairs are so minimal it's like they aren't even there. They must have cost a fortune. The desk is expensive wood, or at least has the veneer of expensive wood. Why is the records room so fancy?

"Can I help you?" the middle-aged woman behind the desk barks, raising her head from behind what Janwar believes is a philodendron. Her lab coat is rumpled, as if she has slept in it. She looks unhealthy, her sallow skin damp and almost grey. She puts down her magazine, which bears the coverline "Bad Mom Sandpapered My Face," and removes her glasses. The copper wires of the nose pads are green with oxidation.

She's not just unhealthy. She's malevolently unhealthy. Janwar's almost a doctor and he sees sick people all the time, but somehow, she's different. His chest tightens.

He struggles to speak. "I'm Janwar Gupta. Med student intern, anaesthesiology. I'm just gathering some data on OR deaths for a project."

"You mean, you're making *me* gather data on OR deaths for a project." The woman's eyes are spiderwebbed with burst capillaries and her nose is running. She wipes it with her sleeve.

Janwar shrugs apologetically. He tries a smile, but it doesn't gain any traction. "I guess so. If I can help in any way..."

"How about you write me a prescription."

"Got the flu?"

The woman laughs, which makes her throat skin quiver, but Janwar gets the sense it is a laugh at him, not with him. His face must have betrayed him, because the woman shakes her head. After her wattles have come to a rest she says, "You don't just come down here. You go into SHROUD and log a research ticket, and then it goes into the queue. Assign it to me."

"Your name is?"

"Venolia Parker."

"If you don't expect people to come down here, why is there a waiting area? Why are there magazines and all those chairs?"

"What, you don't think I deserve a nice office?"

"No, I—"

"Here's the website for SHROUD. You have to have an account to create a ticket." She writes out the web address on a Post-it. It takes her a while. She writes left-handed and her sleeve drags across the ink. It's the same sleeve she wiped her nose with, Janwar notes.

"I don't have an account. How do I get one?"

"You have to put in a ticket with IT."

"Which is, let me guess, also in SHROUD?"

"You got it."

"Can I just visit the IT—"

"What do you think?"

Janwar blows air out slowly through his nose and squeezes his fists together hard enough to feel the skin snap. He looks at his watch and then at the hairline of blood across two of his first knuckles on his left hand. He has to go to his first operation. He hopes the skin cracks won't bleed anymore.

Venolia is already looking back at her keyboard and flexing her pointers.

"What does SHROUD stand for?"

"Oh, honey," Venolia says. She cracks her knuckles.

Janwar leaves the room, his own knuckles pulsating with a woozy heat. He can't put it off. He has to get back on the horse. Horse tranquilizer, he can't help but think. He has to anaesthetize again. Inject drugs that can stop a man's heart—and, which, yesterday, did—into another human being.

The two operations Janwar conducts that morning appear flawless to outside observers, even if internally he's locked into an obsessive loop and suffering microseizure-level panic cthonic breakthroughs. He checks and double-checks and triple-checks the labels of all his vials before and after he draws syringes.

The morning is a success from a medical standpoint, although he would have been happier if Rasheeda was there, to see if she remembered anything he didn't. The fact that she'd made the mixing motion the first time he'd met her, during Mr. Nakamura's operation, makes Janwar think she could be trusted. Instead, the nurses are Henry and an unfamiliar woman, Ashley Penderecki, and the surgeons a new permutation, Gertie and Mildred, who stop talking as soon as they enter the room and see Janwar.

At his break, he decides to visit the IT department anyway. Almost everyone is away, it seems, the room curiously barren. Just one IT guy is drinking something that requires four tea bags out of a travel mug the size of Janwar's forearm, watching code cascade down a vertically oriented screen. His name is Alvin and he has large perky ears like a Boston terrier's.

"One doesn't just *forget* to create a SHROUD account," Alvin says. "You're only here for two weeks, so there's no good business case for us to spend our time on it. You can just ask someone else to make the request for you in SHROUD."

"Oh Christ," Janwar says. "Why does there need to be a business case?"

"Project V."

"V?"

"V for Victory."

"Over what?"

"Overuse of IT resources for avoidable tasks." Alvin points at a World War II propaganda poster tacked up on his cubicle wall. It features two men holding a nutcracker. One man is labelled "Employees" and the other labelled "Management." The title at the top reads, "The Real V for Victory," and the bottom says, "Joined Hands Will Crack This Nut!" In the centre of the nutcracker, about to be cracked, is a caricature of a Japanese man's head, radiator-grille mouth and all. Drawn on the poster with a Sharpie is an arrow pointing to the Japanese man's head and the phrase "Doctors who bring their own tablets to work."

"Trying to make all these third-party apps work on personal devices is a nightmare," Alvin says.

Janwar lets his chin drop to his chest.

"Don't tell me you're offended," Alvin says. "Hitler is the biggest joke there is. The one person you can make fun of without anyone getting upset. All those video remixes of *Downfall*. Why can't I have a poster with Hirohito? Japan did some awful things to the Koreans and the Chinese during the Second World War. Look up 'comfort women.'"

"I don't even know where to start with this," Janwar says.

"Tell you what," Alvin says. "I'll create a ticket for someone to make you a SHROUD account if you get the new server blade for me from Brenda in shipping and receiving. The dead pool server has had a lot of memory leaks recently. We're upgrading to 64-bit architecture. That will reduce the IT task load by one user story, so it'll about balance out."

"Wait, the dead pool with the ER? There's a whole server for that?"

"Of course. What other dead pool is there? We're looking at opening it up outside the hospital. Bringing in some serious cashola."

A blade sounds thin and maybe not that heavy. "I can just say I'm picking it up for Alvin?"

"Alvin Frond. Just forge my signature. It's not hard." Alvin prints "AF" on a Post-it in block capitals.

"Don't they know what you look like?"

"Doesn't matter as long as they have the signature in—"

"SHROUD?"

"Bangarang."

"What does SHROUD stand for?"

"It's just in capitals," Alvin says.

The "blade" is actually an entire server and it weighs 60 pounds. Janwar staggers back into the IT department with it to find that Alvin is now gone. He leaves the server by Alvin's desk and wanders into the next office over, which, according to the sign on the door, is the "Forestry Department." Of course the Ottawa Civic Hospital has the budget for a forestry department, but not enough for adequate tech support. The city is one big park. Now that he looks around, he sees bilingual signs everywhere reminding visitors that the forestry department belongs to the National Capital Commission.

"Where's the IT team?" he asks the forestry receptionist, a boy who seems barely out of his teens.

"Outside," the boy says with a heavy Québécois accent.

"Where outside? Like, in the quad?"

The boy shakes his head. "Outside."

Janwar returns to the IT department and leaves a Post-it on Alvin's monitor bezel: *Janwar Gupta left the new blade. Please get him a SHROUD account and call 778-889-1850 when complete.*

They'd probably just email him anyway, but he might as well try to get a real person on the line.

In the afternoon, Janwar has to face not only another operation's worth of anxiety over the continued existence of another patient, but also interacting with José and Emanda.

José calls him "Angel" again, which, now that Janwar knows more about Dr. M and his experimentation, has accrued a far more sinister valence. Janwar's hands clench so hard he can't let go of his syringe. Dr. Brank would be proud that he's feeling angry, instead of guilty. He leans in toward the smaller man and speaks under his breath. "Can you fucking stop with the Dr. Mengele shit?"

"Listen, Angel," José says. "In 1974, Pinochet's death squads kidnapped my grandfather from his house in Santiago, flew him up in a helicopter, and dropped him in the river. I think I've earned the right to joke about atrocities."

"That atrocity, maybe. But not other people's."

José shrugs. "I don't think Dr. Mengele did any experiments on Indians. Just Jews, dwarves, twins, homosexuals, and Gypsies. So it's not like it's your tragedy, either."

"Don't assume I'm only one type of minority. You don't know I'm not gay and that I don't have a twin."

"Touché."

"Did you grow up in Argentina?" Janwar says.

"Santiago is in Chile, fuckface. And I grew up here. South Keys born and raised."

"What about Henry?"

"What *about* Henry?"

"Did one of his family members go sky-diving?"

"Fuck you. Henry's from rural Nova Scotia. He can make all the jokes he wants because he's black."

"What does his tattoo say?"

"On his arm? That's not a tattoo. That's a scar."

Janwar puts his syringe down. Karan and Mildred are the surgeons in this operation. Janwar wants to get Karan alone for questioning, but he isn't quick enough on the draw, and the man disappears while Janwar's distracted by the sound of Mildred grinding her teeth.

After the operation, Janwar expects Horace to pull him aside, since, as far as Horace knows, Janwar is responsible for getting him in trouble. But Horace doesn't say peep, just closes the flip case on his tablet and walks off. Maybe that's weird, or maybe he's just the nonconfrontational type.

A quick Internet search backs José up—the Rio Mapocho

does flow through Santiago, and Pinochet was the Chilean dictator from 1974 to 1990.

Diego's death probably isn't connected to his Argentinian heritage, or at least, if it is, it's not through José. Although that's not to say José didn't switch the vials back while Janwar was focused on Diego's EKG and before Rasheeda locked the cart. Or maybe he could have switched the vials before the operation, in some way Janwar hasn't yet determined.

Leaving aside the fact that someone would probably have spotted him fiddling, José couldn't have just taken another employee's tablet. A tablet is an identity at the hospital. Each tablet has a fingerprint reader, and you have to launch the app and press your thumb on the metal pad to validate your permission to unlock the cart. You have five minutes to do so before you have to prove your identity again, and unless José had cut off an anaesthesiologist's thumb and kept it on his keychain…

The fact that Janwar doesn't know how the initial switch could have happened and that his whole presumption of innocence rests on someone having switched the vials is worrisome, but he pushes it from his mind. For the time being he has a lot of other questions, and he can't get bogged down in this one detail.

In the hall, Janwar passes Brett Rutan. Instinctively Janwar tenses. But the man looks him right in the eyes and nods, as if they were colleagues. The investigation must be complete from his point of view, and now he's onto the next medical fuck-up, the next pair of scissors left inside someone's abdominal cavity, the next organ theft from the morgue, the next patient getting frightened by Victor's presumably drug-induced situation-independent and overly tenacious erections, which no structureless scrub pant could contain. Janwar could question Brett, but why would he answer? That's the problem with being an amateur detective—leverage.

Janwar runs into Fang when he's about to go to the cafeteria for dinner. She says she's heard what happened, and she's there for him. Like, seriously there for him, if he needs anything. The implication that arises here makes Janwar uncomfortable. When they walked home from the bar, she made clear that they were colleagues, and only colleagues. He wonders what's changed.

He has avoided seeking out casual sex up to this point in his life because he's afraid he'd fall in love. Or, that's what he's told himself, but now Janwar realizes that this is simplistic and is most likely because casual sex has never been explicitly offered to him—a perspective he's kind of been submerging. Regardless, Janwar isn't in any shape to determine if casual sex is what Fang is offering. "I appreciate it." Janwar tells himself he will leave it at that.

Fang suggests they go to Minsky's Diner for dinner. Minsky's is where the hospital staff eat when they get sick of being on campus, about a fifteen-minute walk away. Janwar agrees. "Every once in a while I have to take a break from the embalming fluid they sell us in the Tulip," Fang says.

Mr. and Mrs. Minsky are real sweethearts, a couple in their eighties, and they still run the place, which is pretty much as it was in the 1960s: black-and-white-tiled floors, shiny counters, and blue sparkly seats with curved backs reminiscent of a Corvette Stingray. A framed photo on one wall shows a young man sitting on a stool at the counter, and Janwar can see right away that it is Mr. Minsky, probably in his early twenties. The photo and the actual man have the same smile. There's something life-affirming about the permanence of the smile, even though the man's vitality is fading away.

"Some coffee, love?" Mrs. Minsky says.

Janwar nods.

Fang puts her hand on his forearm. "I'll get your meal. I'm flush right now."

Black liquid pours from the carafe into his mug.

Janwar has to be careful around diners with free refills. He likes coffee, but if he drinks too much his anxiety gets out of control.

"Thank you, 289." Fang bows her head. "Moment of silence?"

Janwar has just killed a man and Fang has won money from the dead pool.

"Is 289…?"

"Oh, fuck. No, 289 was a massive internal hemorrhage. Got hit by a VIA Rail train. Car stalled crossing the tracks, I think. That's so shitty of me, though. I shouldn't have mentioned it."

"It's okay. So Llew won last week, and you won this week?"

"It's been a long time coming."

"But, like, aren't there ways to spend money that have a greater return? After you left the other day, Aspen called me a pussy for not joining. She made cat noises."

"Aspen? What a freak. The dead pool is more of a social status thing. It's like having a polo pony or a golf membership. It's part of the lifestyle. You know, like those rich fucks in the Hamptons who can say, 'Polo is my life,' and mean it. It's what separates us from the patients."

"It's kind of sick, isn't it?"

"It's not like we're killing anyone," Fang says. "Oh fuck.

Sorry."

"Has anything like this happened to you?" Janwar takes a few bites out of his burger, but he isn't hungry.

"Almost. I was about to administer a drug, I can't remember what, and then one of the nurses was like, 'Wait, what are you doing? That's 10 per cent! And I was like, 'Damn yo, when did they change the vials?'"

Janwar's phone rings. A number with way too many digits.

"Hello?"

"Hi?" A woman's voice, Eastern European, with the parking-garage echo that signals an overseas connection.

"Janwar Gupta, speaking?"

"This is Katerinka? I was told to create a SHROUD account for Janwar Gupta?"

"Yes, that's right?" Janwar can't help lifting his inflection at the end of the sentence like Katerinka does. He imagines her as very attractive, in the manner of many Eastern European women he has seen but not known, in the biblical sense.

Janwar takes down his username, which is "jagupta," and his password, which is a random string of digits and letters. Janwar is pretty sure he got them right. In fact, it's easier to tell the difference between 1 and L and 0 and O when dictated by an Eastern European woman than when you see it written down. "Thank you. Can I ask, where are you? The connection makes it sound like you're really far away."

"Georgia?"

"Like, Atlanta?"

"No, like Tbilisi?"

"How did you end up working for—" Janwar catches himself. Fang is looking at him, interested. She could ask him who it is. He could tell her he was talking to the hospital's IT department. He realizes "outside" is in Tbilisi, outsourced, and that in itself probably wouldn't compromise his investigation, but he is a terrible liar, meaning he is terrible at lying, especially when he has to think on his feet, and if Fang asks a follow-up question, he might freeze. He doesn't know if Fang's involved. He hopes she's not.

Katerinka is speaking again. "My manager said something about victory, and now we spend all our time working for this hospital in America?"

"Canada."

"Whatever?"

"Okay, thanks." Janwar hangs up.

"Who was that?"

"The bank. Making sure the credit-card charges in Ottawa are me." Janwar is proud of this lie.

"How thorough. Where was I?" Fang asks.

"Uh, we were at, 'Damn yo!'"

"Right."

"Listen, Fang, how serious is the surgery-anaesthesiology rivalry?"

"It got pretty violent at one point, just over stupid dick measuring, but now just nobody talks to each other. Why? Is someone hassling you?"

"Nah, just curious. How violent is pretty violent?"

"Victor got a black eye. I think he actually cracked an orbit, and Carla lost a tooth—I think that's all. A punch-up in the surgery rec room. It wasn't long after I started here."

"Over what?"

"Like I said, dick measuring. Or, I guess, clit measuring?"

Mrs. Minsky interrupts them with the bill. Fang pays cash and they leave the restaurant.

Fang moves to cross the street against the light, but Janwar balks, so Fang stops too.

"Let's just wait," Janwar says.

"There's no traffic."

"We're in no rush."

Fang's brow furrows and then smooths. "Whatever. What are you doing after work?"

"I'm not sure," Janwar says. His heartbeat speeds up.

"What did you do after work yesterday, Janwar?"

"Honestly?"

"No, Janwar, I want you to lie to me. Yes, honestly."

"I drank an unreasonable amount of bourbon while sitting on the floor of the shower."

"Uh."

"Yeah. But I felt surprisingly good this morning. Like, I had that terrible clarity that—"

"Okay, I feel like you not knowing what you're doing this evening is a bad thing. How about I come over and we watch a movie or something?"

It's probably best for Fang, and everyone else, to think that Janwar isn't investigating anything, is just flying on autopilot, as if he hasn't thought of Gupta's wager.

The white man lights up on the crosswalk signal, and Janwar and Fang cross the street. There does seem to be a sexual element to this offer. Fang is very pretty, and it isn't like he's dating Susan or anything. It's just one date. Janwar isn't really sure how casual sex works, but he has two thoughts about it in rapid succession: one, it is almost certainly better than casual jerking off; and, two, is he capable of performing? This is a time of extreme stress, after all.

Now he is no longer fixated on Diego's death but instead on whether or not his sadness-masturbating has ruined him for women, and he feels driven in the same way that he was driven to analyze the Diego situation. To prove his virility to himself—if sex is explicitly what Fang wants, of course.

"Sure," he says.

Janwar is thankful for the air conditioning in Fang's Lexus. Unmufflered motorcycles bearing leather-jacketed men and women in German military-style helmets shoal around them at a stoplight on Bronson. Each has a patch on his or her arm that reads "1%." Janwar has visions of motorcycle chains crashing through the windows, but the riders don't give them a second look, and when the signal changes, they roar off, each hog climbing through the gears like a walking bass line.

Janwar wonders about the 1% patch. He's seen it a few times. Luckily, he lives in a time where the gap between wondering something and knowing the answer is almost zero, as long as he's above ground. His phone tells him the 1% patch refers to a comment by the American Motorcyclist Association in 1948, in which they said 99% of motorcyclists followed the law. The outlaw gangs therefore took the remaining number, 1%, as theirs, calling themselves one-percenters.

"Funny," Janwar muses. "In 1948, the 1 % were the rebels."

"What?"

Janwar explains what he's just learned about motorcycle gangs, and how that relates to Occupy Wall Street, but Fang's not interested. She's driving, so he gives her a pass.

Fang parks her car in the underground parkade of Dr. Flecktarn's building, and they walk up to the lobby. The concierge is listening to the radio.

"Tune in weekday mornings at six to the *Bobby Dasler* breakfast show, with Bobby and Juliana," the radio says, before the soundbed changes and the program cuts to an advertisement: "Lowell Chilton Real Estate," goes the jingle. "It'll get less real if you decide to wait!"

As Janwar and Fang round the corner toward the elevator, the super is walking down the hallway toward them. Super Giacomo, as Janwar thinks of him, lives in the apartment next door to Dr. Flecktarn's. He is a young man, maybe twenty-five, Janwar's age. His family's company owns the building.

"Hey, buddy. Big night?" Giacomo winks.

"The biggest." Janwar winks back, but his wink is so exaggerated it is like he is sighting down a rifle.

Giacomo laughs. He throws his head back, giving Janwar a look at his strikingly hair-free nostrils. The elevator is mirrored on all surfaces except the floor, which still disconcerts Janwar. Sometimes he doesn't recognize himself and flinches when he catches his reflection in his peripheral vision. For a brief second he imagines sexual positions with Fang in the elevator, Bombay/Beijing Calculus refracted through various angles. No, he doesn't know what she wants from Brown. That's only a possibility, and he shouldn't get himself all worked up.

Dr. Brank told him not to use "should" or "shouldn't" statements, because they foster guilt, but in this case, no, fantasizing about having sex with Fang in the elevator is something he really shouldn't be doing.

"I've always wondered what Ellis's place is like" is Fang's first sentence once they reach the apartment on the fourth floor. She doesn't seem to notice the number of flies orbiting the empty bourbon bottle. "A kind of morbid fascination, I guess. Does it weird you out at all?"

"Why morbid?"

"Oh, I guess that's the wrong choice of words."

"Why would it weird me out?"

She stares at him for a second. "Just…staying in someone else's house when they're not there…"

Janwar files this under "more weird shit that's going on." He'll try to push Fang on it later. "Give me a sec, I just need to send an email."

He withdraws to the bedroom with his laptop and uncrumples the Post-it notes with the URL for SHROUD and his username and password. SHROUD looks like the ticket system he used to report problems with his home Internet. OPREP (Operation Reporting) is the most logical ticket type, and, yes, he can assign it to Venolia Parker in Records. He shudders at the thought of her zombielike skin.

OPREP-9854 Need List of Patient Deaths During Operations Last Five Years.

Hi Venolia! I was down this morning to talk to you.

Can I please get a list of patient deaths during operations in the last five years and access to the files on each?

He sets the priority to "Blocker," meaning it's blocking him from getting work done, because that's true.

There's a field for "Business Case" and a field for "Manager Comments." He has to hope Llew won't get a notification that he filed a ticket, and also that Venolia won't require further approval to begin the task. Maybe these fields are optional, but Janwar has a feeling they're not.

Fang is looking through Dr. Flecktarn's bookshelf when Janwar returns. Medical textbooks. Classics, like the version of *Moby Dick* with the line drawing in various shades of blue on the cover, and that extra-creepy version of *Lolita* with the prepubescent lips.

"So what do you want to watch? Something funny? Something intense?" Janwar rinses the bourbon bottle and puts it in the recycling. Maybe the flies will leave if there's nothing else edible around.

"People always want to watch funny things, so I never get to watch intense movies with other people, which is the only time I want to watch them, because, you know, they're so intense."

"Awesome. We're on the same page, or frame, or whatever."

"What have you got?"

They crouch down in front of the giant plasma television to look at the shelf. As the shelf is deeper than the DVD cases, some DVDs are pushed in more than others. Fang starts pulling them out so they're all equal.

"You really are OCD, aren't you?"

Fang nods. "Let me tell you a story. Once during undergrad I was sitting on the porch of the super-ghetto house I lived in, cramming for a test, and I heard a car accident, like squealing tires and people screaming and shit. I ran around the corner and this chick was lying on the ground and syringes and little plastic bags of powder were scattered around her."

"Coke?"

"Coke, heroin, I don't know. She'd been punched out through the windshield of her car, so there was lots of glass too. And blood. I had no idea what to do."

Janwar raises his eyebrow.

"Come on. I wasn't a doctor yet. I was nineteen. I was studying chemistry."

At nineteen, Janwar was a volunteer for St. John's Ambulance and would have known what to do. Sometimes he forgets not all doctors, or prospective doctors, followed his career path. "Go on."

"She said something and I bent my ear down to her mouth. Her face was totally fucked."

"Totally fucked in what way?"

"Like standard-parts-missing fucked. She said to help her, but all I could think to do was to carefully pick up all of the syringes and the baggies and put them back into her purse and zip it up."

"After calling an ambulance though?"

Fang shakes her head. "Eventually someone came out from one of the other houses and called an ambulance. That's how OCD I am."

Did she keep any of the baggies? Maybe that's an uncharitable thing to think. "And now you're a doctor."

"Doesn't that wig you out a little?"

"Well, you're not in emerg. You've got a bit more control over situations as an anaesthesiologist."

"And thank God. Am I right?"

They look at the DVDs.

"I think I remember hearing about this one." Janwar hands Fang the slipcase.

"'Unpredictable and rich with symbolism, this Argentinian murder mystery lives up to its Oscar.' Sure, sounds dope. But, uh, you down with watching an 'Argentinian murder mystery'?"

"I'll be okay."

Dr. Flecktarn's DVD player looks like it was carved out of a solid piece of metal, but when Janwar touches the glowing red light, a tray separates and slides out. Janwar deposits the disc and it disappears without leaving even the hint of a seam. Janwar wonders how much of the cost of the player went into the precision machining necessary for this illusion and how much went into the actual picture quality. At this moment he feels very much like his father. The first time he bought a jacket that wasn't waterproof he felt a deep sense of shame, probably more shame than he felt at masturbating in the bathroom of the Canadian National Institute for the Blind, post–Thetis Lake.

Janwar folds himself into the couch. A blanket is still out from when he was watching Westerns. He offers it to Fang. Outside the rain starts. Heavy drops streak the windows.

"Thanks." She wraps it around herself and sits on the couch next to him.

The giant screen snaps into life, and Janwar starts the film. It has the predominantly yellow and green colour palette Janwar associates with French and South American films. An older man is writing a novel in the year 2000 about a murder case he was investigating in 1975. He is talking about it with a woman he is obviously in love with, but whom he isn't *with* with. The narrative flashes back into the past.

Within ten minutes, Fang lists to the side like a ferry that has struck a sandbar. She puts her head on his shoulder and he puts his arm around her. She snuggles into him. They stay like this for a while. It's nice. Janwar feels loved in a platonic way, like a dog has fallen asleep on his lap. He tries to head a possible erection off at the pass, and seems to be successful, so far. What he was thinking before about proving his capacity has dissipated in the face of this pleasant feeling. The fact that she is so sleepy suggests that she probably isn't going to suggest they do coke, which is one less awkward situation for him to navigate. Janwar still hasn't determined exactly how he feels about it, but if anyone is going to be conscientious about their drug use, it is an anaesthesiologist, so it isn't likely she's putting herself in a lot of danger.

Fang makes a satisfied noise, mumbles something and pushes her head further into him, starting to arrange herself into a horizontal position.

"Fang, did you want to lie down?"

"Mmmm."

Janwar and Fang adjust themselves so that his spine is up against the back of the couch and her spine is up against the front of him.

Fang says something that sounds like, "It's only for two weeks."

"What?"

"Most importantly, mind which side you're on. Any questions, talk to me."

Janwar doesn't respond to any of her further comments, which all seem to be instructions. Who is she instructing?

Janwar watches the movie in silence for a while. The killer, wearing a garishly patterned shirt, is caught in a football stadium. The woman the investigator is in love with questions the killer's masculinity, in a way that makes Janwar, even though he understands that it is a psychological questioning strategy, uncomfortable about his own masculinity, his strength, his potency, until the killer snaps, hits the woman in the face, says he fucked the shit out of the murder victim.

But this is only halfway through the movie. The killer is set free by the investigator's corrupt boss by way of revenge on the investigator for a previous conflict, under the auspices of the killer's being suitable for spying on subversives, the Dirty War being more important to the corrupt boss than justice.

At one point a series of gunshots ring out, and Fang snorts. Janwar strokes her flank by way of reassurance. He thinks about guys calling her "sweetflanx" by text and nearly laughs, but manages to suppress it. He is feeling sleepy. Her neck looks like a very soft and good place to put his face. He nestles it in there and she starts.

"Wha!"

"Huh?" Janwar assumed that she wanted to cuddle. Is he in fact invading her personal space? Is he being a creep? Does she now consider him a potential abuser?

"You need a shave."

"I'm sorry, I thought—"

"Don't worry about it. I'm kind of a cuddly sleeper. Your neckbeard is just prickly as fuck."

"Really, I—"

"Honestly. This has happened to me before and, trust me, shit got way more awkward."

Janwar starts to stand up, then realizes he is putting himself in a position of power over her. He sits down again, but further away from her.

"I feel like I need to explain. I don't even have an erection—"

"Don't worry about it. But, shit, if I'm falling asleep, I should go home. We have to work tomorrow."

"I'm not sure I'm comfortable with you driving home if you're this sleepy."

"I'm fine."

"Like, I don't mean, stay here and have sex with me." That's the wrong thing to say. "That's the wrong thing to say."

"It's okay. I appreciate your directness. Honestly, this isn't a big deal."

"I mean, stay here on the couch and I'll sleep in my room

and we'll chalk this one up to a misunderstanding and you can leave in the morning."

"No, it's fine." Fang finds her purse. She checks her phone, and her eyebrows go up. She responds right away, angling the screen away from Janwar.

"Everything cool?" Janwar says.

"I'm the worst," Fang says.

Janwar can't very well keep her on his couch, so he lets her go, hoping the nighttime roads, now wet with rain, are forgiving of a sleepy anaesthesiologist possibly going to visit someone she'll regret visiting in the morning.

Janwar returns to his couch alone and goes back to *El secreto de sus ojos*. The investigator learns what has happened: the husband of the murdered woman has kidnapped the killer and locked him in a cell in his shed for twenty-five years. The investigator returns from the husband's property and goes into the office of the woman he has been in love with all this time. They look at each other meaningfully. She says it's complicated, and then she tells him to shut the door.

Janwar tries to examine how he feels about all this, especially being kept in someone's backyard for twenty-five years without them ever speaking to you, but his mind balks and retreats to a less horrifying place, namely, focusing on the psychedelic patterns behind his now-closed and rolled-up eyes. He is asleep before the credits end, but of course he has nightmares until morning.

EXHIBIT E

TRANSCRIPT OF AUDIO RECORDING FOUND ON SUSAN JONESTOWN'S CELLPHONE

SPEAKING: SUSAN JONESTOWN, SHAUGHNESSY O'DEADY, JEAN-MARIE DUFOIS

Saturday, July 5

At the Civic Lazarus. During my break I'll try to track down Dr. Parker.

Shunted Venolia down the priority list. Someone I'd forgotten about is standing in line: the red-haired man who took the therapy dogs from Martina yesterday is waiting to order behind a group of priests.

SHAUGHNESSY O'DEADY: An Americano, please.

SUSAN JONESTOWN: Double shot?

SO: Yes please. Odd there's no Canadiano.

SJ: Probably just as well. The Italians came up with the name Americano during the second world war. It was to make fun of the American soldiers who had to water down their espresso because they couldn't handle the strength.

SO: Glad it's them and not us.

SJ: Hey, I saw you with a couple giant skinny dogs the other day. What do you do in the therapy dog department?

SO: I'm an anaesthesiologist, but I help out here from time to time. My parents raised greyhounds in Ireland. This is my way of kicking back at the pricks.

SJ: In what way?

SO: Being kind to greyhounds and using them to benefit mankind. Imagine how much it would piss off your pig farmer father if you told him you got a pet porker.

SJ: But your parents didn't kill greyhounds, did they?

SO: They sure did. Not for meat, but they'd euthanize them when they'd finished racing, around age two. Or they'd sell them for cosmetics testing. I was pretty gutted about it growing up.

SJ: The silence of the greyhounds. Hey, what's your name?

SO: Shaughnessy O'Deady.

SJ: Susan Jonestown.

SO: Susan, your glove is the sexiest thing I've ever seen.

SJ: I haven't heard that one before. Points for originality. I just picked it for function. The glove, I mean.

SO: What function would that be?

SJ: The espresso machine at my usual location gets red-card WHMIS violation hot.

SO: What do you have on later?

SJ: Not this glove.

SO: Regardless, any chance you fancy a pint?

SJ: You know what, why not?

SO: Seven at the Sir John A?

SJ: I'll see you then.

On break. Inhaled a cigarette so fast that my head feels full of bees. Shaughnessy is obviously a creep but this is my in. If we meet in a public place and I don't go to a second location, I'll be safe.

Heading back in to look for Venolia.

The receptionist at information desk is the baby-faced man from the therapy department, Jean-Marie. He must be a general temp. He's shuffling a deck of Magic: The Gathering cards.

SUSAN JONESTOWN: Excuse me.

JEAN-MARIE DUFOIS: You again. Little Miss Nosy.

SJ: Watch it, pal. I'm taller than you.

JD: But your nose—

SJ: I'm aware.

JD: Well, what can I do you for?

SJ: A woman wearing scrubs named Venolia gave me a twenty for her coffee and walked away. I was hoping you could tell me where to find her.

JD: You can leave it with me and I'll make sure she gets it.

SJ: Not a chance, buster.

JD: What was the name again? Venolia? No, that can't be right.

SJ: Why not?

JD: She doesn't drink coffee.

SJ: How do you know that?

JD: She's more into relaxing. Infamous for it, actually.

SJ: It was decaf. The coffee.

JD: Of course.

SJ: No, don't dial. I'll go find her. Where does she work?

JD: Records. Want me to draw you a map?

SJ: Please do. But stick to this plane, Ajani Goldmane.

Based on Jean-Marie's map, I don't have time to make it all the way to Records, which is in the basement at the opposite end of the hospital, before I'm due back at Lazarus.

Shift is over, but nobody's in the records department. I might as well keep digging on my phone while I wait.

Walking to the bus stop now. Waited half an hour but Venolia never showed up. Just a man with bad acne scars along his jaw who leaned in the door.

Googled Shaughnessy, but he didn't have any online presence. Surprising for a man who looked in his mid thirties.

Maybe he had all the usual accounts under a pseudonym. Or maybe he was only part of that social network where doctors share photos of the insides of people's bodies to help others make diagnoses.

So anyway, unlike the guys I'd met online and creeped before going on dates with them, I didn't have any of the other information about Shaughnessy that people reveal on their profiles.

Digging makes me think of paws, and paws equals paw wax. Frig, I've been so focused on where the drugs came from...

Red Lantern Paw Wax: Official Supplier of the Canadian Rangers and Canadian Junior Rangers.

Canadian Rangers, a.k.a. Northern Rangers: a military force made of aboriginal volunteers. Patrolling the Arctic by dogsled, wearing red cotton sweatshirts. Reminding the Russians that Canada wants the Northern oil once the ice caps melt.

Arctic sovereignty means a possible Harper government connection? Maybe a coincidence. But that's what the newspapers said about Gary Webb and the whole CIA/Contra/crack cocaine story, and eventually the papers admitted he was right. Too bad he'd already committed suicide.

CHAPTER 6

Agent Scully – Double D – Iron Fist – Mistakes Were Made – Hydroplane – Thoughts for Docs – Expressionist Codpiece – Fail – The Big Kiwi – Watching the Insects

Friday, July 11

When Janwar looks at his phone after his first operation of the day on Friday, he sees he has three email notifications from SHROUD. First, Venolia Parker changed the priority of OPREP-9854 from Blocker to Trivial. Second, Venolia Parker assigned OPREP-9854 to Llewellyn Cadwaladr. And finally, Venolia Parker commented on OPREP-9854:

[~*LCadwaladr*] *Can you please approve this request?*

Fuck. He could delete the ticket, but Llew would probably still have a record of it in his email, and then how would Janwar get the information? All he can hope is that Llew, in the manner of administrators everywhere, subscribes to every notification possible, and if Janwar gets Venolia to close the ticket, Llew might miss it among the thousand other emails he gets a day.

Venolia has something he wants—access to the records. She did ask Janwar for a prescription in a way that seemed like it probably wasn't a joke. Janwar isn't too naive to believe that hospital staffers either prescribe drugs to themselves or have friends do it for them. Venolia had laughed when he asked if she had the flu. Flu symptoms are also very similar to symptoms of opiate withdrawal—runny nose, sweating, agitation. So maybe he should just go back down and offer to write Venolia a prescription for whatever she's looking for. She'll get it from someone anyway. And if it isn't okay for medical student interns to fake a supervisor's signature and write prescriptions in exchange for favours, it really isn't okay for them to kill patients, so he isn't getting himself in that much more trouble.

He's got Llew's signature on the emailed letter of offer for the internship. A couple of loops and squiggles. Not too hard. He grabs a prescription pad, checks his pockets to make sure he has at least one pen, and heads for the elevator.

Venolia is reading a different magazine bearing the coverline "See Agent Scully's Pink Tunnel" when Janwar returns to Records. She doesn't put it down when Janwar says her name.

"Venolia."

"What."

Janwar hasn't thought out exactly how to introduce his offer. He looks over his shoulder to make sure nobody is coming and then slams the prescription pad down on the desk.

Venolia looks up. "You again." She looks back down at the magazine.

"Can we leave Agent Scully alone for a minute?"

Venolia doesn't look up this time. "No."

"Remember I asked if I could help you with anything and—"

Venolia drops the magazine, revealing, guess what, Agent Scully's pink tunnel.

"Where did you even get this thing, a corner store in 1995?"

"Oxy," Venolia says.

"What?"

"That's what I want," she says, to the tune of "Money" by the Beatles. "Oh yeah."

Judging by the jittery surgeons, enforcement is fairly lax. And if this helps him dig himself out, maybe it's worth the risk of further punitive action…

"What are you waiting for? Come on, then."

"All right. Don't we need to be subtle about this?"

"Do I look like I want to wait any longer?" Her face is even more ashen than the previous day, and patches of yellow sweat spread under her arms.

"Fair enough. So in exchange for OxyContin you will fill my ticket."

"Yes."

"Today."

"Yes."

A connection sparks in Janwar's brain. "Are you having trouble getting Oxy? I thought there was an Oxy epidemic."

"My usual connection said something is going on, I have to hold tight, just for a couple of weeks."

"That's all he said?"

"Nice try. That's all he or she or they said, yes."

"How much can I get away with giving you?"

"Ninety caps of 30 milligrams."

"Thirty milligrams is a lot."

"I know how much I need. I used to be a doctor. I made some personal mistakes, but there's never been any issue with my work."

Janwar transcribes the amount onto the pad and squiggles his signature along with his attempt at Llew's. "You were an MD?"

"Yes, an anaesthesiologist." Venolia reaches for the prescription.

Janwar jerks back, deciding that withholding the prescription until he has the papers might be a good idea. He raises his arm above his head. “Once you fill the research request.”

“That’s bullying. I’m calling HR.” Venolia grabs for the prescription again, but even standing she can’t come close to the height of Janwar’s hand. A droplet of sweat splats onto her magazine.

“How long will it take?” Janwar says.

Venolia sighs. “Come back at four.”

“So you were an anaesthesiologist? Here?”

“Yes.”

“Were you a Pusher or a Mixer?”

“What?”

“A Pusher or a Mixer?”

“I heard you the first time. I just have no idea what you’re fucking talking about. I’ve been down here for ten years.”

“Why didn’t they just fire you for whatever it was you did?”

“There’s a limit to my garrulousness.”

Janwar waves the prescription again.

“I’m useful in Records.”

“Useful how? To whom?”

Venolia taps her head. “Think.”

“So you’re telling me that even if you fill this request I can’t trust the data?”

Venolia nods. “I won’t change anything from this point. I do owe you. But I can’t guarantee the data is correct as it stands now. And you’d better be back right at four. Remember, even med students have records. You sure do. Whew boy.”

“Can I get a copy of that record too?”

Venolia sighs.

Janwar can’t figure out where the nurse rotation is posted, so he asks the nurse during the next operation if Rasheeda is working again this week.

"She's off," Ashley says. "Holiday in Florida."

Rasheeda's absence is obviously not proof of complicity or lack thereof. It means there are more questions Janwar's not going to be able to answer at the moment. Although taking her out of his investigation feels like scratching off a name in a Clue notebook, it's really not, Janwar has to remind himself. For a second he wonders if she's actually been kidnapped, so she doesn't say anything about whatever she saw during the operation, forcing her to violate OC Transpo Bylaw number 656, which he's noticed is posted on every bus and in every bus stop: "If you see something, say something."

But it's probably easier to kill someone and make it look like an accident than to hold them against their will. And what would happen after? They'd have to kill her anyway, wouldn't they? He decides she probably is in Florida slamming margaritas by a swimming pool.

After the operation, Janwar heads to the Tulip Cafe to re-up on coffee. He hopes Fang won't be there. The business last night wasn't too awkward, all things considered, but still. A cooling-off period would be good. He could go to the Lazarus Coffee by the entrance to avoid her, but that's a long walk.

He's in luck. Carla is sitting at a table by herself, and she waves him over. Janwar doesn't know Carla too well, but she's a human being who can provide conversation and she isn't Fang. He signals with his bandaged finger that he will join her in a second.

His phone rings on the way to the table. He looks at the screen. His parents. If he doesn't pick up, Ajay will keep calling and calling. He picks up. Garati.

"Have you heard anything around the hospital about that anaesthesiologist?"

"Which one?"

"The Ottawa anaesthesiologist. The one that's in the news."

"The Victoria newspapers?"

"No, the Ottawa ones."

Janwar feels a flash of anger. He knows his mother is just interested in his life, and of course reading the Ottawa newspapers is a way to connect, but she's got to realize he's at work.

"The news I've seen is all about OxyContin. There's some sort of crisis." And he's part of it. Janwar Gupta, pusher—with a lowercase P. Venolia better be telling the truth about knowing her limit. If another person dies because of him… Christ, Janwar. He grasps for a topic change. "Some new exciting condo development is going up that's very environmentally friendly. I don't think I saw anything about an anaesthesiologist."

"One of the anaesthesiologists at the Ottawa Civic was arrested and charged with multiple counts of sexual assault a few months ago. And now he's starting to serve his sentence."

"Which one?"

"Fletcher, something like that."

"Flecktarn?"

"I don't think so, but maybe."

It's got to be. "What did he do?"

"Even though staff were standing on the other side of the sterile screen, he put his penis into twenty-nine women's mouths while they were sedated."

"Mom!"

"That's a lot of women."

"Mom!"

"What? Are you upset I said 'penis'? You're a doctor. Or

almost a doctor."

Janwar can hear Ajay shouting in the background, "Provided everything goes well."

Everything hasn't been going well, and Janwar knows that's why he's getting angry, but he can't stop the feeling. He also can't figure out what to say.

"Is everything not going well? You can tell me. Your father and I are here for you."

Janwar holds the phone away from his face for a second. He and Dr. Brank haven't gotten too far into Janwar's relationship with his parents.

"Or is it the 'a lot of women' comment? We haven't heard anything from you about nice girls in a long time."

"I have to go," Janwar says.

Ajay is shouting something in the background. The speaker scrapes as Garati covers the mouthpiece and then uncovers it again.

"Before you go, your father is asking if you can recommend some whisky to him. His new obsession is stocking a liquor cabinet for when people come over."

"I thought he gardened when people came over." Janwar's voice comes out far meaner than he intends.

"Don't use that voice with me, Janwar Aashish Gupta."

"I'm sorry, Mom."

"Anyway, that was last week. I'm trying to get him to socialize. If he has something to focus on—"

"Wild Turkey." Janwar's stomach twists even saying the words. "Okay, I'm going to hang up."

"Son, if you ever want to talk—" Garati says, but Janwar feels his chest seize again.

He says, "I have to go, Mom. Goodbye," doesn't listen to the response, and disconnects.

By now he is at the table, and Carla is looking at him with a quizzical expression.

"My mother just phoned to tell me about a series of sexual assaults conducted by an anaesthesiologist at Ottawa Civic. By the man whose apartment I'm staying in."

Carla breathes out through her teeth. "We were hoping that wouldn't come out. I want to assure you Ellis didn't do anything at home. You never know what goes on in hotel rooms between duvet washings. Think of it like that."

So Janwar had hoped to have sex with Fang in a rapist's apartment. Jesus. In Dr. Flecktarn's own bed, where Janwar has been sleeping.

Trying to quell the rising tide of nausea, Janwar attempts to connect this new fact to his investigation. He fills out a mental index card with the phrase "Anaesthesia Sex Ring" and pins it to his mental bulletin board. He should get this stuff down on paper soon.

"Did you know anything about it?" he asks.

"Everyone in the department was as surprised as everyone else. An unconscious and paralyzed patient doesn't make any noise. And you really can't see what's going on on the other side of the screen."

"Does anyone still talk to him?"

"No, he's in jail."

"But someone must have secured his permission for me to use his apartment."

"Oh, yeah, I guess Llew had someone get in touch, someone from University of Ottawa housing, when we knew you were coming. Thought we'd save you from staying in a hotel."

"Were they friends? Llew and Ellis?"

"They were colleagues."

"I have to ask, Carla, everyone talks about what hot stuff Llew is with GHB. Did he do anything that got him taken out of active service like Venolia?"

"Venolia?"

"The woman in Records?"

"I didn't know Venolia did anything to get there beyond library science. She's been there since I first came to the hospital. And no, Llew's done nothing like that. What's with all the questions?"

"So Llew did do something then?" Janwar tries to look as discreet as possible. It works or, at least, doesn't prevent Carla from giving in after a long pause.

"Honestly, between you and me, he got into his own supply a little. Him and Double D. That's all. If you don't drink at the same time, I've heard GHB can be a fun drug to take in small amounts. And he knew exactly what small amounts to take. But that was a long time ago."

"Double D?"

"Oh." Carla's eyes dart up and back down. "She's not here anymore. You wouldn't know her."

"Too bad," Janwar says.

He takes a sip of his coffee. It tastes like lychee nuts for no discernible reason, so he mentions that to Carla.

"Better lychee nuts than almonds," she says. "Or, wait, no, it's the smell of almonds that..."

Suicide is painless... Janwar extricates himself from yet another conversation about ways to die and heads back to the OR.

On the way, he searches "Flecktarn + Sexual Assault" on his phone and taps the "News" tab, and sure enough, Dr. Ellis Flecktarn, Ottawa Civic Hospital, double-digit despoiler.

After another successful operation, Janwar feels as if he has gained more control over his life. Wearing a mask makes him feel more whole, somehow, like it's keeping his face together, and he begins thinking about next steps. He has two avenues of inquiry while he waits for Venolia to fill his records request: one, the dead pool, and two, trying to get the surgeons to talk, in case they know something or saw something during the operation he didn't. The dead pool is the simplest to explore, so he'll start with that.

Fang said all the doctors played in the dead pool. Wouldn't it make sense that someone would try to fix it, the way promoters fix boxing matches? Meaning that they would try to ensure a certain patient died in order to make sure they got paid? It's a stretch, but now that Janwar is thinking about it he can't stop, picturing medical staff in poorly chosen civvies and big sunglasses slipping envelopes of cash into each other's newspapers at neighbourhood cafes, doctors in the OR calculating dosages twice, once to cure and once to kill. Janwar is now unable to shake the idea that emergency patients' survival is based more on the fluctuations of some secret market than the best efforts of talented and selfless men and women...

Janwar decides to skip lunch and pay a visit to the intensive care unit. He'll say he's interested in joining the dead pool. That'll be more likely to get results than blustering in there and trying to alpha the shit out of everyone.

First he'll ask who he has to talk to about the pool. He'll find out how much money it takes to play, what the average payout is. Whether there's ever been anything suspicious before. How they deal with debt. And if he isn't getting any answers, he'll bring up Diego and see what comes out.

The ICU takes up a massive L-shaped space on the second floor. Janwar shares the elevator coming down with two gurneys and their attendant personnel and wedges himself in a corner.

Exiting the elevator he sees a flash of blond hair in his periphery, which reminds him of Susan. The hair is not atop Susan's scalp, however—and why would it be, in the hospital?—but atop that of a bulky, tanned, middle-aged man.

"Hi," Janwar says to the receptionist, a fiftyish lady who, unlike Venolia, is so comfortable at her station that she's not merely painting and filing but actually clipping her fingernails, which shoot off into the metal garbage can next to her desk with loud pinging noises that put Janwar's teeth on edge. Her name plate reads "Teresa Galway."

"Hi, Teresa? My name is Janwar Gupta. I just joined the anaesthesiology department and—"

"The dead pool, right?" Teresa makes a second snap with the clippers to remove a stubborn thumbnail.

"Right. How—"

"One second, please." She presses a button. "Paging Dr. Miroslav. Dr. Miroslav to the front desk about the dead pool."

"Aren't you worried about what the patients think, mentioning the dead pool out loud?"

Teresa scrunches up her face. "Not really." She nods at someone behind him.

Janwar turns. A Slavic man with a strikingly handsome face and a ridge on the top of his skull like a dinosaur, which Janwar can see only by virtue of his own height and the man's thinning hair, stands with his hand out.

"Anton Miroslav. You want to talk about the dead pool?"

"Janwar Gupta. Yes. I just joined the anaesthesiology department and I'm interested in learning a little more."

Anton doesn't recognize Janwar's name, or he's doing a good job hiding it. "Doing your due diligence."

"Right."

"Good plan. You can never be too careful, whether you're risking your Porsche upgrade budget on a preconstruction condominium, or taking part in more traditional gambling. Like our little racket here. So what are your questions?"

Janwar learns from Anton that the pay-in is $100 a week, the average payout is $7,000, Anton "rules the ICU with an iron fist," and he doesn't tolerate any funny business. Moreover, people have to pay cash to play; Anton isn't into trying to collect money after the fact. If anyone is in hock over the dead pool, it isn't to him.

Anton's phone rings.

"One sec," Anton says. He turns away and speaks softly but Janwar can make out the words *victory* and *outsource partner* and *Georgia* and *agent* and *server cluster*.

Janwar listens as hard as he can without obviously appearing to be listening, but he can't make anything else out until the end, when Anton turns back to him and he hears the telltale uplift of Katerinka's voice on the other end. "Goodbye?"

Anton shakes his head. "IT problems. It's good you're looking at all the angles. But let me assure you, we run a tight ship."

"Do people who leave the ICU but remain in the hospital stay in the dead pool?"

"Yes. But nobody bets on them, because once they're out of the ICU, they're out of the woods."

Diego was never in the ICU in the first place. The muggers beat him in the knees, not the head. He was admitted to the emergency room and wouldn't have been eligible for the dead pool. Fuck.

With that, Janwar's dead-pool investigation bottoms out. He hasn't found anything to firmly indicate a conspiracy. He still could've given Diego the wrong dose. He could have wagered wrong. This could be all in his mind. He has to sit down for a while and breathe in and out and focus on the sound of the ventilation system before he realizes he hasn't explored the surgery connection yet. Could the surgery-anaesthesiology conflict have resulted in Diego's death?

When Janwar tries the surgery department, the receptionist says she'll go see if Karan is there, but Gertie Toledo comes back instead. In comparison to the chilled-out vibe of the anaesthesiology department, the scene behind Gertie is frenetic—a couple of surgeons Janwar hasn't met doing dishes, one washing, one drying, so fast Janwar thinks the wheels are going to come off and plates shatter at any minute. The turning on and off of the tap is accompanied by the drill of fuzzed-out punk rock, the singer yelling something about the American dream. Janwar can also hear the rolling squeal of a rowing machine moving at tremendous speed outside his line of sight.

"He doesn't want to talk to you," Gertie says.

"Can I come in and speak with you for a second instead?" Janwar says.

"This is our rec space," Gertie says. Her eyes sport dark circles. "No anaesthesiologists. Nothing personal. Some things happened a ways back. Heads got heated. Mistakes were made. And after that, well, rules is rules. Security set 'em. For all our protection. Though odds are against the exact same thing happening again. Anyway, Karan said he doesn't want to talk to you. I'm sure he's got a good reason." She's talking even faster than normal, her eyes darting back and forth. She swallows, licks her lips.

"What about Victor?"

"Victor's not here today. If you think Victor or Karan will believe you didn't make a mistake, drop it. Every doctor kills someone sooner or later. Take it like a man. If you fail out of med school, you weren't meant to be one of us anyway. You're not one of us anyway since you're going into anaesthesiology, but you won't get to be a doctor, is what I meant."

"I got that," Janwar says. He strains to unclench his teeth.

Skipping lunch turns out to have been a poor choice. Janwar has removed another possibility, plus Gertie's attitude, when she'd seemed so nice in the earlier operation, suggests something is up, beyond dexedrine-dependence irritability. But he feels awful for the rest of the day in a corporeal sense. In the future he'll have to better balance food intake with detecting.

Now his afternoon operations are over, a couple of cakewalks. It's four o'clock and he has to go see Venolia. He is hungry almost to the point of tears. Dr. Brank would have told him to put his own needs above those of others, but Janwar, a believer in harm reduction, doesn't have the heart to deprive an addict of their fix any longer. Janwar will survive a few more minutes without food.

On his way to the Records department, Janwar debates tearing up the prescription and going home, but Venolia is going to get Oxy somehow anyway, so he might as well commit.

When the prescription and photocopies have changed hands, Janwar heads to the closest place for quick food off-campus, a submarine sandwich shop, where he braves the chemical-bread smell and orders from the bored teenager at the counter. As he finishes his foot-long, Janwar reads through his own report. Everything is as Llew said, and as he saw before—accidental death, at fault: Janwar—although Venolia did intimate that information could have been changed after the report was filed. He spreads out the photocopies along the counter by the window and tallies the number of OR deaths at which each anaesthesiologist was present, regardless of reason. Shaughnessy's is the highest by a small margin. Victor and Karan, on first glance, weren't present at any more OR deaths than anyone else.

Janwar quickly becomes overwhelmed by the amount of data. Now that he sees how the data is organized, what fields are present on each printout, what options are available from drop-down lists, he knows exactly how he should have asked for it to be provided. But Venolia has gone home for the day and is probably fucked on Oxy, and he's not sure he can get anything else out of her anyway. So he's stuck with a stack of paper he has to analyze manually. It's too much. He won't be able to see a pattern until he tabulates all the data, and it will take him hours using Microsoft Excel. He might as well take the one finding he's already come to, that Shaughnessy has a high number of OR deaths, and do some old-fashioned gumshoe work. That is, follow Shaughnessy around. Shaughnessy has gone out of his way to be mean to Janwar anyway. If anyone's up to something, it's probably the Irishman. And the logic behind Gupta's wager still holds. He might as well keep digging because he'll have a complete meltdown if he admits his guilt.

Janwar returns to the hospital and checks the schedule in the anaesthesiology department. Shaughnessy's next operation is done in an hour. A series of red streaks that weren't there when he looked at the schedule first thing in the morning catch his eye. Fang's operations have been crossed off for today and assigned to other anaesthesiologists.

Peter is watching CBC News in the common area, sprawled on the couch, his limbs like rubber. His breathing is slow and he has a faint smile.

Janwar sits down next to Peter. "Where's Fang today?"

"Nobody told you?" Peter says, even more slowly than usual.

"No?"

"Her car hydroplaned last night during the rain and it slid into the side of someone's house."

A kick in the gut. "Is—"

Peter increases his muscle tension enough to pull himself up into a sitting position. "She's fine. Walked away. The people who owned the house were in the bedroom at the back, and they ran out as soon as they heard the crash, so they're fine. The front of the house isn't. Fine, that is. Neither is Fang's car. *Especially* neither. She hit the gas line, so a few minutes after she got out, everything caught fire. The fire department got there before the fire spread, so the neighbours are fine. But seems like between home insurance and car insurance all the damage is covered."

"Jesus."

"So four 'fines' out of six. Not bad. Whole thing was an act of God, really. She took the day off to deal with the paperwork."

"So no legal issues?"

"Doesn't seem like it. She was driving the speed limit. If it speeds, it bleeds. Point is, she'll be back at work tomorrow."

"I'm not sure that's the expression," Janwar says.

With forty-five minutes to go before he has to be lurking outside OR II, Janwar is in a minivan cab going to the nearest thrift store. If he's going to follow Shaughnessy, he's got to have a disguise. Or, at least, he's got to wear something other than scrubs and hide his nose. He tries to convince himself he had nothing to do with Fang's accident. She would have been that tired anyway. He couldn't have kept her at his apartment. And maybe sleepiness wasn't a factor. Maybe it was an act of God.

Janwar doesn't really know what makes up the average man on the street's wardrobe in Ottawa or anywhere else. It would have been much easier to be a private eye in the 1940s, when every man wore a trench coat and brimmed hat. And was white.

Where they are now, along Carling, there are no pedestrians for Janwar to appraise sartorially. Just car after car, bus after bus. And it's summer. Everyone shows so much skin. Choosing a disguise would be a lot easier in the winter. Black toque, scarf, big coat—you could be anyone in a parka.

He takes note of how the cab driver is dressed for the heat. Cab drivers never stand out. Saleh Azam, according to his registration card, is wearing a short-sleeved button-up shirt in ochre. It's way too large for his tall and skinny frame, and open enough to reveal copious chest hair. Okay, Janwar can do that. Cheap sunglasses. Yep. Unshaven. Well, it's almost 5 p.m. Baggy acid-washed jeans from the 1990s. Doable. Scuffed leather casual shoes. Sure. Baseball cap with a local company logo (the driver's is grey and has the Corel logo on it). Yeah. This won't fool anyone who looks closely, but from a distance if he dresses like Saleh he could be as close to a winter-parka-clad everyman as he could get in the summer. Janwar relaxes back into the bench seat. The Impala's body wallows in its bagged-out suspension as the driver changes lanes.

When Janwar and Saleh pass a road sign that reads, "Normal Speed Meets Every Need," Saleh snorts. "Normal means average. Everyone goes at least sixty here. If they wanted people to stop speeding, they should say something else." He steps on the accelerator, and Janwar's seat sinks toward the rear axle.

"They do. It's that sign that says fifty kilometres per hour."

"You suggesting I slow down? Be direct, man." Saleh stands on the brake pedal and laughs when the driver of the car behind them honks.

"I didn't mean to come across as a snark. You drive your own speed," Janwar says. He remembers a handout from cognitive psych class, and the words spill out unbidden. "It takes higher-level cognition to understand why the speed limit is there, consider the risks, and then break it, than to see the sign and follow the limit. I mean, higher level not in a moral way, but in an early childhood development sort of way." That's not helping. He gives up, hoping Saleh won't bother responding. He's surprised he remembers that fact. It's not even interesting. The class was a grade booster in first year; "Thoughts For Jocks" was how it had been known colloquially, although a lot of his classmates had been pre-med like him. Maybe one day the balance would tip enough it'd be called "Thoughts For Docs" instead.

"Are you calling me a highly developed child?" Saleh says.

"Aren't we all?"

"Right on, brother," Saleh says. "Hey, do you smoke pot?"

Janwar never has. He shakes his head. "Not my thing."

"The prime minister sure does," Saleh says. "Loves him a big ol' jay and a bag of McChickens."

Canada's sweater-vested prime minister seems like the least likely person imaginable to smoke a joint and get takeout at McDonald's, let alone multiple burgers, but who knows, cab drivers talk to everyone. Maybe some public servant with a taxi chit had a few too many at a diplomatic function and ran her mouth.

"How do you know that?"

Saleh taps his nose.

They pull into the Value Village parking lot, which is attached to a strip mall that could be anywhere in North America. Janwar retrieves his bag from the trunk and taps the trunk lid twice to send Saleh on his way.

After dashing up and down the men's aisle a couple of times, Janwar's able to find a pretty close approximation of the taxi driver's outfit—ochre Ralph Lauren shirt (two sizes too big, making for extra chest hair exposure), toy-plastic aviators, Wrangler relaxed-fit jeans, brown Sears-brand loafers, black TVOntario baseball cap—which makes it extra-awkward when Saleh Azam's cab is the one that picks him up again once he's done. In deference to the social contract, Saleh doesn't say anything about it, only raises a furry eyebrow and continues to sing along with the country music on the radio without shame.

Upon returning to the hospital, Janwar looks for a bathroom so he won't have to leave his post while waiting for Shaughnessy. The men's washroom has a "Closed for Cleaning" sign, so Janwar turns to the handicapped one across the hall. Despite all the talk among eager med students of constant hospital hookups, Janwar has yet to encounter any—either offers or accidental exposures. Until now, that is. He opens the door to the single-occupant bathroom, and, lost in thought, his ears full of the sound of the fan, he's already well into the room before he notices the two people he's interrupted are in the middle of vigorous intercourse. The man is seated on the toilet, his wrists bound together with oxygen tubing. The woman sits on his lap facing him.

She turns to look at the source of the noise, which is Janwar. Her head snaps back around and she covers her eyes with one hand while climbing off of her partner. With nowhere to hide in the square room, she moves to the corner. But it's too late—Janwar has seen it all. He's processed her identity: Teresa Galway from the emergency room, the middle-aged receptionist with the fingernail trimmer. Brett Rutan takes the opposite tactic, leaving his face exposed; his bound hands scrabble around and settle on one pointy boot as the best item to cover his genitals, which once installed looks like an Expressionist codpiece—the codpiece of Dr. Caligari.

Brett winces. Something drips out of the boot and onto the concrete floor. "I guess we forgot to lock the door," he says, his voice thick. One of his nipples is much hairier than the other.

Teresa snorts from the corner.

"What's that supposed to mean?" Brett says.

"What's it to you? I'll snort if I want to," Teresa says.

Janwar breathes out through his nose. "We all make mistakes. I'll leave you two to it."

"Or not to it, as the case may be," Teresa says.

"Don't look so horrified, kid." Brett looks over from Teresa back to Janwar. "Middle-aged people need to burn off stress too. Did you think only the young and beautiful have sex in intense environments?" He pinches his belly flab.

"I hadn't thought about it, really. I've never had sex in an intense environment." The first image that comes to Janwar's mind is the end of *Speed*, when Keanu Reeves and Sandra Bullock, after finally getting off the bus, get off with each other. Janwar moves to open the door and pauses. Something's dinging in the back of his mind. Position. Leverage. "I have a question for you, Brett," Janwar says.

"You've got me at a disadvantage."

"You know who I am, right?"

"He was asking about the dead pool earlier," Teresa says from the corner, where she's trying to reach her clothes with one foot without turning around or bending over. "I knew he sounded familiar."

"You're the boy who killed a patient a few days ago," Brett says. "Johnny? I almost didn't recognize you without your scrubs. You should come by my office for some civilian-clothing tips."

"Janwar, not Johnny. I do like those boots," Janwar says. "I don't want them though. Given the circumstances. Listen, was there anything ambiguous about what happened? In Diego's death?"

"Ambiguous in what way? Can we talk later? This isn't the right situation for a serious discussion." Brett's circular gesture takes in both the boot and Teresa. "And, actually, we shouldn't be talking about this anyway. We already had our official conversation about it on the record. The report is final. It's closed. Finito."

Janwar shakes his head. "We're going to talk now. It's not like this is going to get any more embarrassing for you than it already is, unless I open the door. Which I'll do if you stonewall me. Was what you found the same as the report you filed?"

"Yes," Brett says, seeming honestly surprised. "Why wouldn't it be?"

"Nobody leaned on you?"

"No."

"Keep in mind that I can open the door wide right now," Janwar says. He cups his ear to the door. A large group of people are standing outside, talking loudly in Japanese. Janwar's private school in BC made Japanese mandatory in Grades 4 to 6, but all he remembers is that the Japanese word for *four*, *shi*, is the same as the word for *death*, so whereas North American buildings skip the thirteenth floor, Japanese buildings skip the fourth.

"We wouldn't like that," Brett says.

"We," Teresa repeats.

Brett ignores her.

"What was the finding in your report?" Janwar says.

"There was a vial of the correct solution that was unopened and there was a vial of the stronger solution that was missing enough to have killed the patient. You were the only one injecting anything into the IV. It all seemed pretty straightforward. I talked to everyone present and I filled out my report. The legal counsel and I both signed it and then it went straight into records."

So the report hasn't been messed with, despite Venolia's warning, if Brett is to be believed.

"Did you fingerprint the vials?"

"Who do you think I am, a cop? I'm a bureaucrat."

Janwar sighs. "Oh, one more thing?"

"Yes?"

"Does anyone care that the surgeons are all on 'drines?"

"No." No inflection to his voice, no hesitation.

No leverage to use on Victor then. Balls. Janwar opens the door a crack.

"Ready for round two?" Brett says.

"As if. No, we're done here. The moment is finito," Teresa says. "You wanted to get caught, admit it. You were on the edge for so long and then finished in your boot after he was already in the room. You're a sicko."

Janwar squeezes himself out through the door.

Three priests screech by Janwar on a golf cart. Fair enough. Not all priests are in good enough shape to spend the day running around the hospital.

As Janwar returns to the centre of the hallway, a shadow blocks out the overhead light. Janwar turns. Karan's turban puts him a good eight inches taller than Janwar.

"I thought you specifically didn't want to talk to me," Janwar says, ruining his disguise.

Karan seems to have seen through it anyway. "Meet me outside the psychiatric care department in five minutes," he hisses.

"Why?"

"No surgery or anaesthesiology there."

Karan is sitting on a bench when Janwar arrives.

"Okay, what's the deal?" Janwar says.

Karan's body is rigid. "Did you hook up with Fang?"

"What? No. We're just friends. I thought you hated each— Oh."

"She texted me she was with you at Flecktarn's pad last night and she hasn't texted me back or picked up her phone since."

"Oh shit, no, she didn't stay with me. Nothing happened. We watched a movie and then she left. Peter said she got in a fender-bender. But she's okay, everyone's okay," Janwar adds quickly.

"You sure?"

"Promise," Janwar says. "She's probably got too much shit to deal with, insurance and everything. I mean, how serious are you two?"

Karan appraises him. "Not that serious."

"You don't seem happy about that." Janwar remembers Fang saying, "Shit got way more awkward before," and wonders if whatever she's got going on with Karan is also a result of unconscious sleep-cuddling.

"Just because we're outside the psychiatry department doesn't mean you can psychoanalyze me."

"Sure," Janwar says. "Hey, speaking of Dr. Flecktarn's apartment, nobody told me dude was in jail before I moved in. Couldn't they have rented me a hotel room?"

"That'd be reasonable. Civic anaesthesiologists always take the sleazy way."

"So you guys keep saying."

"Because it's true. Except for Fang. She's on the up and up. But, what I told you about me and Fang, don't repeat it."

"I get you. Surgio and Anaesthesiette."

"Thanks," Karan says gruffly.

"Now you gotta do something for me."

"What?" Karan adjusts his scrubs, revealing his kirpan in its scabbard.

Janwar continues anyway. A kirpan is a ceremonial weapon and if it's anything like his Sikh friend Manavinder's, it's dull as fuck. Although a surgeon would know how to keep a blade sharp, and might even take pride in it. Well, fuck it. Bombs away. "Was there anything off about the operation where Diego died?"

Karan makes a face. "No. And so you know, everyone knows you're going around playing detective. People are telling jokes about it now. 'Why did Janwar drop his cell-phone? So he could crack the case.'"

"That's brutal."

"I didn't say I was the one telling that joke. Accept you messed up."

"You know I've got your thing with Fang over you. Victor wouldn't be happy to hear about it."

"I'm telling the truth," Karan says. "I didn't see anything other than you mixing up your vials. All you whiny Gen Yers can't accept responsibility for failure. You call everything bad 'fail,' but you can't deal with failing."

Janwar thinks about revealing the Karan-Fang affair to the anaesthesiologists and the surgeons out of spite, but he doesn't want to fuck over Fang, or for anyone to get their orbits cracked or lose a tooth.

Anyway, he has to run to be outside the OR when Shaughnessy gets out.

"I've got to go." He stands up and almost runs into a gurney.

"Check your blind spot, taxi driver," Karan says.

"You talkin' to me?" Janwar shoots over his shoulder.

Once he gets into position outside the OR, Janwar passes the remaining few minutes of lurking focused on a bug crawling slowly across the bench. A silverfish, he thinks it's called, a many-limbed sonofabitch. The fact that he's able to hold his attention on something so mundane for so long suggests his caffeine tank is nearing empty. He wants to get coffee, but then he might miss Shaughnessy. He weighs the options and decides the thrill of the chase might wake him up enough to hold off making a dark roast pit stop.

It doesn't, because rather than leaving the hospital, Shaughnessy leads him no more than fifty feet. Janwar is stuck looking like a taxi driver where he'd stand out less if he'd kept his scrubs on. At least Shaughnessy led him to the Tulip Cafe, where he could get coffee. The Irishman eats alone, taking far longer than he needs, checking his watch every five minutes. Janwar reads today's *Ottawa Citizen* and drinks his coffee fast enough to make his skin crawl. The newspaper is full of ads for the football team playing in Lansdowne Stadium, by Dr. Flecktarn's condo. They're called the Ottawa Redblacks, which Janwar can't help feeling uneasy about. Sure, it's not technically racist. But the name seems like it's purposely pushing the boundaries of political correctness. "The Nepean Redskins had to give up their name? Fuck bleeding hearts. Let's denigrate two minorities at once," Janwar imagines the owner saying to his business associates.

Shaughnessy stands right as the clock strikes eight, and leaves his tray on the table like an asshole. Janwar keeps an eye on the man as he deposits his coffee cup into the appropriate receptacle, and then follows him up the stairs at a discreet distance. Shaughnessy's next stop is back in the anaesthesiology department. The lights are off but Shaughnessy slips inside. Janwar follows him in.

Janwar hears Shaughnessy's voice, rising and falling, under a lot of stress, coming from Sylvie Dalsgaard's office, but he can't make out the words. Janwar pauses outside the office, flattens himself against the wall, and listens. Four shadows are visible through the frosted glass. One is short and squat: Shaughnessy. Another tall and thin, presumably Sylvie, who Janwar has still not yet met. The third is too indistinct to tell. And the fourth is massive, a football player gone to fat.

"What the fuck, Shaun?" the woman snaps.

"You and Llew used to do it," Shaughnessy says. "Don't get on your high horse."

"That's the seventies. We did all sorts of things we regret in the seventies. And we didn't have something else going on. Something that affected other people besides ourselves. Get the fuck out right now and shut it down. Don't talk to him until this is all over. We can't let it break down even for a second. You never know who's watching."

"But—"

"Do it, you paddy shitstain," the fat man rumbles, with a clipped accent that might be from New Zealand.

Janwar doesn't have time to duck out of the way, so he holds himself still as Shaughnessy storms out. His luck, perhaps aided by his earth-toned disguise, holds: Shaughnessy turns left, not right, and Janwar is able to creep after him undetected. Do what? Do what, Shaughnessy?

But Shaughnessy gives him the slip, stepping into the elevator alone and facing out, meaning Janwar's disguise won't stand up if he joins Shaughnessy in there. Despite Janwar's running down the stairs, sliding his hand down the bannister fast enough for it to tingle with heat, Shaughnessy is gone by the time Janwar reaches the main floor.

Janwar gets off the bus at Bank Street and the 417 and stops at the art store to buy a corkboard, pushpins, and index cards, like a real detective. The OC Transpo app tells him the next bus isn't coming for ten minutes, so he decides to walk the rest of the way back to Dr. Flecktarn's; he'll plan out the corkboard as he walks. He'll put a card with Diego's name in the centre. And then around it cards for Shaughnessy, Henry, José, Aspen, Venolia, Ellis, the whole sick crew, including the presumed New Zealander who had berated Shaughnessy. The big Kiwi.

There's a liquor store across the street a couple of blocks back. Janwar makes an about-face, turning down a request for change from the panhandler outside for the second time. The panhandler gives him the cut eye.

He purchases another bottle of Wild Turkey to replace the one he almost polished off the other night.. The act of finding the bourbon takes far more effort than he'd anticipated. Eventually he locates it not with the other whiskies but in the middle of the Argentinian wine shelf, which he has to tell himself isn't a clue. He also purchases a bottle of Kraken spiced rum for himself. As he enters his PIN, he realizes he's buying a replacement bottle of whisky for a convicted rapist, but he's already partway through the transaction and he can't face stopping now.

Janwar climbs the stairs to the fourth floor of Dr. Flecktarn's building with his supplies.

Once in the apartment, he first has to confront the fact that not only have the flies not left, they have multiplied, sprayed across the cupboards like birdshot. He flattens a few with a rolled-up copy of the *Ottawa Sun* and then jettisons the bloodstained newspaper and makes a flycatcher—pours whisky in a glass, covers the top with cling wrap, and pokes holes in the thin plastic. Better the whisky go to the flies than to Dr. Flecktarn. The insects circle the glass warily at first, but soon one lands, and the fact that it can't get out doesn't seem to worry the other flies, who are also drawn one by one to the sweet liquor. Janwar, also drawn by liquor, pours a glass of rum for himself and watches the insects die, until Ajay and Garati inevitably call to check up on him again, asking if he's okay, which he obviously isn't.

EXHIBIT F

TRANSCRIPT OF AUDIO RECORDING FOUND ON SUSAN JONESTOWN'S CELLPHONE

SPEAKING: SUSAN JONESTOWN, SHAUGHNESSY O'DEADY, ALEJANDRO MONDRAKER

Saturday July 5

I'm sitting on the patio of the Sir John A, ready for a quick escape. I kept the bottle of 50 even though the waiter poured it into the glass. Self defence.

I can see Shaughnessy coming down the street. He's wearing a gross fedora.

SHAUGHNESSY O'DEADY: How was the rest of your day?

SUSAN JONESTOWN: Oh, you know. Smile, grind the coffee, tamp the coffee, brew the coffee, repeat. How about you?

SO: Similar. TKO after TKO.

SJ: I guess you don't ever want a partial knockout.

SO: You sure don't. That's when you wake up partway through surgery and you can't move and can't scream.

SJ: Horrifying.

SO: That sort of thing is pretty rare now. We've got the technology. But let's not start with work. Where'd you grow up?

SJ: Nova Scotia. Dartmouth.

SO: Pardon my ignorance, but where's that?

SJ: It's across from Halifax and cheaper. Like, as Oakland is to San Francisco, Dartmouth is to Halifax. What about you?

SO: Kilkenny.

SJ: Like the beer.

SO: Kilkenny ale is shite though. Ireland's not exactly known for its ales. If I wanted to drink nitrogen I'd just steal it from work.

SJ: Speaking of steal—

ALEJANDRO MONDRAKER: Sir, can I get you something to drink?

SO: Do you have Delirium Tremens?

AM: Good choice, sir.

Frig, Siri must have thought she heard her name in there somewhere and stopped recording. Quick recap while Shaughnessy is in the bathroom before I forget:

Didn't learn much in the first couple of hours. He wasn't a stunning conversationalist. Went back to my J-school training and asked the open-ended questions that make people want to talk about themselves. His mom was really into gardening. Which maybe explains—no, Susan, don't go there.

After three pints of Delirium Tremens, I managed to get him talking about stresses at work. He was going on and on about surgeons before he excused himself.

SHAUGHNESSY O'DEADY: Where was I? They just don't understand the importance of anaesthesiologists. The anaesthesiologist is the most important person in the room, no matter what the surgeon or the patient says. A surgeon can fuck up virtually anything and the anaesthesiologist keeps the patient from pushing daisies.

SUSAN JONESTOWN: Right.

SO: Do you do anything besides drink?

SJ: I've only had two beers.

SO: That's not what I meant. I was talking about drugs.

SJ: I smoke a couple cigarettes a day, and I smoke pot maybe twice a year.

SO: What about pills?

SJ: No, no pills. But when I was a teenager, I enjoyed being mangled on codeine for a week after I had my wisdom teeth removed. And when I was recovering from my knee surgery and the doctor prescribed Oxy, it was a pretty good way to waste time. I like doing things, so I never felt the need to take downers for fun. I can see how other people could enjoy it though.

SO: That's good.

SJ: Which part is good, that I like doing things, or that I enjoyed Oxy?

SO: Forget it. I'm more used to asking for patient histories than small talk. I suppose it shows.

SJ: Is it true that doctors in hospitals are all heavily into drugs? Like prescribing speed for themselves?

SO: Not all doctors. On-call doctors are the ones who get hooked on amphetamines. Anaesthesiologists have a more regular schedule and don't depend on uppers. Some doctors at the hospital take speed for sure. But not yours truly.

[PHONE RINGS]

SO: It's work. Do you mind if I...?

SJ: Sure, take your time.

Update while Shaughnessy is on the phone around the corner: He's on his fourth pint and his lips are getting more and more mushy. If I can keep him talking about Oxy, he might be drunk enough to give something away, especially if I suck it up and touch his arm from time to time. Too bad I'm not wearing my glove.

SUSAN JONESTOWN: Bad news?

SHAUGHNESSY O'DEADY: Just working through a stupid departmental conflict at the hospital. I forgot to do my part.

SJ: Surgeons causing trouble?

SO: No, within my department, with some other anaesthesiologists. Jesus, Mary, Joseph, and the donkey, the hospital is like a

schoolyard sometimes.
SJ: Do you need a hall monitor to step in? I handed out a lot of demerits when I was eleven.
SO:...maybe you can help us out.

CHAPTER 7

Convenience – Babylon – The Creepshots – Mens Rea – Sirens

Friday, July 11

Janwar gets rid of Ajay and Garati in a few minutes. It seems like a matter of life and death to focus the conversation on them, heading them off every time they try to ask about him. Today Garati went to aquacize at the Oak Bay Rec Centre, and even though all the ladies were much older, she had a great time splashing around with them and they all went for coffee at McDonald's after. And the coffee itself was surprisingly good, Garati says. Ajay test drove some different cars at Glenoak Ford with no intention of buying any of them and got his bimonthly haircut at Status Barber Shop.

Like his father's, Janwar's facial hair is as thick as his head hair, so he shaves a second time before meeting Susan. He shaves against the grain this time without cutting himself or raising more than a couple of bumps. He flosses with precision, threading the floss through a blue plastic loop to get in between his front bottom teeth and the retainer that his childhood orthodontist said was supposed to fall out at some point in university, but which the university dental clinic told him needed to stay in forever and glued back on. Janwar has never had much trouble with the blue floss threaders, after a dental hygienist who called herself the Ayatollah of Tooth Care expressed several dire warnings about the consequences of not doing so.

Soon his teeth and gums are broccoli-free and the clothes he is wearing are in order. Next up are his thoughts.

He has determined that Shaughnessy is involved in something, although there isn't anything to suggest Shaughnessy himself is responsible for the higher percentage of OR deaths at which he was present. That's a lot of progress. Tonight he will devote himself to making progress with Susan—although, he remembers now, Susan already knew about the Pushers and Mixers. "Are you a Pusher or a Mixer?" she said, which means she might be involved somehow.

Even if she is involved, he still wants to have sex with her. That's why femmes fatales are so *fatale*, of course. He tucks in the sheets on his bed and makes sure the condoms in his toiletries kit haven't expired (six months left). On second thought, he puts some of the condoms into a Band-Aid box and puts the Band-Aid box into his shoulder bag, which also contains earplugs, the book *House of God*, and his cellphone charger. Best to be prepared in case he goes to her house. It's creepy to be prepared with condoms, but it's only creepy if Susan doesn't want to have sex and sees them. If she does, it'll just be convenient.

This reminds Janwar of the George Costanza test: if a good-looking man says something to a woman that would be creepy coming from shirtless George Costanza, it's likely still creepy, no matter how good-looking the speaker is. Janwar's not sure about the morality that drives the Costanza test. It sounds demeaning to women to assume they're blinded by firm abs and chiselled features, and also demeaning to poor old George, who just wanted to find love and get a job with the New York Mets. But George does date way above his level, pulling models and so on, so, go, George, go.

Come to think of it, Janwar hates when people talk about someone dating above or below their level, maybe because it's a privilege belonging to the kind of people who don't regularly go a year or more at a time without having sex.

Babylon doesn't have a sign; the entrance is an unmarked wooden door with a porthole, underneath a pool hall. Janwar has to ask the neatly bearded man at the end of the line if he is there for the Trillaphonics.

He is. Janwar steps in line behind him.

"Have you seen them live before?" the man asks, pushing up his glasses with excitement.

Janwar admits he hasn't.

The man says he's got something to look forward to. "This is my third—no, fourth—time. They were all part of an improv group together for years and they're big on audience interaction. They're like no other band touring these days. Superpositive energy. Not sure why the Creepshots are opening for them, though. Short notice, I guess."

"What are the Creepshots like?"

"Really grimy rock and roll. They're from Montreal, but they play here all the time, especially at Rock and Roll Ice Cream Tuesday."

Before Janwar can ask what Rock and Roll Ice Cream Tuesday is, his new friend has reached the bouncer and passed inspection, disappearing into the bar.

The bouncer weighs a good 250 pounds and has a long stringy beard and a grey ponytail. He's wearing a T-shirt that reads "Support Crew 81," and on his leather jacket, which is draped over the tall chair behind him, Janwar can see a "1%" patch. A girl in line who is maybe nineteen addresses the bouncer as Daddy and touches him fondly on the thigh.

Babylon is clearly a dive bar, nothing like the concert venues he's been to in Vancouver. Though it is still a step up from Big Bad John's in Victoria, where the floor is made of sawdust and peanut shells—Janwar's Jewish friend Nick having joked that if his friends took him there, as he was allergic to peanuts, it would be like taking him to the gas chamber.

The walls of Babylon, where they aren't covered with posters from punk shows past, are flat black. A couple of pool tables are squirrelled away in the back, surrounded by bench seats from different models of minivans. A movie is playing on the old CRT television above the U-shaped bar. Janwar watches it for a minute. Some white men dressed as baseball players with carnival face paint are fighting a mix of white, Latino, and black men dressed as Native Americans, maybe in the 1970s.

Janwar is glad that he decided to dress down, and that his Vancouver EMS T-shirt and paramedic-issue combat boots are black. He doesn't fit in—everybody is wearing either logo-less shirts or shirts with the name of a band with "the" in front of it, including one that spells *the* with two Es—but at least he isn't wearing a striped dress shirt and oxblood shoes, his usual date attire, or his taxi driver disguise or his scrubs.

"What can I get you?" the bartender asks. She is short and well-proportioned and Janwar can tell that her voice is always this strident, sending sound waves crashing into your eardrums like a cheap radio turned up a little too loud. She is wearing a black T-shirt with the words "Kein Sex Mit Nazis" and, in a red "forbidden" circle, a pixelated swastika.

"I have to ask. I can't speak German—"

"No sex with Nazis." She holds out the image, and Janwar can see now that the swastika is not in fact pixelated but instead made up of drawings of stick figures enjoying various carnal positions.

Janwar nods. “Story checks out. What do you have on tap?”

She points at the chalkboard.

“What would you recommend?”

“Sweetheart. Beer is beer. This is what’s on sale.” She drums her fingers on the navy-blue tap.

“Okay,” Janwar says. “A pint of that.” Buying beer that isn’t on sale doesn’t seem like it is a recommended course of action if he wants to fit in.

The beer has a weird, sharp taste; not the sharpness of a Pilsner, but like something is wrong. Vitamin P tastes like nothing, so drinking it’s a neutral experience. This is actually bad. It burns the back of his throat. Maybe some kind of weird preservative. Beer isn’t just beer, but Janwar isn’t going to start an argument. He’ll drink his pint and maybe if Susan orders something else he’ll try that.

Janwar leans against the bar and examines the crowd. Many people have packs of cigarettes in their hands as they file past him out the door. That’s something major he’s noticed about Ottawa compared to Vancouver and Victoria: most young people smoke here. He can understand the appeal of pot, but cigarettes don’t make you feel any better than a jolt of caffeine, plus you cough a bunch and can’t run very fast.

A hand touches his back. He turns. Susan is standing behind him. She smells good and he can feel the heat of her body travelling through him, pooling in his thighs, where the major arteries are.

“Hi, Susan,” Janwar says.

“Oh hey there, Big Cat.” She stands on her tip toes and kisses Janwar on the cheek in the continental manner, her lips warm and soft, as lips often are, and his ear gets really hot.

He kisses her cheek, also in the continental manner. He debates kissing her on the mouth but it doesn't seem to be time for that yet, Mister Wolf. She relaxes her calves and returns her soles fully to the ground. She's tall for a lady, but not as tall as he is.

The sound guy turns the level of background music up, signalling that the concert will be starting soon. "I—I—I," the singer's voice slurs from the speaker pillars over a choppy guitar riff.

"Want to get into a good position?" Susan says.

"And how," Janwar says, and then blushes.

The singer for the opening band has a shaved head and a giant Victorian moustache, the kind a weightlifter in the 1890s might have. Though he is muscular, it is more ropy Clint Eastwood sinew than power-lifter bulk. All the band members wear black denim and leather and most have visible tattoos, the drummer even up to his neck. Janwar wonders if Susan has any tattoos. He doesn't have any himself.

"I'm Gizzard," the singer says. "This degenerate behind me on the drums is Wrongo Starr, and this villainous monster on bass is Crash Testes, and together we're the Creepshots." He leers into the microphone. "All right, Ottawa, let's fuck!" he shouts, "One, two, three, four!" And before his pick makes it across all six strings of his Flying V, the first five rows have become a roiling mosh pit.

"That bass player is monstrous," Susan screams in Janwar's ear. "I can feel every note in my diaphragm."

Janwar thinks about asking "Which one?" but doesn't. First, that'd only make sense in, like, 1940, when diaphragms were a popular method of birth control. And second, Janwar has learned that flirting, for him at least, is more complicated than just making oblique references to sex. The mosh pit is maybe 60 per cent male and 40 per cent female. Probably none of the women present use diaphragms, given that it's the twenty-first century.

A tiny girl falls and a giant bald man holds back the rest of the pit while she stands again and gets right back into it.

"Martín is from Argentina," Gizzard howls. "His apartment needs a cleaner / 'Cause the inside of his head / Sprayed right out, all grey and red."

The tiny girl has made it to the stage. Several leather jackets in the front row have boosted her up.

"Anita, Martín, Fleming, Dean / It's all part of the American Dream / Anita, Martín, Fleming, Dean / It's all part of the American Dream."

The tiny girl spreads her arms and dives into the waiting arms of the crowd. Janwar and Susan put their hands up and pass her over their heads. Susan's hands extend to almost the same height as Janwar's.

"That was 'American Dreamer,'" Gizzard says. The crowd ceases its motion and catches its collective breath. The tiny girl returns to the ground.

"Hey, Ottawa, what's the Canadian dream?" Gizzard says.

"Beavers," some comedian in the crowd shouts.

Gizzard nods. "For some, sure. But please dream respectfully. Just because you're dreaming of beavers doesn't mean beavers are dreaming of you. That makes a good segue, actually. Consent is really fucking important, you guys, so we wrote a song about it and it's hard as fuck."

He chugs the rest of his beer and the crowd cheers.

"All right, Creepshots, 'The Bad Things That Happen to Women'—let's go!"

Susan leans into Janwar after the Creepshots bow and leave the stage. "What did you think?"

"I'm really awake now," Janwar says.

"Nothing like punk rock to get your heart going."

"It's the—what do you call it, the two paddles—zap?" Janwar's mind is completely blank. He mimes using a defibrillator.

"A defibrillator. Shouldn't you know this?"

Janwar feels his face heat up. "It's been a long day. But yeah, punk is the defibrillator of musical genres." A connection sparks in his brain. He'd been pretty drunk during their first conversation, and only now that he's drinking has it come back. "Speaking of medical procedures, when we met, you asked if I was a Pusher or a Mixer."

"And you said you were a Mixer. And I was into it. I mean, not that I wouldn't have been into you anyway."

Janwar rubs her shoulder. "And that's why we're here." He chances it and kisses her hair just beyond her left temple. She is okay with it, because she doesn't move away, but she doesn't do anything by way of reciprocation, which is a signal for him to dial it back, physical-contact-wise. His mouth keeps going.

"But, yeah, no. I was invited to join the Mixers because of the way I blended drugs together before an operation. Some guy named Shaughnessy, another anaesthesiologist, was getting all up in my face, and pointing me out to others. They all give me dirty looks whenever they see me. Later I found out they called themselves the Pushers. And then, in the middle of all this—" Here Janwar is about to tell Susan about Diego, the closeness of this beautiful girl and the preservative-laden beer in his gut moving his real concerns further and further away, but that's way too heavy a thing to drop on a first date. Now he's thinking about Diego again, his covered body rolling out of the OR...

"And what?" Susan is still looking at him.

"Oh, nothing, lost it." Not quite a lie. He can omit details far more easily than he can lie outright. "How do you know about the Pushers and Mixers?"

"I have a friend who's a nurse who told me about it."

Janwar could call her bluff, ask the nurse's name, but he hesitates. "Why are you excited I'm a Mixer?" he asks instead.

"Oh. She said the Mixers were the cool ones. Like the Mixers were the rebels and the Pushers are the establishment, the system, the Man."

"After that set, I have a pressing desire to go find the Man so I can burn him down."

"Like an anarchist Where's Waldo?"

"I guess the Pushers would be a good place to start."

Susan doesn't respond.

Janwar retreats into joke territory. "Also, when I take a break from burning down the Man, I'm thinking I should give myself a stick-and-poke tattoo."

"As an anaesthesiologist you've got access to all the clean needles you want, I'm guessing?"

"Definitely. There'd be no risk at all. What should my tattoo be?"

"A jaguar?"

"Not bad. If I did it myself it'd probably just look like a kid's drawing of a cat, though."

"That'd be really attractive. It'd show your childlike playful side. Chicks would be all over you."

"Would you trust someone with terrible refrigerator art on their skin to anaesthetize you, though?"

"It's not like you have to do it so it's visible when you're wearing scrubs. You can be a secret punk."

"Doctor above the belt, punk below."

"Every girl's dream."

Janwar's not sure where to go with the conversation. The jokes aren't coming thick and fast anymore. He could go somewhere with that, but... No, it's too much.

Susan's not holding a drink anymore. Maybe a quick trip to the bar will give him time to come up with a plan. "Anyway, can I get you a mixed drink?"

Susan punches him in the upper arm. "They don't do old-fashioneds here. Can you get me a whisky sour?"

As he forces his way through the crowd toward the bar, Janwar wonders, are the Pushers willing to set him up to kill someone just to make trouble for the Mixers?

The house music between the Creepshots and the Trillaphonics is a medley of cheery Top 40 from years past, some songs that Janwar, more an aficionado of minimal electronic music than anything else, even recognizes. Janwar got into electronica in high school because its steady tempo helped him be productive—he mostly listened to music while studying to block outside noises and his own subconscious, but he's never seen any of the artists in his music library play live.

The playlist culminates in "Bohemian Rhapsody," as the Trillaphonics finish setting up their equipment on the stage: two drum kits flanking two tables, one with a keyboard and the other covered in hundreds of different wires of varying colours plugged into almost as many metal boxes.

The Trillaphonics open with a noise like Janwar's parents' bathroom fan when it was broken, in between the keening of a scared animal and a grain thresher. Somehow Janwar finds it pleasing.

The singer is a bearded, portly man wearing a bandana. He picks up a microphone from the nest of cables and leads the crowd through activities as the drummers pound away and the keyboard player builds up loop after loop of wavering scree.

"Everybody crouch down and follow my hand movements," the singer says. The crowd obeys, and Susan loses her balance and ends up sitting, or leaning, on Janwar's angled lap. She laughs. "I don't think I can get up again. This chick in front of me is sitting on my foot."

"I don't mind," Janwar says, but she can't see his smile from where she sits.

A few songs later, over a whooshing keyboard bass line, the portly man points at the exit. "Hey, you two over by the door. Can you... I don't know if this is going to work. Is there... Oh, I got it. Okay, you all, you see the small flight of stairs going up from the floor? You there, in the blue hat, and you, with the big smile, put your hands up like this, but each other's, like, yeah, okay, you got it. Now, you two on the other side, yeah, you"—he is pointing at Janwar and Susan, now standing again—"you do the same."

Janwar puts his arms up and Susan threads her fingers through his, forming an arch.

"Now when I say 'go,'" the singer continues, the bass line syncopating underneath his voice, "if you're on the left side I want you to go under the arms of the people by the stairs, and once you've gone through, put your arms up and make an arch with the person who came through behind you. And the same on the right. Got it?"

Drumsticks crash into drums.

"Go!"

Janwar becomes aware that he is enjoying himself, even beyond the fact that he is holding Susan's hands. As people duck under his and Susan's arms and the archway becomes a tunnel that snakes around the hall, he feels part of something good and human, and when the last person on the dance floor has gone through, Janwar follows Susan into the human tunnel. The music is hypnotic, the two drummers laying down a complicated tribal rhythm. Lights paint everyone's skin in primary colours. Janwar has to crouch down so low that his head is far forward of his legs, and he follows the man in front of him through the tunnel, feeling like the contents of an IV tube must feel going into a vein.

When the song ends and the tunnel breaks up, Janwar and Susan are on opposite sides of the room.

"All right," the singer says. "Now, everybody, let's get into a circle. Put your hands on the shoulders of the person in front of you and close your eyes."

This isn't Susan, it's a different woman. Normally Janwar would feel uncomfortable with this—dance with the girl who brung ya and all—but any sort of concerns about himself seem petty compared to the positive energy of this joyous communal event. Janwar feels *human*.

"Okay? Now, start to turn to your left. Slow. Slowww."

The strobing bathroom fan sound from the start of the show returns, the keyboard wheezing into an almost orchestral melody overtop of it, but when the drums and keyboard kick in, the singer shouts "Break!" and the crowd surges forward and crams together, spasming in ecstasy.

Janwar spots Susan near the front of the mosh pit. He inhales deeply and works his way toward her.

As he gets closer to the speakers, someone taps him on

the shoulder: a stocky man wearing a thin-brimmed fedora that doesn't go with his Euro-fit blue jeans and tight T-shirt.

Shaughnessy reaches up and puts his arm around Janwar's shoulder and screams in his ear. "I was just trying to warn you before, lickarse. The Mixers are bad news. You don't want to get involved with them. And you killed a patient this week? You should've stuck with what you learned in school."

"That's my problem, not yours," Janwar says

"It's everyone's problem. And you make everything worse when you run around playing guard."

"Buddy, just back the fuck off. The more people tell me not to dig, the more I'll keep digging. I'm a goddamned terrier."

"You're too goddamned naive, is what you are. Everyone's got shite going on that they want to keep to themselves, that's got nothing to do with any of this."

"So there is a 'this.' And something else on top of that? Something else you're personally invested in? Does the something else perchance involve OxyContin?"

"Shut your fucking mouth."

"Maybe if Venolia gets desperate enough she'll tell me what's going on."

A vein throbs under the brim of Shaughnessy's pushed-back fedora. He swings a roundhouse punch right into Janwar's sternum, and Janwar is too slow to get out of the way of Shaughnessy's Fist Express. All the air rushes out of Janwar's lungs. He can feel them sucking inward, sticking to each other. He knows he is wheezing in great whoops and gulps but he can't hear anything. He wants to throw up. His stomach is an elastic band.

"Don't you fucking dare," Shaughnessy says. "Lay off

Venolia or the next time you find yourself in the ER you'll be looking at the ceiling. Oh, and say hi to Susan for me. Did you really think a bird like that would go for a gowl like you?"

Janwar wheezes in response. He turns his head to look at Shaughnessy and, probably without mens rea, spews lager and bile all over him. Now his lungs are inflating again. Did he hear Shaughnessy right? How does Shaughnessy know Susan? Have they slept together? He'd feel sick at the thought if he didn't already feel sick from Shaughnessy's punch.

Shaughnessy releases Janwar. Janwar breathes in, white dots exploding behind his eyes, and grabs at the pain point by Shaughnessy's collarbone. Shaughnessy pulls back and paws at his eyes. Janwar figures Shaughnessy must be wasted or on some heavy prescription narcotics, otherwise he'd be screaming, so he summons all his strength, makes sure his thumb is outside his fist, which is one of the two things he knows about punching people, then swivels on his right foot like he is grinding out a cigarette and slugs Shaughnessy in the face.

"I'll look at whatever I want," Janwar says. Each word throbs in his chest. Not exactly a zinger, but accurate, covering both the ER and his amateur detective work.

Shaughnessy's head snaps back and he stumbles and falls, his boot soles unable to gain purchase on the beer-slicked floor. Blood sluices from his nose, turning the bird logo on his shirt into a cat victim. Janwar doesn't have a ton of muscle, but at least he has leverage.

Shaughnessy's elbows hit the ground first, then the brim of his fedora, and finally the back of his head. Probably not hard enough to cause any permanent damage; Janwar well aware that if the circumstances had aligned differently, Shaughnessy might have hit the ground headfirst at exactly the wrong angle and died, becoming Janwar's second murder of the week. But he's thrashing around right away. And what else could Janwar have done? Shaughnessy started the fight.

The bouncer holds the crowd back while some other concertgoers help Shaughnessy up. He pushes his way to the back of the crowd, his face barely missing the flailing feet of another crowd-surfer.

Janwar should have asked Shaughnessy how he knew Susan, instead of coming up with a lame action-movie retort. He's too full of adrenaline to have a chthonic breakthrough, but it'll get him later. Ignoring the pain in his chest, and now his knuckles, Janwar pushes his way toward Susan.

Susan is still on the other side of the mosh pit, but now the pit has doubled in intensity. A crust punk crashes into Janwar, right about the time his adrenaline starts to subside. Vertigo washes over him. He's got to sit down immediately. He staggers toward the entrance and leans against the door frame. A quick scan for Shaughnessy comes up empty. Janwar sits on the curb and puts his head in his hands. A couple of minutes later, he pulls his phone out and, with the stiffening, swollen fingers on his right hand, texts Susan: *Getting some fresh air. Just outside.*

1:43 am—New message from Susan: I'll join you, one sec

The bile Janwar threw up earlier burns in his esophagus. Susan sits down next to him and puts her arm around his back. She leans her head, hair soaked with sweat, on his chest, and he twitches away violently. His ears are still ringing. It rained while they were inside. The ground is slick and reflects all the lights: street lamps, headlights, cigarettes.

"Are you okay, Big Cat? One second you were there and then I couldn't find you."

"I got hit really hard in the chest."

Susan leans back.

Janwar pulls up his Vancouver EMS shirt; he already has a bruise right on his xiphoid process, an oval that shifts from grey to deathly purple as the xenon headlamps of luxury cars flash by.

"Aw, Janwar. Did some asshole try to fight you in the pit?" Susan says. "Your shoulders don't hurt when I touch you, do they?" She lifts her arm.

"Yeah, someone really *pushed* me around." Janwar feels a bit of relief, knowing he is, at this very moment, in control. He knows something she doesn't, so she doesn't know how to act.

"What happened?" she says, but she knows already. She must. If Shaughnessy knows her, she's playing a role in this whole business. Her voice, hollow and bony, drifts toward him from farther away than the ringing in his ears would account for. She reaches into her purse and produces a pack of Camels and a red BIC lighter.

"It was Shaughnessy," Janwar says.

Susan inhales a deep breath of smoke, and it curls out from her nostrils. "Is that the guy from the hospital you were talking about?"

"Oh, come on," Janwar snaps. It feels good to snap. He never gets to be mean, so when it's justified, he enjoys meanness like a vice. "He mentioned your name."

Susan's expression remains blank. "What did he say to you?"

"He said I was mixing with the wrong people at the hospital. And to say hi to you. And—" Janwar's throat stops up, leaving him unable to repeat the presumed insult to his manhood, regardless of the fact that he has no idea what *gowl* means. The image of Shaughnessy's sweating red face inches from Susan's passes across Janwar's vision like a cloud of smog.

Susan takes another puff, and the cigarette crackles. Janwar is anti-smoking, but he can't say that there isn't something sexy about it now that he's watching a pretty girl do it, even if she's a pretty girl who might have asked him out at the behest of a Eurotrash wannabe mobster.

Susan grinds out the end, which features a carmine imprint from her lips. "I can't say any more about it. I didn't mean for you to get hurt. Believe me."

"Things aren't looking good in the 'you're interested in hanging out with me because you're looking for a nice man to spend good times with' department, Susan. You were interested when I said I was a Mixer. Somehow, you know Shaughnessy. And you invited me here, where Shaughnessy tried to beat me up."

Susan looks off at the partygoers clogging Bank Street, climbing into cabs, stumbling down the sidewalk, at the calf muscles straining against high heels. A beer bottle someone has snuck out of one of the bars explodes against a fire hydrant, spraying shards of glass.

Janwar doesn't move his gaze from Susan. "That's not fucking cool. Do you want to explain?"

"I can't right now."

"You can't or won't?"

"I should go. I'm sorry." She stands and waves her hand. A cab swoops to the curb, and she climbs inside.

Janwar slumps against the newspaper box. Two a.m. has come and gone. Susan has changed from being an exciting diversion to a bubble on his mind-map connected by dotted lines to the other bubbles that read "Pushers" and

"Shaughnessy." He'll have to do some serious mapping soon, but not tonight. He's been awake for twenty-two hours straight.

He pulls out his phone: *Gowl* is a derogatory Southern Irish term for female genitalia.

He begins to stand up, but a boot crashes into his ribs and he falls back, his phone skittering across the concrete. The boot's toe slams into his sternum again, and the nebula with yellow edges comes back and takes over his vision. He struggles to rise, but the blob hangs between him and the outside world. His attacker shoves him back down. Janwar's head bounces off the front glass of the *Ottawa Citizen* box, right where the headline reads, "Bronson Slope Condo Development LEEDer of the Pack," and the last thing he hears, before blackness claims him, is the wail of sirens.

EXHIBIT G

TRANSCRIPT OF AUDIO RECORDING FOUND ON SUSAN JONESTOWN'S CELLPHONE

[RECORDING REDACTED BY ORDER OF BRIGADIER GENERAL SILUK TUPIQ]

PART III: THE CRUNCH

CHAPTER 8

Cohasset – Suspira – OK Corral – Pushrods Forever

Saturday, July 12

When Janwar wakes up, he's in a hospital bed and everything is beautiful: the light coming in the window, the view of Dow's Lake beyond it, the reflections on the waxed floor, the crisp white of the sheets. He moves his eyeballs over to the left. An IV sticks out of his arm. Probably a mix of hydromorphone and sufentanil, based on how he feels.

Although he's also been badly beaten, and he has no idea how badly, he feels a weight off his shoulders. Because he's been beaten, in fact. Since Shaughnessy warned him off and then presumably came back and stomped him, he almost certainly picked the right side on Gupta's wager. Even if he hasn't come anywhere near clearing his name, something criminal is going on here and Diego's death has to be related.

The weight is gone, but now he feels guilty. Dr. Brank would tell him that even as he lies here, he's reinforcing negative neural pathways. His obsessive commitment to determining the responsibility for Diego's death at the expense of his own health, to, like, a really serious degree, now that he's lying in a hospital bed, has been borne out. And in future, Dr. Brank would say, he will have that much more of a reason to disregard his own personal health and follow his own anxious thinking, and that's not a positive outcome for his development into a functional person.

"Aye, awake are you?" a voice says from outside of his field of vision. "Here's what it is. You have a minor concussion, a gash across your chest, a couple of cracked ribs, and significant bruising and swelling. And you opened up a proper nasty cut on your knuckles. But we mixed you up the good stuff. Never let it be said that we Mixers don't protect our own." The voice wobbles and reverberates in his ears so much that he can't tell who it belongs to. Llew drifts in from Janwar's left with the fluidity of motion reserved for film, until he stands at the foot of Janwar's bed.

Janwar tries to nod but all he manages is a slight inclination of his head, which means he can now see that Carla is standing in the doorway. His muscles feel like they belong to a housefly stuck in a glass of liquor. He can move his lips a bit. Air flows over them and strings of saliva connect his upper lip to his lower lip as his mouth parts.

"Uh," he says. His tongue feels dry and alien. "Thhhh," he continues, the Hs dragging on far longer than he wants. He isn't concerned and he isn't troubled. That's the nice thing about opiates. Chemicals can counteract pretty much any kind of thought pattern, especially blunt-force heavyweights like hydromorphone. He concentrates, trying to make his Jell-O mouth form one syllable at a time. "Thanks," he manages, or something close to it that takes a long time to say. He closes his mouth again.

Someone knocks on the door. "Never, Father," Llew says. "He's right as rain."

Llew turns back to Janwar.

"I expect you figured out that the conflict between the Pushers and the Mixers isn't just a matter of professional disagreement. But don't fancy we're a gang of ruffians. There are two reasons we 'beef,' as Fang puts it. First off, mixing drugs helps our patients. I wanted you on board because I heard you were beyond a dab hand with a syringe and I didn't want the experimentation flattened out of you by the Pushers. I thought they'd leave you alone because you're new, and that not telling you the whole story would protect you. The second reason is a larger political one."

"Mm?" Janwar manages. He's conserving energy. He'll form words again only when necessary.

"The Mixers mix drugs in one syringe. The Pushers use separate syringes. They get kickbacks from Syrinx because they use three to four times as many syringes as we do. Syringes are made of plastic. And plastic is made from oil. Syrinx gets kickbacks from Cohasset Oil and Gas. And you must be familiar with Cohasset—they're trying to build a pipeline from Alberta across British Columbia, which is bound to cause an environmental disaster."

Signs saying "Stop the Pipeline" have sprouted up all over Vancouver over the last year, so Janwar is very familiar with Cohasset.

"Maybe you won't credit this, but we're very ethical, we Mixers," Llew says. "So I hope you can understand and that you'll keep on mixing. We won't let Shaughnessy near you again; one of us will be here around the clock until you're mobile again. It goes through me that this happened to you. So, can you forgive us, boyo?"

Janwar shrugs as much as he is able, which is not much.

Llew picks up on the movement. "Aye, sometimes it takes a while to forgive. I can appreciate that. But we aren't the ones who gave you a belting. And if you're ambivalent about forgiveness right now, that's okay."

Janwar looks to Carla, but she is facing the hallway.

Llew's jaw hardens. "I have to tell you: nobody's going to

let you leave with a good reference if you go in for an exit. It’s early days yet. You’re sticking with us, boyo.”

This isn’t a question, but Llew seems to be waiting for a response.

“Yes,” Janwar says.

“Good. You’ll come up a treat in no time.”

Llew fiddles with the IV drip, and Janwar’s eyes roll back. Llew’s warm, firm hand on Janwar’s forehead is the last thing he feels as he slips back into darkness.

When Janwar wakes up, the first thing he registers is blond hair. Why would Susan be here? If Susan is here, will Shaughnessy come back and finish the job? But as his vision swims into focus, he sees that the hair is Emanda’s, not Susan’s.

Peter is dozing in the visitor’s chair. Emanda puts her finger to her lips, upends both her palms, and pats herself down to show she doesn’t have anything hidden on her person.

She bends down to Janwar’s ear. “Don’t worry. I just want to make sure you know something. And then I’ll go.”

Janwar nods. His ear brushes against her lips. “Is he—?” he whispers. He can form words that don’t drag on forever again.

“Drugged? No, he’s just asleep. If you shout, he’ll wake up.”

Janwar tries to engage his vocal cords. It doesn’t go well. He goes back to whispering. “So what do you want me to know?”

“The Mixers aren’t innocent either.”

“In what way?”

“Thiopental has traditionally been the best induction drug.”

“Yes, and?”

"Because it's cheap and it doesn't go bad for a long time. You can open a vial for one operation and use it again a month later."

"Right, but—"

"But the Mixers can't use it because it doesn't play nicely with other drugs if you inject them all at once. It can crystallize and kill the patient."

Janwar sees Diego's last minutes again, the flatline, the crash cart, the drape, the orderlies, but he's still too tranquilized for the tightness in his chest to return.

"Right," he says.

"And instead, you use..."

"Propofol. I'm not sure about the others."

"They do too. Even now that it's generic, propofol is expensive. There are often shortages, and it goes bad six hours after you open the vial. So you have to keep throwing it out and buying more."

"That's true. I—"

"And who makes the generic propofol we use here?"

"Suspira Labs?"

"Bingo. What I'm trying to say is that if you look closely, there's a lot of Suspira merch floating around."

Peter snorts in his sleep, and Emanda startles.

"I'd better go. Just think that over before you make any serious decisions."

Janwar is offline right now and there isn't much he can do, research-wise, when he can't make it out of bed. Something is bothering him, though. It's nice of Llew to give him "the good stuff," but it is presumptive of him to assume that Janwar likes being whacked out on morphine derivatives, which he doesn't really. Is that all they gave him? What day is it? How long has he been drifting? Where is his cellphone? Are they going through his messages?

Soon he's asleep. The fat-man silhouette from Sylvie's office lumbers through his dreams, a supermassive man-shaped black hole, every piece of matter in the hospital drawn to him, sticking to the outside of his body as his shadow grows to encompass the entire universe...

When Janwar wakes up this time, the lights inside the room are off and so is the radio. The door to the room opens slowly, letting light in from the hallway. Fang has replaced Peter, Janwar can see now, but she doesn't stir. Two figures in scrubs and surgical masks pause in the doorway, waiting for any signs of alarm, then tiptoe into the room, followed by two more figures, then two more, their Crocs squeaking at an almost sub-audible level. Maybe they've added skins to the bottom, fabric layers like Janwar used to climb hills on smooth telemark skis while backcountry skiing on out-door club trips.

"Fang!" Janwar hisses. She doesn't move. "Fang!" He feels shame at having spoken out loud in the silent room, but on the plus side, at least his lips are working properly.

The first figure in the door drops something into the sharps container attached to the wall, and Janwar's shame ramps back up into fear. "Don't bother," Shaughnessy says. "She's in lotus land for a couple of hours. And I don't mean BC."

The second figure looks out along the hallway. Dr. Aspen Tanaka.

"All clear." She shuts the door and turns the light on.

Two further figures are Dr. Tariq Hadad and another woman Janwar doesn't know, slight and with one eye that seems less real than the other—and then last, Henry and José. They crowd around him.

"Nurse! Can I get some twins? Stat?" Henry says.

"Hand me that dwarf!" José holds out his hands behind him.

Shaughnessy is unimpressed. "Shut up, you goons."

"Come on, we're a reasonable Paraguays."

Shaughnessy rolls his eyes. "I don't even get how that one's connected to Dr. Mengele."

"And you're a fascist," Janwar says. "Paraguay was where Dr. Mengele eventually died."

Henry and José look at each other and then at Janwar with a modicum of respect.

The thin woman's eye seems unreal because of the way it wobbles vertically. Either it's a very slippery glass eye, or something is going on with her extraocular muscles.

"So, blue-eyed brown boy, have you given any thought to your situation?" Shaughnessy speaks with a hypnotic cadence, but that might just be whatever's clamped onto Janwar's neurons, making him think that.

"Lots. I can't do much besides think. Though it's been going very slowly on account of whatever Llew shot me up with. Which particular thoughts do you want to know about?" He surreptitiously flexes some muscles, but although he might be able to raise himself into a sitting position, he isn't in any offensive or defensive shape.

"What's your best guess?"

"You want to know whether I want to stay a Mixer or become a Pusher or somehow assert my neutrality, which nobody seems to think is an option," Janwar says.

"Right. It's not. It's an all-or-nothing deal," Aspen says. "Fuck an excluded middle."

Shaughnessy pulls on a pair of gloves. "Now, don't waste my time and thrash around."

"Waste your time?" Janwar says.

"I have patients to get to. This is a hospital."

"Ah. Have to keep helping people because it's in your blood." His heart hammers.

"That's right."

"It's not the only thing that's in your blood from the looks of your pupils."

Shaughnessy's pupils are black pinpricks. He's also been hitting some heavy opiates.

The door opens and the Mixers file in, Llew in the front, holding his hickory bat by his side.

But before the drama can play out, unskinned Crocs squeak outside the door and someone clears their throat. Llew and Shaughnessy exchange glances. A message transmits between them.

"Come in," Llew says.

Emanda holds up her hands again to show she isn't packing anything. "Rat Fink Patrol's just down the hall. Thought y'all down here at the OK Corral would want to know that."

Llew crosses his arms. "Which of us are the Earps?"

"Fuck if I know." Emanda shrugs. "Actually, no, wait. You're all Doc Hollidays."

"Nice," José says. Henry nods. Aspen mouths "mew" at Janwar and holds up her fingers to her face like whiskers.

Llew scowls at Emanda. She blushes and withdraws, which Janwar, even in his addled state, thinks is a strange response.

The Mixers step away from the door to let the Pushers out.

Fang's eyes pop open, unclouded, as far as Janwar can tell from his bed.

Llew turns to Janwar. "Thanks be to security. Expected we were going to have a scuffle. Boyo, you're going to be safer at home. I thought we could protect you better here. But we botched it. We have too many operations to do to give you more than one guard, and all it took was one quick stab and Fang was out."

"How did it happen, Fang?" Janwar says.

"I don't think I remember."

"They must have hit you with something that causes amnesia…"

Llew holds up his palm. "We can draw a blood sample and send it to the lab in a minute. But Fang's awake now and she seems right enough. We have to get Janwar home."

Peter circles into Janwar's field of view. "One of us should run you home. You may be awake but your judgement is probably still off. Dr. Louisseize, do you want to do the honours?"

"That's plain Dr. Choi again," Horace says.

The corner of Peter's mouth twitches. "You mean…"

"She wants a divorce."

"I'm sorry we messed with you the other night."

Horace waves Peter's apology away.

"Does she—" Fang starts, but a warning look from Llew shuts her up.

"Ready to go, Janwar?" Horace says.

"Yes, thank you. Hey, I have a question, though." Janwar looks over at Llew as Horace disconnects him from the IV tree. "The woman with the weird eye. I didn't recognize her. She's not an anaesthesiologist, is she?"

"Deadeye Dalsgaard," Peter says.

Llew nods. "She's the head Pusher. She's an administrator like me, head of the department."

"Oh, Sylvie Dalsgaard, with the office next to yours."

"Righto. No end of grief."

"What's with her eye?"

"No idea, but I credit whatever it was. She deserved it," Llew says. He fishes in his pocket. "Here's your cellphone. I forgot to give it back to you. The paramedics picked it up from outside that bar."

Janwar swipes across the screen to unlock it. It's fully charged. Nine missed calls from Ajay and Garati. He texts Ajay *Still alive. Everything cool. Don't panic.* He'll pay for this later, but for now he just can't deal.

Horace's car is a blue-flake sixties Corvette Stingray, painstakingly restored.

"Didn't figure you were a classic-car guy." Janwar folds himself into the passenger seat, still drugged enough that the vinyl feels amazing against his legs. Little bursts of pleasure shoot up and down his thighs.

Talking about cars allows Horace to pass his sadness in the left lane, and he responds in a far cheerier tone. "I grew up in California, which is nothing but muscle cars and muscle beaches. And I don't look good in a swimsuit. My back makes my jawline look airbrushed," rubbing his acne scarring, "so muscle cars it was. I restored her myself." Horace turns his key in the ignition, and the engine growls. "Are you into muscle cars?"

"Sort of. Mostly because of old cop movies and shows. *Bullitt*, *The French Connection*, *The Rockford Files*. Speaking of which, your Corvette is pretty close to Rockford's Firebird. I'll bet you could do a beastly J-turn. Start in reverse, jam on the e-brake, and swing it around so you're facing forward and going in the same direction."

"I'm not big on risk, to be honest," Horace says. "I like driving fast cars slowly."

They drive in silence for a couple of minutes. "You doing all right?" Janwar asks.

"I'm just having a rough day. A little distracted." Horace turns onto Bronson, leadfoots the accelerator, and darts around a funeral procession. What would happen if nobody claimed Diego? Janwar doesn't know if the city will pay for embalming and a coffin, or just for cremation. He assumes cremation is cheaper, although maybe it's only cheaper in bulk...

"Do you want to talk about it, Horace?"

"Not really. We can keep talking about cars, or something else."

"I was meaning to ask, why's Llew got so much hate for Sylvie? What he said at the end—it seemed like a giant leap in cruelty for him."

"They were friends before."

"Just friends?"

"Yes. Just like me and— Yes, just friends."

"It seemed almost like a jilted lover sort of vengeance-anger."

"No, he probably just feels bad."

"Feels bad—like he's been bad, or bad like he's sad their friendship is over?"

Horace shoulder-checks and changes lanes. "The second one."

"Wait," Janwar says. "Deadeye Dalsgaard. Double D."

"Right."

"Carla said when Llew was really into experimenting with drugs on himself, a woman named Double D was also into it with him."

"Carla would know better than I would."

Janwar watches the sidewalk scroll by as they pull up to the light. Another advertisement for Lowell Chilton Real Estate, on a bench this time, the man's upper body wearing an XXL hooded sweatshirt and holding up boxing gloves: "Don't throw in the towel. Throw in with Lowell."

Janwar never thought he'd get sick of puns, but these Lowell Chilton ads are really pushing the limits. Slant rhyme isn't playing fair.

Something's ringing in the back of his mind. Lowell Chilton reminds him of someone. Something to do with the slant rhyme, maybe.

"How did the whole thing start?"

"What?"

"The division between the Mixers and the Pushers. Did it start because she's the head of the department and he's the dean? Some sort of turf thing? And people chose sides?"

The engine races, and Horace looks down at the gearshift. "Actually, can we talk about my wife?"

"Are you sure?"

Horace says that he's sure, but he speaks slowly, thinking about every word. "It had to do with children. We loved each other—we do love each other. There was nothing wrong. But we disagreed about children. I didn't want them because I thought I'd be too absent and she wanted me to quit my job so that we could have them. I thought she would change her mind and she thought I would change my mind."

"Fuck, man." Janwar isn't really sure what to say, but his mouth is, apparently. "For what it's worth, philosophically, I think I have the same position you do. I understand that there's an evolutionary imperative to pass on your genetic material, but I have no interest in creating something that looks a bit like me and a bit like my partner, just for the sake of it. The world is overpopulated and fucked in so many other ways. I can make a positive difference in the world by being a doctor, which is what I feel I was born to do, or I can spend eighteen years raising a child and hoping that she will want to make a positive difference in the world, which is just putting off making a difference, and gambling that the sort of difference the child wants to make and is able to make then is more beneficial than the difference I'd make. I mean, the kid could be a white-collar criminal, which would be a net drain on the world, but I'd still be committed, because she'd have my nose. And if I tried to do both—raise a kid and be a doctor—I know I'd just fuck up one or the other. I don't think I can do anything at less than 100 per cent. And in the end, I think being a doctor is more valuable."

"I've never heard that justification for not having children before. I think about my own gratification and work and the impact on one child's life, and you think about the entire world."

Janwar shrugs. "Do you have a place to live? Outside where you live with your wife, I mean?"

"I can go stay with my brother. The condo isn't ready yet."

"The condo? You move fast."

"Oh, it's— Yeah, I do. All about that Craigslist. Speedy Louisseize. Speedy Choi." His face crumples.

Choi Division, Janwar thinks. Much sadder than Bombay Calculus.

They pull up in the lot outside Dr. Flecktarn's building in the Glebe and Janwar climbs out.

"Thanks for the ride, Horace."

Horace nods. He looks ready to weep. As he reverses, Janwar sees Horace's hand hover over the e-brake, as if he's considering a Rockford turn, but maybe that's just wishful thinking on Janwar's part. The Stingray rumbles off, the exhaust note from its big-block V8 taking several intersections to fade from earshot.

Janwar spends the elevator ride alternating between looking at his reflection, which has seen better days, and trying to psych himself up to face the mammoth task of transferring his mental mind map to his index-card map—adding "Suspira," "propofol," "Syrinx," and "Cohasset"—but by the time he gets up into Dr. Flecktarn's apartment, his bed beckons, and he barely has the energy to make sure his phone is plugged in and the alarm is set before blackness claims him again.

CHAPTER 9

Animate and Otherwise – Nothing But Butchers – Sneaking Around – La Chasse – Dirty Bird – Body World – Fat Man – Year of the Glad – I Don't Know, Are They?

Monday, July 14

In the morning the glass on the counter is now full of a grey-brown liquor-fly slurry. The insect corpses under the Saran Wrap have started to decompose, but despite the presence of death, the trap keeps attracting more flies. Are they coming into Dr. Flecktarn's unit just for the whisky now? Or for the other dead flies? Janwar commits the flies to a mass grave in the kitchen garbage and washes the glass. On his way out of the apartment, he throws the garbage bag down the chute. His phone tells him he has three missed calls from Ajay's cellphone. He texts Ajay back *Can't talk now, sorry.*

6:30 am—New message from Ajay: That's now. What about last night, huh?

Janwar turns his phone off.

As he approaches the hospital, his heart rate begins to climb. Last time he was here, only the quick action of the Mixers prevented Shaughnessy's injecting Janwar with an unknown substance. The Irishman has already sucker-punched him, stomped him, and now tried to introduce a foreign agent into his bloodstream. Where will he escalate it next?

Two police officers, a man and a woman, are speaking with one of the information-desk personnel as Janwar crosses the lobby. They stare at him unashamedly because they're cops and he's looking a little worse for wear, more like he should be lying on pale cotton than wearing it.

Even though Janwar has broken very few laws in his life, having won a citizenship award and all, and even though Canadian police are miles away from, say, Haiti, on the corruption index, police officers still make him nervous. He can trace this feeling back to the time when he was eighteen and a Victoria police constable at a drunk-driving checkpoint stopped Janwar in Ajay's Navigator. She asked for his driver's licence, looked at it, then took a step back and put her hand on the butt of her 9 mm. Janwar can remember the woman's name still, Constable Diane Phelps, from the adrenaline-spiked, hyper-aware moment during which he stared at her as she appraised him, before realizing that she had misread the beaten-up card, which Janwar had once dropped in a sewer grate and managed to rescue with a convenient branch, a couple of bulldog clips, and a piece of string. The constable thought it said "Jairam Aashish Gupta," one of the three men who made up the notorious Gupta Brothers gang, when in fact it said, "Janwar Aashish Gupta."

The Gupta Brothers aren't part of Janwar's family, or if they are, they're so far removed he hasn't met them—and he's met everyone, Garati has made sure of that—but he'd seen them at Hindu community events when he was a teenager, with their shiny SUVs and sports cars and bombshell girlfriends and sharp suits and expensive sunglasses, and he admired them. Ajay, in a rare display of social intelligence and good parenting, saw young Janwar coveting their chattel, animate and otherwise, and told him that the Gupta Brothers were criminals and that he,

Janwar, could have all the same things they had by becoming a medical specialist, and that being a specialist came without the risk of getting shot in a crowded restaurant or while walking out of a mall or dancing in a club or doing anything else anywhere else, really.

The presence of the police officers jacks up Janwar's heart rate even more, and reminds him that Diego was brought into the hospital as the result of a crime. He turns his phone back on, swipes away the notifications for more messages from Ajay, and calls the police communications phone number to ask about Diego's mugging.

The communications officer isn't going to be too scary to talk to. She just works there, and over the phone, she can't point a gun at him.

"Ottawa Police Service, Callie Sjostrom, speaking?"

"I'm Ganesh Agrawal, a journalism student at Carleton," Janwar lies. Ganesh was the first word that popped into his head. He always liked Ganesh, the elephant-headed god. If the God of Detectives had an animal head, what would it be? "Is there a public report about the mugging of Diego Acosta on July 9 that I can access?" Janwar says.

"Is it a class assignment or something? You're the second journalism student to call about this."

"Scooped again," Janwar says. "Nuts!"

"I've got the brief here," Callie says. "Do you want me to email it to you?"

Receiving an email is obviously not compatible with Janwar's previous lie unless he's able to sign up for a new email address before she sends the file—Janwar.Gupta@ubc.ca is pretty clearly not the email address of Ganesh Agrawal at Carleton. "Uh, if you have a minute can you just give me the Coles Notes?"

"Sure. A man in a red hooded sweatshirt approached Mr. Acosta and asked him for money. He told the man he didn't have any change. The man said he wasn't asking and to hand over his wallet and cellphone. But as Mr. Acosta put his hand in his pocket to get his wallet out, he turned and saw another man with a baseball bat, also wearing a red hooded sweatshirt, was standing behind him. This second man smashed Mr. Acosta in the kneecaps. Then the first assailant held him down while the second took his wallet and cellphone, and then they left him on the ground and the two of them took off. A cab driver who turned the corner a few minutes later called 9-1-1. We're encouraging people to call in if they witnessed anything."

Still seems like a straight-up mugging, but maybe that's just what they want Janwar to think—whoever they are.

Shaughnessy seems rather obviously to be the key to this whole thing, given his leadership role in both the beating and the OK Corral standoff. Janwar decides to follow the Irishman again. He did okay *mano a mano* with Shaughnessy when they sparred in the nightclub, he reassures himself. Both times Shaughnessy came out on top; he had the drop on Janwar. If Janwar follows *him*, the element of surprise should be on his side. But first he's got patients to attend to. He returns to active service, inducing and intubating with his usual efficiency, though he's still feeling a little light-headed, his forehead is tender, and his ribs ache dully. You can't do anything about cracked ribs anyway, besides avoid strenuous exercise, and anaesthesiology isn't a heavy-lifting-based profession.

Both Karan and Victor are scheduled for one of Janwar's operations this morning. Victor and Janwar are in the operating room alone. Even though he's got no leverage on Victor, Janwar wings it. "Victor, about the other day, can I—"

"I'll give you one free answer: the anaesthesiologists killing my patients joke? Was a joke."

"But—"

"That's all. Our issue with the anaesthesiology department is personal. They're insufferable. 'You'd be nothing without us,' they say. 'Nothing but butchers.' But we're the ones doing what needs to be done. If you anaesthetize people and don't perform surgery, that doesn't get you anywhere. They just go to sleep for a while and when they wake up their femur is still sticking out of their leg."

Karan walks in.

"If you conducted surgery without anaesthesia," Victor continues, "the patient would be in a lot of pain, sure, but they'd have had the operation they needed. So, surgery trumps anaesthesiology."

Janwar opens his mouth.

Victor holds up a hand. "Our personality conflict has got nothing to do with that man's death. Don't pull us into your little hard-boiled wonderland." He turns away, removes something from his pocket, and dry-swallows it. Karan's arms are crossed and the muscles in his biceps twitch underneath his scrubs.

Karan sees him looking. "And anaesthesiologists are all about counterproductive drugs. It's unprofessional. The only moral position is to take drugs to make you work faster and harder. Oxy just makes you boneless." He scratches the edge of his turban.

"And, coming full circle, if you're so bored by what you do that you need downers to get through it, your job isn't that important anyway," Victor says.

Victor turns back to his instruments. Karan does the same. With no cart to occupy himself with yet, Janwar studies the patient's chart.

Henry walks into the room pushing the anaesthesiology cart. He looks from one man to another. "Did I just interrupt concentration camp?" he rumbles.

"Just give me the damn cart," Janwar says. He swipes his tablet at it to unlock the drawer.

Back in his taxi-driver disguise, his vision tinted blue by the amber sunglasses, Janwar follows Shaughnessy. This time Shaughnessy does leave the hospital. Janwar maintains twenty feet between them and makes sure to swing wide to stay in Shaughnessy's moving blind spot as the man looks both ways before crossing the street, his shitty little fedora turning side to side to be sure that a red Miata and maroon Explorer will slow enough to let him through.

Janwar waits for the two vehicles to pass and then darts across the street himself. A cyclist flying by skids her rear tire when she sees him, and Janwar feels a little bit bad about it, but it isn't a safety issue, just a being-an-asshole issue. Shaughnessy doesn't turn.

Janwar lets a couple of people pass him to distance himself from Shaughnessy, though if Shaughnessy looks back, he'll see Janwar's head bobbing above them, like a hot-air balloon wearing a TVOntario hat.

Shaughnessy speeds up and turns left on Irving. Janwar has to abandon his confident approach to shadowing and dive behind a newspaper box in order to avoid being seen. At least the traffic noise along Carling is loud and big trucks make the ground vibrate as they pass. One semi has spikes on its hubcaps like something out of *Mad Max*, which can't possibly be legal, even in Quebec, which is where the truck's licence plates say it's from. The word *Quebec* tickles something in the back of Janwar's mind...

Now that they're on a side street with trees and cars and elevation changes, Shaughnessy looks around furtively. He does this at every street and driveway crossing, and Janwar begins to enjoy finding pieces of cover to aim for, to plan his route like Billy in *Family Circus* with a series of dotted lines and vector changes. He lies prone next to a Dodge Caravan, dives into the shadow an elevated set of steps casts on a sun-browned lawn, crouches next to a garbage bin that smells like the intestinal flora of several dogs with diverse but equally unhealthy eating habits, and slides onto a park bench and scoops up an *Ottawa Citizen* ("Stephen Harper Close to Finding Lost Arctic Ship from Franklin Expedition"), as Shaughnessy tacks and leads Janwar down side streets. Turning left on Norman, Janwar is a little too slow to take cover, and Shaughnessy spots him, stiffening and breaking into a run before disappearing around the corner.

Janwar stops. Maybe Shaughnessy is waiting for him, syringe in hand.

If so—Janwar turns right, cuts through the alley next to Capital Cutlery Sharpening Ltd. East, hoping the fence will be vaultable without incurring too much damage to himself. The fence is chain-link with a hollow pipe across the top. Not barbed, not purposely sharp on top, but the pipe is affixed to the links with bands of metal. Janwar strips off his exterior pair of scrub pants and wraps them around his hands before taking a running jump at the fence.

The last time Janwar examined a fence this intensely was when he was in Grade 9, freshly arrived at the senior school campus, and a few Grade 12s lured all the Grade 9s to the

Nelly McClung Pavilion with the promise of a surprise, which turned out to be more, stronger Grade 12s who seized them and zip-tied their wrists to the fence.

After his Grade 12 captors had released him and the rest of the future class of 2008 and trooped off to the headmaster's office to face the music, Janwar and Nick had gone to the computer lab to research how to get out of zip ties. One method required having the presence of mind to hold your hands out in a certain way to be bound, another required your hands being bound together no matter the way and having the ability to raise your wrists above your head and then bring them down again as if you were trying to make your shoulder blades touch, and the final method required a second person who was able to reach your zip ties with a fingernail or credit card.

He feels the pants tear, but they don't catch, just rip right through. Metal brushes against his fingers, maybe drawing blood, but he's already over the fence and running with Shaughnessy, who's slowed down to a walk, in his sights.

Shaughnessy stops in the parking lot of the Natural Resources Canada building. Janwar is now able to observe him from the bushes just around the corner of the south wing. Something furry rubs against Janwar's leg, and he really hopes it's a cat. By the time he looks down, it's gone deep into the underbrush, but he thinks he catches a glimpse of a pink tail.

Shaughnessy raises his phone to his ear and lowers it again.

A Lincoln Continental with no front licence plate pulls up next to Shaughnessy. It's matte black like the Trans Am of the Apocalypse.

A familiar leather-jacketed Quebecker opens the door to let Shaughnessy in. Jacques. But Jacques is Horace's patient? Regardless, Jacques doesn't look happy. And Jacques was wearing a "1%" T-shirt in D'Arcy McGee's. Meaning, Jacques is a Hells Angel, or a member of another motorcycle gang. A Bandido, or a Red Devil, or a Rock Machinist... But probably a Hells Angel. The Angels are so big, especially in Quebec, that they have a legitimate merch store that sued Zappos for copying their logo.

The car purrs to life and swings out of the parking lot, revealing the *Je me souviens* license plate of *la belle province*. Janwar sprints around the corner and races after the Lincoln, trying to at least get an idea of where the car is going.

A van cab pulls up alongside him. Janwar waves it down, slides into the back seat.

"Where to?" Same company as last time, but the driver isn't long tall Saleh.

"Follow that—"

"Hold on, guy. Are you police?"

"I'm a doctor. Or, almost a doctor."

The cabbie shakes his head. "Not good enough. I have wife and kid in Bangladesh. No car chases for me. I'm not risking collision." They're at least going in the right direction, albeit very slowly. The Lincoln is idling at the corner of Rochester and Carling, waiting for the light.

"I'll pay," Janwar says. "What do you want?" He doesn't mean to have such a hard edge in his voice.

"Don't blow your short fuse at me, sir."

"The only reason I have a short fuse is because you cut it." A bon mot lost on the driver.

"You tell me somewhere to go, I take you there," the cabbie says. His name card reads "Ahmid." "But at my own law-abiding speed. Do you have any idea how much debt I took in order to own this car? I crash it, my wife and kid never come here." The Lincoln swings right onto Carling.

Janwar breathes in through his nose, which takes a long time on account of the pollen in the air having constricted his nostrils. "Okay, first you turn right on Carling."

"Nuh-uh," the driver says. "I see what you're doing. Tell me where you're going and I decide how to get there."

Janwar makes a shaking-a-baby motion with his hands, then, abruptly, his adrenaline runs out. "Okay, just take me home."

Janwar needs to think through what had happened over the last couple of days, but now that he's home it's 9 p.m. and his brain is mush.

He plugs his phone into Dr. Flecktarn's speaker dock, skims through his library until he finds some calming, measured electronica, and shuffles into the kitchen, where he examines the flies hanging on to the cupboard doors and, at a loss for what else to do, gathers the materials to construct a second flytrap. There's still a couple of inches of bourbon in the bottom of the old bottle of Wild Turkey. He doesn't have to open the new one yet.

Susan laughs. "What kind of drink requires Saran Wrap? Also, can I have one?"

She's sitting at the dining table, staring out the window into the darkness and playing with her lighter, flicking the flame into and out of life.

"Jesus fuck."

Last time Janwar saw Susan, he got beaten to a pulp. Is Shaughnessy about to pop up and shit-kick him again? Will Susan try to injure him? Should he attempt to restrain her? How? He looks around wildly. With the cord from the vacuum cleaner? He'd have to cut it first. With a tea towel? It might not be long enough. And plus he'd be tying her up in a rapist's apartment, the thought of which makes his stomach somersault. His nervous system whines in his ears. He picks up the whisky bottle by the neck and brandishes the base at her. She can leave if she wants. He's protecting himself in case Shaughnessy is here. No coercion is taking place. She is closer to the door than he is. He's not blocking her way out.

"Chill your boots. It's just me." She stands and turns her pockets out, holds her hands in front of her.

Janwar peers into the other rooms. No Shaughnessy. "How did you get in?"

"I told the super I was your girlfriend. I might have implied that we were looking for a third."

"With Giacomo? Ugh."

"If he knocks on the door later, just don't let him in," Susan says. "Now can I have that drink? It's been a hell of a day."

Janwar shakes his head. "Why would you think that's on the table?"

"I'm a guest. People offer guests alcohol. I can see that you have some and that you were planning to drink it."

"I was planning to catch flies with it. Guests in general, sure. But specifically, you—why would I give you anything after you left me to get curb-stomped by Shaughnessy outside Babylon?"

"Hold up, he came back?"

"I ended up in a hospital bed with a concussion and cracked ribs. Among other injuries."

"I'm so sorry. I had no idea. He said he was just going to warn you off. But you're okay now?"

Janwar pulls up his shirt to show her the gash on his chest. "This'll go away, but you never know about the long-term effects of concussions."

"Again, I'm really sorry," Susan says. She looks genuinely concerned, but Janwar's going to need a lot more information about what happened to decide if he can trust her.

Susan must have at least some of that information and Janwar's not in any apparent physical danger. Susan is also super attractive and doesn't look disgusted by his bony, hairy chest. As long as he stays alert, it can't hurt to keep talking, and to give Susan what she wants. "Whisky or rum?"

"Whisky."

"I have Wild Turkey." He surveys the counter. "Not sure where I put it though."

"It's in your hand."

Janwar lowers the bottle. "Right."

"And you're holding it wrong."

"Wrong?"

"Hold it by the other end, because if you smash—"

"Whatever," Janwar says. "Okay, I'll pour you a drink, but then you're going to answer some questions."

"You'll pour me a drink and then we'll talk about it."

"We'll talk about you answering my questions."

"That's right."

"I'll go with that."

"Make it a double."

Janwar pours a tumbler for Susan. He could get the rum for himself, but it's easier to just pour a second whisky. He empties the dregs of the bottle into his glass. "Here's your dirty bird."

"Dirty bird for a dirty bird?"

"How dirty are you?"

"Depends on what kind of dirt we're talking about."

"Let's start with legal hygiene. Now's a good time for you to spill. Or come clean, I guess, if we're keeping the dirt metaphor consistent. What's your angle on all this?"

"You tell me exactly how Diego Acosta died," Susan says. "And I'll see what I can do about answering your questions."

"How do you know about Diego?"

Susan doesn't say anything.

"And how do I know you'll tell me anything after I tell you what I know?"

Susan's smile fades away, leaving nothing but Susan, a reverse Cheshire cat. "You don't. But you don't have any choice. Look at it this way. We both have information the other wants. It's in our mutual interest to share."

"So why do I have to go first?"

"Because I've got the power in this situation."

"Do you?"

"You were brandishing the whisky bottle earlier. Would you really have hit me with it?"

"I—"

Susan picks up the whisky bottle from between them and smashes it on the edge of the table. Amber liquid arcs through the air, carrying with it tiny shards of glass. The jagged edges of the neck point toward him.

Janwar jumps up and backs away instinctively, his forearms in front of his face, facing out, as he once heard you should do in a knife fight, to protect the arteries on the inside.

"QED." Susan puts the bottle back down again. "I'll clean up the glass later. If everything goes well. Now, tell me about Diego Acosta."

"How much do you know?"

Susan looks pointedly at the bottle and its sharp teeth. Amphora dentata, Janwar thinks.

"Okay. Diego Acosta was a middle-aged man. Originally from Argentina. Some sort of building engineer. He was mugged and the muggers got a little feisty with his kneecaps. That's why he was in the hospital."

"I know that part. Walk me through the operation. Who brought in the drugs?" Susan asks.

"One of the nurses. José Almeida."

"Who filled the syringe?"

"I drew it. We call it drawing a syringe. Can I ask a question now?" Janwar says. He could lunge for the kitchen and try to grab a knife, and then they'd both have sharp items, but whether or not she'd actually injure him, she knows he'd hesitate. And she's not exactly holding him prisoner. "Who the fuck are you, besides a badass lady?"

"A journalist."

With the hanging lamp above the table unlit, Susan's face is in shadow, but the fluorescents in the kitchen light her from behind, turning her short blond hair into a bent halo.

"So I'm guessing this means you're on the side of good."

"I like to think so."

"Or, at least, not the side of Shaughnessy."

"Correct."

"Are you a journalist or a journalism student?"

"Same thing."

"Didn't you say you were doing your MA? Do you work for a newspaper?"

"A journalism student."

"So you're the one who called the police to find out more about Diego's mugging."

Susan wrinkles her nose. "How—? But yeah, that's right.

Listen, can I smoke on the balcony?"

"Only if we agree to put the broken bottle away."

"All right," Susan says. "I just always really wanted to do that, anyway. To be honest, I didn't think I was going to do it until I did it. It's been a weird couple weeks. Do you have a cardboard box for the glass?"

Janwar locates a wine-bottle box and and a roll of masking tape, and Susan places the bottle and shards inside it. Janwar seals the box, which is branded "Dark Tower," and places it by the door to dispose of in the garbage chute. He opens the sliding glass doors. The cool air of Dr. Flecktarn's apartment swirls out into the humid night, visible as a fine mist. Susan follows it out. She leans against the railing and her lighter clicks. The cherry flares at the end of her cigarette and a couple of sparks crackle off into the darkness.

Janwar joins her at the railing. Down below, he can see the young professionals walking their backpack-wearing, hypoallergenic dogs along Bank Street, stooping and picking up their dogs' shit from the sidewalk in compostable bags and depositing the bags in trash cans outside organic cafes—safe despite the hour. In this neighbourhood, the yuppies own the night. But this is where Dr. Flecktarn lived and fantasized, if not, to Janwar's knowledge, acted. One after another, pigeons dive off the roof of the building across the street.

"What are you looking at?" Janwar says.

"Glass fell off this condo building and killed someone last year," Susan says.

"For real?"

"Just walking along. Cut him right in half like one of those Body World exhibits. Freak accident. Totally painless, at least." Susan takes a drag on her cigarette.

B, A-B, A, B, A... "Speaking of accidents, and things that aren't accidents, I'm starting to think the mugging was really a targeted assault to get Diego into the hospital," Janwar says. He hasn't been able to articulate any of his theories out loud to anyone, and although he can't fully trust her, this is a good venue for him to try to get his thoughts in order.

Susan exhales through almost closed lips, the smoke eddying upward through the still air in a perfect ribbon. "Yeah, seems like it."

"Why?"

"Maybe he knew something about the Pushers they didn't want him to know. Still hazy on that."

"I'm slowly putting together the pieces here," Janwar says. "The Pushers are maybe connected to the Oxy epidemic in the news? They're actually pushers?" Uptalking like Katerinka.

"Bingo. At least, that's what I think."

"And maybe that's where Jacques fits in?"

"Wait, Jacques who? A Jacques popped up in my investigation too. Wonder if it's the same one."

Janwar fills her in on his Jacques: a Hells Angels–type dude the anaesthesiologists spoke to in the bar the night he and Susan had met, but it was Horace, a Mixer, who recognized him and interacted with him. And today Janwar saw Shaughnessy and Jacques meeting in the parking lot of the National Resources Canada building.

"Could be the same guy," Susan says. "I saw a drug mule threaten a biker-looking guy named Denis by saying she'd tell Jacques on him."

"Okay, now, your turn, for real this time," Janwar says. "Why did you get involved in Shaughnessy's scheme?"

"It seemed a reasonable enough thing to play along with

if it led me to the Oxy ring. Ah—I'll start at the start."

A couple of army-green trucks rumble by.

"Shoot."

Susan watches the trucks until they disappear from view before she begins.

Now that her story's over, Janwar stops looking at Susan's lips, which are very red. He's heard men are attracted to red lipstick because it reminds them of engorged, hot-to-trot ladybits. He returns his gaze to her eyes.

"So..." Janwar says.

"Bottom line is I think the Pushers are shifting Oxy out of the hospital with these therapy dogs," she says. "Then at least one dog walker, maybe more, is transporting it around the city and eventually passing it off to the Angels. Like I said, the dog walker even mentioned a Jacques to Denis. Maybe the Angels smashed Diego's kneecaps to get him into the hospital?"

"But, Horace, the Mixer, was the one who knew Jacques, because Jacques was his patient."

"Maybe he was Horace's patient, but he also met Shaughnessy at the hospital."

"Maybe," Janwar says. "Yeah, that could be it. Horace and Jacques were talking, though, like having some sort of meeting at the bar. And, I don't think I said, Jacques seemed angry with Shaughnessy when he let him into the car."

Susan grinds her cigarette out on the railing, and looks around for an ashtray.

Janwar examines his now-empty glass. "Just put it in here."

Susan's fingers brush his as he passes her the glass, and then again as she hands it back with the butt sitting at the bottom like a compressed tequila worm. His fingers have really taken a beating this trip, between the dry air and the stress and the fight with Shaughnessy. At least they look relatively clean now, with the wounds all adequately bandaged.

"Give me your phone," Janwar says. "I have an idea."

"Come on, Janwar. You should know better than to ask for a lady's cellphone. It's the twenty-first century 'don't look in a lady's purse.' Plus, I'm a journalist."

"Journalism student."

"Fuck off. Anyway, sensitive material."

"Do you have Shaughnessy's cell number?"

"Of course."

"Read it out to me."

"One sec." Susan fiddles with her phone. "Six one three—"

Janwar snatches the phone, hits dial. He backs up into the apartment. Any possible weapons are behind him.

"Not cool," Susan says. "Not cool at all." Maybe this was a mistake, but now is not a time for Janwar to have second thoughts. He holds his finger to his lips. Susan arches an eyebrow and crosses her arms.

"Susan?" Shaughnessy says, suavely.

"Heeeeeeere's John G!" Janwar's voice riding a crest of inappropriate laughter he hopes makes him seem dangerously unhinged, rather than imbecilic.

"What the sainted fuck? I told you to stay—"

"Listen, I know the fat man told you to lay off and I know you're still doing it." Janwar rushes through his words, afraid Shaughnessy will hang up, meaning his use of Susan's cellphone would come out a net negative.

"What the shite are you talking about?" Shaughnessy says. "What fat fella? What am I doing? What did he tell me to lay off?"

Janwar hasn't thought this far ahead. Position. Leverage.

"I saw you with Jacques."

"Who?"

"Jacques. The biker. The Hells Angel."

"Whatever."

But this isn't an "I don't know" whatever. It's a "You don't scare me" whatever.

"I'll tell the fat man," Janwar says.

"You don't even know who he is."

"So there is a fat man."

"Somewhere there is a fat man. Obesity—"

"The fat man is..."

Janwar looks at Susan. She's lighting another cigarette and pretending to ignore him.

Janwar has a bolt of inspiration. "The real-estate developer."

He's not sure why he didn't think of this before. It was too easy, somehow. But maybe that's it. Silence on the other end, but somehow by the quality of the silence Janwar knows he's hit home. "Lowell Chilton."

"Keep guessing," Shaughnessy says.

"No, it fits," Janwar says. "Diego was a structural engineer. Chilton is a condo developer. And fat."

"Do you know how insane you sound?"

"Paddy shitstain," Janwar says through his nose, aiming for a New Zealand accent.

"What?" A thrum of panic in Shaughnessy's voice.

"You heard me."

"Okay, fuck. Fuck. What do you want?"

"Blow the whistle. Tell me what the fuck is going on."

"I can't."

"Won't."

"Can't. Can't make the words come out of my mouth. I'm

not scared of the fat man. But there's someone else I'm a lot more scared of."

"But you don't want me to tell the fat man."

"No."

"You've got to give me something. Let's start at the start. José switched the vials, right?"

"..."

"Right?"

"Fuck."

"Like, José and someone else?"

"In a way. Listen, just...think about the drawers. Think about how it could have happened."

"For real? I've been trying to figure that out this whole time. If you don't tell me more I'm calling that number on all the Lowell Chilton advertisements. Come to think of it, Dr. Flecktarn even has a Lowell Chilton mug here. The number's probably on that."

"Go ahead. He'll be mad, but I'd rather have him mad than end up like Diego."

Shaughnessy disconnects. Janwar tries to call back but gets Shaughnessy's voice mail: "This is Shaun's answering machine's answering machine. Shaun's answering machine can't come to the phone right now—" Janwar hangs up, thinking, Christ, what an asshole. Then he realizes that if the line is busy, who is Shaughnessy calling?

"Impressive," Susan says. She holds out her hand. Janwar steps back outside and returns the phone. Their fingers brush again, and Janwar has to tell himself not to grab her knuckles and run his fingers around the bones, even if he wants to show he's interested, because that probably isn't appropriate right now. "Although, you could have just told me your plan," Susan continues. "What did he say, besides, I guess, confirming José was involved? And what does Lowell Chilton have to do with anything?"

"He's the fat man."

"Which means…?"

"My brain's getting pretty fried. Not just mush but fried mush. This might take me a while. Just going to get another drink." He goes back inside to fill a new glass with rum, but Susan follows him and stops his arm before he pours. She points at the unopened bottle of bourbon on the shelf.

"Drink whisky," Susan says. "Let the dirty bird raise you from the ashes."

Janwar sighs and fills a new glass with Wild Turkey. He gives her the rundown on the meeting he overheard in Sylvie's office. "And like I said to Shaughnessy, a condo developer and a structural engineer are both in the same industry, sort of. Which isn't exactly a motive, but it's, I don't know, a commonality. Maybe Diego was blackmailing Lowell over something? And I don't know what Lowell's connection is to the Pushers, except that he was talking to them."

"Right."

"And so what Shaughnessy said at the end was 'Check the drawers.'"

"What drawers?"

Janwar tries really hard not to say anything about his or Susan's drawers here and, amazingly, succeeds. "On the anaesthesiology carts."

"Why?"

"I'm thinking. Someone switched the vials in one cart, probably José somehow. Whoever set me up had to know I'd use one particular drug from the cart."

"Would you normally use that one drug? What did you call it?"

"Lidocaine. No, there are a bunch of different options. Oh, no, scratch that. Shit. I'm an idiot." Giant forceps clamp around Janwar's head. "There was a shortage of the coinduction agents that weren't lidocaine, so they knew I'd use lidocaine. But I still don't know how José switched them. The carts are electronically locked. Only an anaesthesiologist can unlock them."

"With what?"

"One of these..." Janwar holds up the tablet on the kitchen counter. He opens the app, presses his thumb against the metal pad, and a green light flashes.

"Now it's authenticated for five minutes."

Outside a car's tires squeal, which reminds Janwar—"Wait, fuck, when José was bringing the cart down the hall, Llew told him to watch out."

"So you think José almost hit Llew with the cart?"

Janwar nods. "Maybe that could have let him use Llew's tablet to unlock the drawers, if Llew's tablet was still authenticated. Maybe that's what Shaughnessy meant. That's a long shot, but I can't think of what else he was getting at. I'll go look at the carts tomorrow and see how close the tablet has to be to work." He smiles at Susan.

She smiles back. Usually running out of words feels like a personal failure, but there's something behind this smile exchange that transcends rational meaning.

Susan is the first to speak. "So, until then."

"Until then?"

"I—" Susan hiccups.

Janwar laughs.

Susan takes a step closer to him. "Hey, you're a doctor, or practically one. How do you cure hiccups? I've heard hold your breath, drink a glass of water upside down..."

"It has to do with spasms in your diaphragm, so yeah, try to hold your breath, and then do a few squats to work it out."

"All right." Susan breathes in and closes her mouth, and looks him in the eye.

Janwar feels a giggle rising in his chest. He fights it down. "Okay, now squat! Squat! Squat!" he shouts.

All of Susan's breath comes out in a rush. She laughs until she's crying, and Janwar laughs because Susan's laughing, and by the time they stop laughing Susan's hiccups have disappeared.

"So until then?" Janwar moves closer to Susan.

Susan puts her head on Janwar's chest. He kisses her hair and things take their natural course.

"Watch the ribs," Janwar mumbles into her mouth, and then he doesn't say much for a while after that, until he has to get up to turn off the speaker dock because his phone has changed from playing electronica to 1960s soul, and the soul singer is so macho that Janwar feels a bit awkward and emasculated. Later he says that he has condoms, and Susan is glad, and Janwar is glad too.

Susan is a very dirty bird, at least in terms of what she says over the next hour or so. While Janwar hasn't been into that sort of talk in the past, in this case, because of the proximity to death, the edginess of the whole situation in which they find themselves, it seems appropriate, part of the drama they are playing out. Janwar gets into it, taking control to a degree that he has rarely done in the past.

"Are the pants coming off?" he says, which is probably not the best possible phrasing for the situation. He needs to verbally make sure that consent has been given without trying to seem as if he's unsure of himself.

Susan pulls her head back to look at him. "I don't know, are they?"

He does experience a couple of stabs of fear when his erection is not initially as tenacious as he'd like, but he gets there in the end. And after it's over, he doesn't panic at all about his performance. In fact, lying in his bed with Susan, their bodies together like a fleshy jigsaw puzzle, the play-roughness having dissipated, Janwar becomes aware of the fact that although he is in a ridiculous situation, and has been for some time, he isn't panicking. Maybe it's just because the situation hasn't been resolved yet, and his panicking usually comes after, or maybe it's because he's just had athletic and satisfying sex with an attractive woman and has possibly conquered some leftover feelings of inadequacy from past relationships, but he thinks it's something more than that, something deeper. It's like the feeling he had at the concert when the Trillaphonics were playing, that feeling of being part of something greater than he was, of knowing what he needed to do. A feeling of loyalty and community.

He pries himself out of the Susan-Janwar puzzle and pads to the door naked, checks the lock, and attaches the chain, just in case Giacomo gets any ideas. Taking this precaution is not just paranoia; it's actually reasonable, Janwar tells himself. If Dr. Flecktarn was doing anything untoward at home, by virtue of being his neighbour, Giacomo could have also been involved. Men of Ottawa are not to be trusted, Janwar has learned. Women too, but especially the men.

CHAPTER 10

Onside – Thundercoat – Drawers – Pure Reptile – Déja Vu – The Boogeyman Closet – Staying Awake – Hickory Wood

Tuesday, July 15

When Janwar's alarm wakes him just a couple of hours later, Susan's fingers have found his. They have been holding hands like otters who don't want to drift away from each other during the night. He does not, under any circumstances, repent his fornication. He rubs her knuckles.

"Susan, I didn't tell you before. I'd kind of forgotten because I was so fucked on hydromorphone at the time. Both the Pushers and the Mixers told me that the other was part of some giant political thing involving kickbacks—from syringe companies, for the Pushers, or from the company that makes propofol, for the Mixers."

"That's some heavy pillow talk. How about we have sex first and then you run that by me again?"

Janwar doesn't have any problem with that. Afterwards, Janwar reiterates. "That's not what you think they're into, is it? It sounds ridiculous, telling you here in the light of day."

"What the fuck time is it anyway?"

"Six o'clock. But, my question. What do you think?"

"No. I don't think five anaesthesiologists could use enough syringes to make a difference in the profits of Cohasset, or enough propofol to make a difference to whatever company owns propofol."

"Suspira Labs."

"I think it's just Oxy. The Pushers are into selling Oxy, with the whole dog walker thing, and they were framing you for murdering Diego. And they got you to kill Diego for Chilton. For some reason. I don't know why the Mixers are making that shit up about plastics though. Maybe they don't know anything and they were just trying to get you onside."

"I'd like to get on your side," Janwar says. Susan ignores him. They've already done that, scant minutes ago, and now it's business time. Janwar has, however, remembered that one reason he likes having been physically intimate with someone is that he's able to create innuendos out of almost anything they say.

"Llew talked about BC, right? Maybe it was just an appeal to your caring for your homeland."

"Maybe. What about the real-estate connection? That seems more promising."

"I need to go to work. Split shift today. I'll try to do some digging into Chilton when I'm off. When do you finish your shift?"

"Seven."

"Okay, come by the Lazarus Coffee at Wellington and Caroline?"

"Deal. Susan, you know what? I don't know your last name."

"Jonestown."

"Jonestown? Really?"

"Sort of."

"Sort of?"

"My grandfather's last name was Zhukovsky when he immigrated from Ukraine. But because there's no Cyrillic *zh* character in English, immigration officials changed the name to Jukovsky. Grigori's co-workers on the Canada

Pacific Railroad changed his name from Jukovsky to Jewkovsky to Jerkoffsky. Eventually he got sick of the taunting, at which point Grigori Jukovsky moved down the line one stop and signed up with a boring Canadian name. And Greg Jonestown's name stayed boring until that business with the Peoples Temple."

Janwar likes that Susan also answers simple questions with long stories. "I'm glad I met you, Susan Jonestown."

"I'm glad I met you, Janwar Gupta."

He gives her a solid hug and kisses her, and her lips feel good against his lips and her body feels good against his body. After she closes the door, he turns on the speaker dock again and dances around the room, strumming in the vicinity of his genitals, even though there are no guitars in this track, just wailing organs. He still might have killed someone, but at least he's had emotionally satisfying sex with a girl who was even sexier out of her tights and boots than in them. Her legs could wave at him from below a cliff any time and it would be worth the danger... She lives in Ottawa and he lives in Vancouver, but he reminds himself it's too early to think about things like that. He turns the speakers up and heads into the shower to wash Susan off, although he kind of doesn't want to, just wants to roll around in her scent like a dog.

After the shower, he suits up. This time, instead of putting his paramedic shears in his scrub pants pocket, he tapes the holster to his leg. Concealed carry, what's up, he thinks.

Outside the entrance to the hospital, Janwar stops to pet an unbelievably tall and narrow dog. He's always liked dogs but finds the idea of paying for a living being that's obligated to be friends with you discomforting. Janwar is used to seeing greyhounds in flight, as it were, on the sides of buses, all four legs extended in full gallop, and so it takes him a minute to realize this gangly alien thing standing quietly is a greyhound at rest. He isn't sure what it's doing tied up outside at 7 a.m., or why it's wearing a backpack that looks empty. Its owner, a neon-jacketed runner, comes out of the lobby and sees him staring.

"Why the pack?" Janwar asks.

"It helps him feel safe. It's like a Thundercoat but cheaper."

"Thundercoat?"

"You know how animals sometimes get scared in thunderstorms?"

"Yeah? I guess you guys do have a lot of thunderstorms here."

"Pismo's scared all the time when he's outside. Skateboards, plastic bags, you name it. He's got an anxiety disorder." She unties Pismo from the post. He doesn't move.

"He seems okay now."

"That's the backpack, that's making him okay. Who's a good neurotic?" she asks the dog as she rubs his hairless belly. His rear leg jerks.

"How does it work?"

"You tighten it around his body, so he feels like he's always being hugged. Come on, Pismo."

When the woman and her dog are gone, Janwar tightens his belt, but it doesn't have the same effect. He loosens it again and takes in a deep breath.

He needs to clear his head before following up on his hunch. He's never been up to the roof of the hospital. Maybe he'll do that. He sets a timer for ten minutes and takes the service elevator to R. When he steps outside onto the gravel, the noise of the air-conditioning system's fans reminds him of the Trillaphonics. The machine bears a sign that says, "Do Not Fork Under Coil," whatever that means. Janwar, who has recently forked for the first and second times in a good couple of years, has a nice trip through last night's and this morning's experiences, but the closed-eye viewing of his private reel doesn't relax him; it just raises his heart rate even more.

Janwar looks southeast over the arboretum and Dow's Lake. It's too early for kayakers. Morning joggers are running along the canal path. Soon he will be gone, back home to British Columbia, away from polluted, hot, criminal Ontario, back to clean air and evergreens, away from dead pools and GHB wizards and rival gangs of surgeons and anaesthesiologists... Though he still has to solve a complicated and far-reaching mystery first.

And Janwar has been playing detective since the start, he can see now. His trip to Ottawa began with a dark-haired woman handing him an envelope as he sat in an office chair, his feet up at his desk—even if the woman was his mother, the letter told him he'd been assigned a two-week placement in anaesthesiology at the Ottawa Civic Hospital, and the desk was in his childhood room in his parents' house.

The timer beeps on his phone.

After the carts are done being used for the day, they live in the storage room in the anaesthesiology department. Nobody is in the department when Janwar lets himself in. He turns the lights on, and the fluorescents buzz to life.

There's a man standing in the corner. Janwar reaches for his shears, then realizes it's the cut-out of young, unbearded, dark-haired, bespectacled Llewellyn Cadwaladr that Llew used to send to parties in his stead. Janwar turns it around, but it's double-sided.

The carts are lined up against one wall. Janwar pulls out his tablet and replicates how he imagines the José-Llew collision in the hallway went down. He walks past the cart, passing within one foot. Nothing. The drawer's lock's light doesn't even flicker, let alone flash green. He moves within six inches. No dice.

Rubber squeaks against the floor behind him. Janwar spins around, right into another person. A solid Welsh person.

"Sorry," Janwar says.

"Didn't mean to scare you, boyo. I thought I heard some noise. What are you doing by here so early?"

"Oh, hi, Llew. I was just checking…" Janwar's vocal cords freeze.

"What were you checking, Janwar?"

Janwar points at the drawer of the cart.

"The drawer, is it? You don't have to worry about it. Everything's in its right place."

Janwar's voice module reactivates. "What about those cops yesterday morning?"

"Filling in some paperwork on an emergency-room patient."

"You're up-to-date on what's going on."

"Take me at my word, boyo, you have nothing to worry about regarding the carts."

"I'm not worried about what's in there now. I'm worried about what could've been there. And how it got there."

"I do get moithered in my old age, boyo. Can you run that by me again?"

"I think someone switched the vials."

"I get why your confidence in yourself as an anaesthesiologist is shook. I know you put in that SHROUD ticket, but I'm willing to ignore that breach of trust. It's all squared, boyo. You can go by me."

Janwar could give up for now and come back later, when Llew isn't there. Something feels off, and his instincts are telling him to get out of there. But now that he's started, he has to figure it out, and there's no way to do so without revealing his investigation to Llew. Who had told Janwar that there was a shortage of ketamine and other coinduction agents that weren't lidocaine? None of the other coinduction agents could have caused instant death the way lidocaine had.

"I understand that and I appreciate it, Llew. But, listen. Here's what I think. Right before Diego's operation, I heard José run the cart into someone in the hall. I heard a squeak of wheels and someone tell him to watch out. So, if he ran into an anaesthesiologist, maybe he got the lock close enough to their tablet to open it. And it would've been easy for someone to have switched the bottles back after."

"That was me he ran into," Llew says.

Janwar has given Llew an out, but Llew hasn't taken it. What does that mean? Is he trustworthy, or just playing a higher-level game?

"I'm proper interested now," Llew continues. "What are you trying to figure out by there?"

"How far away the tablet would open the cart from."

"Let's have a look." Llew covers one eye and squints at the cart.

Janwar repeats the distances he tried earlier, to no effect. Finally, he holds the tablet against the receiver with his left hand and, after a full second, the drawer snicks open. There's no way it could have happened by accident. Maybe Janwar was wrong and José's running into Llew was a red herring, but—

Carla told him about the shortage of coinduction agents. A Mixer.

Had Shaughnessy been on the phone with *Llew* when Janwar tried to call him back?

Janwar's thoughts tumble together, too fast for his conscious mind to process. Faces flicker and merge. Jacques and Horace and Shaughnessy and Llew and Fang and Carla and— Llew darts to the door, closes it, and flicks the light off. Janwar scrabbles for the paramedic shears taped to his leg. But before his eyes can adjust to the darkness, a sharp pain blooms in his thigh. He folds and sinks to the floor.

When Janwar wakes up, he's lying on the table in the anaesthesiology department meeting room with his shirt off and sensors attached to his skin. He's shoeless and his leg stings where the tape holding his paramedic shears has been ripped off. The conference table is cold on his back, which means he probably hasn't been in this position long. His hands and feet are bound with zip ties. He tests their strength, but they are looped through the cable holes for the conferencing system and will not give. Their microribs dig into his flesh, bringing him back to the fence at the Nellie McClung Pavilion.

Because his arms and legs are spread apart like the universal man, zip-tie escape options one and two are out. Llew is the only other person there; so is option three.

Llew is wearing scrubs and a cap, and his mask is hanging around his neck. He sits at the head of the table, near Janwar's feet. His gloved fingers twirl a vial like a helicopter rotor. The halogen track lighting on the ceiling is focused on Janwar, and he half closes his eyes against the glare. Janwar's glasses are still on his face, so whatever Llew's doing probably requires that he be able to see what's happening.

"What the fuck, Llew?"

"What did you expect, boyo?" Llew's pupils are pinned out, like Shaughnessy's. Now that Janwar's all tied up, Llew has taken something to calm down.

"You can't just keep me here. I have operations today. Someone will find out."

"Fang and Shaughnessy are filling in for you."

Shaughnessy? Why would Shaughnessy—

"So, boyo, who knows about this?"

The plot has expanded far beyond Janwar's imagination. What's Llew's angle? Why would he have killed Diego? Were just he and José involved? Do Fang and Shaughnessy know why they are filling in for Janwar? Why would Shaughnessy do a favour for Llew? Are Horace and Shaughnessy working together on the Oxy smuggling with Jacques? Is that even related?

Janwar has nothing. No evidence. Just that Llew thinks Janwar knows something he doesn't and has flipped out, and now Janwar is tied to a conference table.

"Nobody," Janwar says.

"Your eyes are giving you away. I can make life proper unpleasant for you if you don't tell me. You're not a fool, boyo, now are you. You must have told someone if you figured out this much."

Janwar is telling the truth. Nobody knows, but he isn't protecting Susan by saying that; he's making himself useless to Llew, which doesn't augur well for his longevity.

"Okay, yeah, I told someone. About Chilton. About Diego. About Denis and Jacques."

"Who?"

Janwar presses his lips shut.

Llew rocks his chair forward. "Tell me, Janwar."

Janwar declines. At least he knows that no matter what

Llew does to him to find out, Llew is a doctor, and while it might be painful, it probably won't kill him.

Llew circles the table and disappears from Janwar's field of view. When Janwar arches his neck backwards to see behind him, he sees upside-down Llew, his mask now on, picking up a syringe with a red label from the anaesthesia cart. An anaesthesia machine and two IV trees are also present, Janwar is thankful to see, though who knows how far Llew is going to depart from standard protocol during this operation. Just because he's monitoring Janwar's signs doesn't mean he's committed to keeping them vital. Janwar also can't see if any surgical implements are laid out. This being a conference table, not a surgical bed, there's no standard swing-out tray to put them on. They could be anywhere outside of Janwar's eye line.

"Know what I'm holding, is it?" Llew says, waving the syringe.

"Roc. Rocuronium."

"So you know what I'm going to do to you if you keep on being contrary."

"You're going to put me in the boogeyman's closet."

"So there for you. Who've you been spouting to?" Llew holds up a vial of GHB. "You can tell me, boyo. You won't even remember now, will you. It'll be like you didn't do it."

"Not telling," Janwar says.

Llew takes a vial of fentanyl from the cart, and draws a syringe combining GHB and fentanyl.

At least it won't hurt when Llew intubates him. Llew is anaesthetizing him, which makes any sort of pain-based physical torture pointless, although some serious psychological damage would probably ensue from eyes-open surgery of any kind, even if it didn't hurt. Like if Llew showed him his ripped out fingernails, even if he couldn't feel it... And it's not like the boogeyman's closet will be a walk in the park, by any stretch. Llew could do some pretty serious damage to him without cutting him up, either by withholding oxygen or injecting God knows what into him.

"You think I'll be so traumatized I'll cave and tell you who else knows."

"Doesn't that sound square?"

"Llew, I'll just be traumatized. It won't make a difference."

"I carn't just take your word for it, can I, boyo?"

GHB, Janwar thinks. There was GHB in that syringe as well. Which means—

"You think you're such hot shit with GHB, don't you, Llew? You think you can make me forget everything that just happened."

"And everything that's going to happen."

"So..." Janwar has to fight to keep an insane grin from spreading across his face. "So why don't you tell me how it all went. Give me the full rundown. So I can appreciate how well you executed it."

"Not a hope in hell."

"Wait, so I *won't* forget everything?"

Llew says nothing.

"You don't think you're a good enough Mixer?"

What Janwar can see of Llew's face darkens behind the mauve mask. Janwar is getting somewhere, but not fast enough, because now Llew is standing over Janwar.

"Enough talking." He rubs alcohol onto the inside of Janwar's left elbow, swirling the hair around into a Milky Way pattern. "Now clench your fist or I'll clench it for you."

At least Llew's doing his part to avoid infection. Janwar clenches his fist, then clenches it again, until the median cubital pops out nice and blue and ready for the IV. Llew's going to stick him no matter what, so Janwar might as well help Llew get a good connection the first time.

Once the IV is in, Llew tapes the tubing down and picks up the syringe. "Having fun now, boyo?" He taps out a couple of drops and injects the roc into the IV.

The first part of his body Janwar loses control of is his left big toe. He tries to wiggle it and nothing happens. He's lost his fingers, too. Roc paralyzes small fibres before large ones. After about a minute, when Janwar's body attempts to breathe, it can't.

Llew holds up the clear tubing. "Open wi-i-de."

The paralytic has taken care of Janwar's gag reflex, and the tube slides down his throat.

Llew's gloved fingers in Janwar's mouth remind Janwar of the Ayatollah of Tooth Care giving him a tough-love flossing lesson as a child.

The tube slides into his esophagus, not his windpipe. Does Llew know? The ventilator turns on. Air bubbles into his stomach. Janwar can't indicate to Llew that the air is going into the wrong place.

Janwar's lungs stick together. The white blob with yellow edges that has been his frequent companion over the last few weeks covers his vision again.

The halting of the ventilator brings Janwar back. Now he feels the tube slide back out, then, a second later, down into his windpipe.

"Just kidding," Llew says. "Remember how rough I can make it for you, boyo."

Janwar hears the ventilator begin to whirr again, and air rushes into his lungs, but Llew is touching his forehead and he can't move away. Llew removes Janwar's glasses and tapes his eyes shut. The fear catches up with him. The rational part of Janwar's brain switches off, and he is pure reptile.

A visceral feeling of relief shoves Janwar's reptilian brain back for a second. He focuses on the feeling. When he tries to articulate it into words in his head, the feeling is that he has been here before.

The memory coalesces: as a child, when Janwar had nightmares, sometimes he'd wake up and not be able to move his muscles or call for Garati or Ajay. At the time, he thought it was something that everyone experienced, that it was scary but ordinary. One of these nightmares, in fact, being of a grey-bearded man bending over him...

But in medical school, after he'd forgotten he'd experienced it himself, he learned his symptoms described a condition called sleep paralysis, which is the failure of the natural human function that paralyzes skeletal muscles while sleeping—to avoid rolling over onto a child, or acting out one's dreams—to wear off upon returning to consciousness. The nightmare was caused by the paralysis and not vice versa. Janwar had been strong dealing with it as a child; he could make it through this experience. He has no idea what is going to happen, but it's more likely to turn out all right if he's able to focus on what Llew's saying now.

"Here's what it is. Doctors are proper bad with investments: we have money and no time. Whole companies of financial planners exist that work only with doctors to try to prevent us from making investments in shady condominium projects, like the one we all invested in..."

Under the influence of the anaesthetic cocktail, Llew's voice recedes from Janwar's ears, and the story passes in front of Janwar's eyes at twenty-four frames per second, in high-contrast black and white.

Llew's sitting by a hotel pool in Miami with a martini and a crime novel. A fat man in tiny swimming trunks has taken the chaise next to him. When Llew finishes his martini and gets up to refill his drink, the fat man asks if Llew can get him another drink as well. He hands Llew a twenty. As Llew opens his wallet to put it in, the fat man says in a deep, South African–accented voice that he can't help but notice that Llew has an Ontario driver's licence.

Llew nods. "Are you also from Ontario?"

The man says he was born in Cape Town, but now lives in Ottawa and spends most winters in Miami. He's a condo developer, name of Lowell Chilton. They talk investments.

Llew flies back to Ottawa. A week later he brings the other anaesthesiologists to an information session Lowell Chilton is holding at the Château Laurier. Everybody is jazzed about the project: a condo complex on the site of the Bronson Centre. Since the centre is a charity, it can't afford to stay in its current location as the neighbourhood gentrifies. It's moving out to Tunney's Pasture, and Bronson Slope will be built in its place.

The plans show a LEED-platinum-certified tower sharp as a scalpel jutting up into the Ottawa skyline. The mock-ups of each condo's interior look like they're from Los Angeles, all clean and white, decorated in an art-deco revival style. In a city full of concrete apartment blocks, rich federal bureaucrats who believe they have taste and care about the environment will gobble them up like taxpayer dollars, Chilton says.

The entire anaesthesiology department gets in on it.

Between them, they own almost the whole building. The units start selling, and life is good.

Then, a few months later, Chilton calls Llew at 3 a.m. There's a small problem. One of the prospective residents, a man named Diego Acosta, is a structural engineer, and when he walked by the build site to see how it was progressing, Diego recognized that the builder had made substitutions that weren't in the plans. These are substitutions Lowell had instructed the construction company to make. In fact, Chilton has paid off the LEED inspector with the doctors' money. Llew gets red in the face.

Chilton tells Llew to hold on. This isn't a black-and-white situation. These structural changes—they're not dangerous. They're just saving some money. Putting in thinner insulation, mostly. The building's not really going to be LEED platinum certified. But who cares? The tenants pay for hydro, and if it's a little higher than they expected? They're buying the idea of LEED certification, so that's what Chilton is selling them. Canada is built on property scams. It wouldn't be an economically sustainable country if the government lived up to every promise. Chilton's just continuing in that tradition, but he's scamming everyone equally. Isn't that progress? And Acosta isn't some shining knight, because he's shaking Chilton down for money. A lot of money. He's going to tell the press unless Chilton pays him off.

"So what are you going to do?" Llew asks.

They're all in it together, Chilton says. If Llew squeals to the papers that the building's not LEED platinum, all the tenants are going to back out.

"Then we'll sue you for our money back, won't we."

Chilton says that's not going to happen. The doctors are welcome to try but they won't get shit. Chilton didn't get to be a real-estate mogul without the civil courts and city council in his pocket.

"What are we going to do?" Llew says. "Scare him? Hit him sick?"

There's only one way to get rid of a blackmailer, Chilton says.

"You want to put him in the ground."

He's not a nice man, Chilton points out. Diego's bleeding them of hundreds of thousands of dollars, and he won't stop unless they take action. If he were a nice man, Diego would go straight to the papers. And nobody will miss him. Chilton did his research when approving Diego to buy the unit. Diego's from Argentina and he doesn't have any family here. He moved here in the 1980s. He was probably involved in the Dirty War.

"That's a bit far, Lowell," Llew says. "That's like saying you likely left South Africa because apartheid ended."

Chilton waves that away. They're talking about murdering a blackmailer. Chilton's racial politics aren't relevant. They have to stay focused on the problem—which the anaesthesiologists, with their easy access to narcotics, could solve. And Llew's the dean of anaesthesiology. He's got to be able to pull strings.

"First we'd have to get him under the doctor," Llew says.

Chilton says his goons could follow Diego and accost him, and if they did it close enough to Civic, the man would end up by there instead of General. He looks to Llew for confirmation.

Llew nods.

And Diego would go along with the mugging narrative when he talked to the police, because even if he suspected something else, he couldn't risk having the whole story come out before he got all his money, Chilton continues.

"I have to mull it over and talk with the others, don't I," Llew says.

Chilton breaks character. His anxiety can't handle this much longer. He's already Xanaxed to the tits. Llew has to let him know tomorrow.

Llew calls a meeting at Minsky's. Over eyeball-rattling amounts of caffeine and artery-busting piles of doughnuts, Llew sketches out the situation and tells the rest of the department that he's going to pitch something that might sound heartless. "What if we get a poor lamb of a med student to administer a lethal dose of a medication to Diego by accident?"

It's beyond heartless, it's straight evil, the other anaesthesiologists bluster at first. But when Llew explains the impact of not taking action, they have second thoughts. A guaranteed tripling of their money is going to turn into total financial ruin—their all-time sure thing will go bad, real bad. Or they could suffer through a couple of weeks of moral turbulence and then it'll be like nothing ever happened.

Some of them have killed people by accident in the past, Llew continues. Over years of putting people to sleep with narcotics, it's unavoidable. This isn't that much different—it doesn't take a tectonic shift, just a minor push in morals. Sylvie is the biggest opponent, and she takes the opportunity to remind Llew that their last excursion past the restrictions of the law resulted in irreparable damage to the muscles in her left eye. Llew reminds her that it was her own fault, for not wearing the eye protection he had provided. Above everything else, Sylvie is a rational person, a scientist, and she gives in: this is the least risky play to make in a very ugly situation.

It's early summer at this point. The department will be getting a medical student in July. They'll select one from out-of-province, so he'll return back home once their placement is over, minimizing the chances of an in-depth investigation.

Right before the operation, one of the nurses will run into Llew in the hallway, and Llew will swipe his tablet across the sensor, unlock the drawer, and drop in a more potent solution, enough to kill the patient.

Next the anaesthesiologists have to figure out how to make the medical student use the right solution, and believe that he'd messed up, rather than that the drugs had been switched.

The solution comes from Carla. She says they could convince the student that there were two factions of anaesthesiologists. They'd then cast the groups as violently opposed to each other and make it appear that under no circumstances would they ever work together outside of the OR—like the surgeons and the anaesthesiologists in real life. Fang looks away.

Some of the anaesthesiologists mix their induction agents and some don't, Peter says. Maybe that could be the division. Shaughnessy thinks the med student would be suspicious. In Fang's opinion, that's non-issue. They need to remember that the student would be coming from med school and he'd have no idea how the real world worked.

Carla jumps in: Peter's idea would solve both problems. The mixers always use thiopental and the other group always uses propofol. The two drugs require different coinduction agents. As long as the anaesthesiologists knew which agent the student would use, they could swap the vials and increase the potency enough to kill.

Llew suggests that he and Sylvie watch the student during his first operation through the two-way mirror. If the student used propofol she'd congratulate him and invite him to be a Pusher. If he used thiopental, Llew would induct him into the Mixers. José and Henry would aggravate him if he mixed, and Carla would aggravate him if he pushed. They'd play out a whole *West Side Story* charade so that the student believed in the conflict and it wouldn't occur to him that both groups could've been in league.

With unanimous agreement, Llew goes back to Chilton the next day.

"Okay," Llew says, "we'll do it. Have your lads break his kneecaps late on the night of July 8, and do it somewhere close to Civic. Make it look like a mugging that went wrong. I'll have the emergency-room doctors get him to surgery."

Chilton says he knows how to stomp a nosy son of a bitch without getting pinned. Llew shouldn't assume he hasn't done this before. But he has a deal.

Llew tells José and Henry and Rasheeda and Emanda just enough to play their roles, and pays them off. The department writes a letter of offer to Janwar, and right on time, Diego turns up in the emergency room.

The screen fades to black and Llew's voice-over returns.

"And you know the rest. Diego was scheduled for surgery the next day. José had the cart filled at the dispensary for the audit trail. José ran into me in the hallway. I switched the vial. Rasheeda switched it back. You killed Diego.

"Oh, and Shaughnessy: that half-soaked paddy almost botched everything. He was supposed to recruit some piece to play the femme fatale and get you out to the bar so he could give you a warning, to make the whole conflict seem more real. But he wasn't supposed to give you a belter, let alone stomp you. We had to switch our plan up a bit after that, since I wasn't expecting Shaughnessy to let loose. And we certainly weren't planning on you being a patient. Then this week Sylvie told me she found out Shaun has been running an Oxy scam with Horace: they'd been writing ghost prescriptions and paying off Brenda in shipping and receiving to redirect packages for them, somehow involving dog walkers. The Hells Angels in Gatineau bought all the Oxy. I expect you caught on to that and that's why Shaun clobbered you, boyo? Sylvie and Lowell pulled Shaun apart and as far as I understand Shaun and Horace were calling it off. Shaun managed to tell the Hells Angels they were getting out of the deal without them dropping him in the Rideau River with heavy shoes. So, thank the Lord the police didn't come down on us for that Oxy business, or for anything else.

"I think that's about everything. Any questions? No? Now we just have to figure out what to do with you."

Janwar doesn't, in fact, have any questions. Llew has pretty much laid it all out on the table. The problem is that Janwar is still laid out on the table. And now that Llew has stopped talking, Janwar has nothing to focus on outside himself. His world has shrunk to just him, in the closet, paralyzed.

Another voice speaks, a female voice. "What's going on here? Janwar, are you okay?"

"He collapsed. Must be all the stress. I had to act fast now, didn't I."

"Why's he got his eyes taped shut, then? And why the fuck is he zip-tied to the conference table with a tube sticking out of his mouth?"

"Are you an anaesthesiologist?"

"No, I—"

Then Janwar hears the sounds of 60/40 poly-cotton lab-coat sleeve against lab-coat pocket, the scuffling of feet, and a thud.

"Stupid girl," Llew says. Drug-preparation noises. Janwar's muscles start to come back under his control; Llew shot him up with sugammadex to reverse the paralyzing effects of the rocuronium. Why? So Janwar can talk? What's Llew done to Susan? Janwar must have been willing himself so hard to thrash that as soon as his muscles can accommodate it, he spasms and bucks epileptically.

"Easy." Llew yanks the tube out of his throat. "Was this piece who you told, you crot?"

"What did you do to her?" Janwar slurs. His throat is on fire.

"Buck up. I just shot her with a tranquilizer. She's right enough, but she won't be if you keep at being contrary."

"What's your plan now?"

"Putting you back to sleep now, aren't I?"

"I am so goddamn sick of going to sleep," Janwar says. "When this is over, I'm going to stay awake for days."

When Janwar wakes again, he's in a dark room. His wrists are zip-tied together behind his back, his ankles are also bound, and his mouth and eyes are taped shut.

Somehow, despite all of these concerning elements to his environment, he's calm and his head is clear. He's not anxious at all. He's in a problematic environment, but he can still act. He can perform one action after another until he is out of the situation. It might be too much to assume that the boogeyman's closet has cured his anxiety, but maybe now that he's in a physically dangerous situation, his adrenaline is doing what it evolved to do in primitive homo sapiens. That is, making him more alert and able to act quickly and correctly, able to fight sabre-toothed tigers and chase mammoths—not just revving his motor in neutral like it normally does in a standard chthonic breakthrough. Or maybe there is going to be a permanent benefit to all this. Now that the worst has happened—he's visited the boogeyman closet—he can move on. Unintentional aversion therapy, Dr. Brank would say.

Janwar can hear breathing.

"Mmm?" he ventures.

"Mmm." A female voice. "Mmm mmm mmm."

Janwar humps his body over toward the voice. Susan. He can tell from her body that's who it is. Good thing he is so familiar with it now. He feels further along Susan's body with his face, the only part of him he really has dextrous control over, until he gets to her hands, which are also zip-tied.

"Mmm," he says, he hopes reassuringly, and then twists his body around so he can get his hands near her hands. He tries to picture the video of how to get out of zip ties with a credit card and translate how the zip ties feel to how they look. Thank Christ he hasn't trimmed his fingernails in the last few days.

He manages to locate the tab that holds the zip tie shut and digs his fingernail into it, which is a strangely sexual process. He suggests through grunts and thrusting his back against her back that she try to pull to the right, which, after a few tries, he manages to communicate, and after a few tries of his lifting the tab and her pulling to the right, the zip tie slides open. Susan reaches forward and rips the tape off her eyes and mouth.

"Amazing," she whispers, as she attempts to locate his

face in the dark. "How did you know how to do that?" She rips the tape off his eyes and mouth.

"Ow. Bullying."

"You were a bully?" Susan obviously a little woozy still.

"No, I was bullied."

"You can fill me in later. What are we going to do now?"

"I'm going to get your ankle zip tie off so at least one of us is fully mobile, and then you can do me. I'll walk you through it."

"Can we turn on the light?"

"Someone could see from outside the door. Pull your feet to the right."

Now Susan's feet are free. "How do I get you out of these zip ties?"

"What holds the zip tie closed is a bar that rests against the ribs. You just need to get your fingernail between the tie and the bar, and then it will slide out."

"Okay."

But before Susan has a chance to get her fingernail in the right place, Llew swings the door open, illuminating the room. They're in the storage closet. Janwar scans the room for a weapon. He catches a glimpse of wood. Llew has returned his bat to the tub in the corner. Janwar jerks himself to his feet with the world's largest pelvic thrust. "Susan, grab the bat—in the Rubbermaid."

He hops toward Llew, who backs away, closing the door. Janwar crashes into the door and falls on Llew. With neither his hands nor feet, free he can't put Llew in a wrestling hold. Llew rolls on top of him. Janwar's face is in Llew's side, which smells of sandalwood, presumably aftershave. He can't see anything, but he hears and feels the impact of hickory wood against old Welsh skull.

CHAPTER 11

Bobby Dasler – Ball and Chain – Body Count – Manville

Wednesday, July 16

A detective-constable from the Ottawa Police took his statement bedside. Now, Janwar's in the Ottawa General Hospital, which is eleven kilometres from the Civic. Kurt Rickenbacker spoke in rapid-fire bursts, and as far as Janwar could piece together from the bald detective's telegraphic delivery, Llew was going downtown for kidnapping and assault for sure, but unless he had a snitch jacket on under his lab coat and rolled over on the rest of the anaesthesiologists in order to reduce his prison term, this would likely be a "Forget it, Kurt, it's Civichospitaltown" sort of deal with respect to the Diego business. Rest assured, Kurt would keep an eye on the Civic Hospital from now on, and Janwar was certainly welcome to leak the real-estate scam to the papers if he thought it was defensible—given slander and libel and all that.

Janwar knows the man's right; he doesn't have any hard evidence of a criminal conspiracy. Connecting Llew to Diego's death would be very difficult to prove beyond reasonable doubt in court. Kurt is the one straight shooter Janwar has met in the entire city, and Janwar is effusively thankful for him, possibly to the point of making Kurt uncomfortable, but then again, what detective wouldn't want to be thought of as a straight shooter, even if it's by a dark, handsome East Indian med student and not a leggy blonde?

How's his leggy blonde doing? Janwar doesn't have his phone near him. He reaches over to the bedside table and switches on the radio, and, against all odds, the newscasters are talking about Susan.

"Now, here in Canada we live in a just and democratic society. Ms. Jonestown herself is facing charges of assault for concussing Dr. Cadwaladr, while allegedly freeing Mr. Gupta."

"Does she play baseball, Bobby?"

"I'm seeing here she played on a rec team at university called— Oh, no way."

"What?"

"The Bunter S. Thompsons."

"Don't stop here, this is—"

"Although she did a heck of a number on him, there does seem to be evidence that it was self-defence."

"Dr. Cadwaladr paralyzed Mr. Gupta against his will with rocuronium."

"That's one of the drugs, which, correct me if I'm wrong, Juliana, one of the drugs that the State of Virginia recently started using as part of their lethal injection procedure?"

"That's right, Bobby. Although as far as I understand, it's not the drug that stops the prisoner's heart. It's the drug that stops him or her from twitching and spasming, for the sake of the observers."

"Isn't that messed up, Juliana?"

"It sure is, Bobby."

"Anyway, Ms. Jonestown claims that Dr. Cadwaladr was withdrawing a syringe with an unknown substance in it from his pocket and threatening Mr. Gupta with it when she grabbed the baseball bat and hit him in the head. A spokesperson for the police said that a syringe containing

GHB was found in Dr. Cadwaladr's hand, which lends some truth to her story."

"Why was there a baseball bat?"

"I think that—"

"Sorry to interrupt you, Bobby, but Dr. Cadwaladr is now in stable condition, I'm hearing from the hospital."

"That's good, Juliana. Nobody deserves to die for their crimes without due process."

"I thought nobody deserved to die for their crimes period. This is Canada, Bobby."

"Sorry, Juliana, just having a back-home moment there, I guess. We at the *Bobby Dasler Show* are firmly anti–death penalty. We'll keep you posted as new developments reach us. And that's it for the news on CHEV 95.3, Ottawa's best country. Now here's some Johnny Cash, with 'Twenty-Five Minutes to Go'—"

Janwar turns off the radio and closes his eyes. His anxiety hasn't come back yet. He focuses on the hum of the machinery and lets his mind drift like a continent.

Susan is still being held at the main police station, near the Pretoria Bridge.

"Why's she still there? Hasn't she had a bail hearing yet?" Janwar asks Detective-Constable Rickenbacker.

"Above my pay grade." He's managed to wrangle Janwar a visit first thing in the morning on Thursday, however. "Ten minutes," the man says. "All I can."

Susan's saying goodbye to a long-haired man wearing overalls as Janwar arrives. Who's that? A brother? An ex? He feels a twinge of jealousy.

She looks okay. She's wearing her usual clothes—that is, boots, tights, denim shirt. Janwar isn't sure whether he expected an orange jumpsuit or just imagined it that way.

"Hi, Susan," Janwar says. "They were talking about you on the radio."

"Oh yeah? Who was?"

"The hosts on the country station. CHEV."

"What did they say?"

Janwar's mind blanks.

"Janwar?"

"That you played on a baseball team."

"Well, that's true. Speaking of which, everyone seems satisfied that I swung at Llew in self-defence."

"So why haven't you had a bail hearing yet?"

"Red tape, I guess. Or maybe all the justices of the peaces got shit-faced last night and didn't show up for work? Legally it's got to happen today."

"And if they all agree it was self-defence, you'll get to go home soon. I can't imagine why they'd deny bail. We have to make this quick, but here's what Llew told me while I was paralyzed. I don't have any evidence at all, but I figured you had to know."

"Hit me up."

Janwar tells an abbreviated version of the story, trying to cover all the bases. "The whole anaesthesiology department killed Diego because by jeopardizing the condo project he was risking their investments. And the Oxy was just Shaughnessy and Horace initially, but when Lowell and Llew and Sylvie told Shaughnessy he had to shut down the trade and couldn't work with Horace while they were play-acting the Mixers versus Pushers thing, Shaughnessy got the other Pushers involved instead, because they were supposed to be seen with each other. Which Llew still doesn't know about. I just figured that out myself. So, you were right, in the end the Pushers did become pushers."

"Okay, so—"

Someone clears their throat behind Janwar. The constable who escorted him down here has returned. "Time's up."

"One sec," Janwar says. "Go on."

"It'll take me a while to figure out what to do about the Oxy and the dog walkers, but as soon as I can call someone I'm blowing the whistle on the Bronson Slope condos. It shouldn't be too hard to find out who did all the shoddy insulation."

"That's good. At least you get your story." The only person Janwar feels any sympathy for is Fang, but she's still been involved in premeditated murder.

"When do you go back to BC?" Susan says.

"This afternoon. But maybe I'll come back out here."

"Am I supposed to say, 'I'll be waiting for you when you get back out here?'"

"BC isn't jail. I could visit."

Susan laughs. "I like you, Janwar, I really do, but you should find a nice girl in Vancouver. Come on, you don't want a ball and chain with a ball and chain."

"But you'll be released today."

She holds out her hand.

Janwar squeezes it. His throat feels thick. Dr. Brank would tell him that there is no pattern, that each failed romance is its own unique circumstance, and it's just bad luck that things haven't truly aligned with him and a lady, like, ever. But it's human nature to see patterns. And what's the constant here? Good old Janwar, and an endless series of emotional investments that haven't gotten Janwar what he wants, which he thought until now was an equitable long-term relationship with a pretty girl who cared about him, and who he could care about in turn, but which he has now redefined as "any sort of relationship involving Susan."

Sad-face emoji, he thinks: a frowning yellow blob looking down and to the side. He distracts himself by pondering the fact this is the first time he has thought in pictograph form. He really is a millennial. This is also depressing.

He follows the constable back up the stairs. A group of military policemen in red berets push past him, going in the opposite direction.

Police officers have invaded the hospital by the time Janwar returns to the Civic to get his stuff, which has been left for him at the information desk. Most of the people in line for the Lazarus Coffee by the door are wearing blue and they look tired enough that coffee might not do any good. A few are priests and they don't look tired at all. Their driver idles the cart across the hall.

The two cops Janwar saw the other day, the ones who stared at his beat-up face when he returned to work, are standing outside the ER entrance where the ambulances pull up. Janwar's about to ask them what's going on, but as he approaches, he overhears what the man is saying, which is, "Glad I wasn't on duty there when buddy got snuffed."

Janwar freezes and backs up until he is mostly hidden behind a potted plant. He lowers his bags to the ground and stands still.

"The boys and girls of the Ottawa PD look out for one another. Niles'll be fine," the woman says. "He doesn't have any priors."

"He out hacking a dart?"

"Peeing."

"Maybe the sergeant should have borrowed some catheters from the Civic if she wanted a single officer to stand watch over a perp who was probably going to roll over on a bunch of others."

Janwar's knees start to ache. Someone killed Llew while he was under police custody. That's why the hospital is full of police. He rotates his head so his right ear is slightly closer to the officers and curls his hand into a tube.

"Have you ever had a catheter, Richard?"

"That's a little personal, eh?"

"Don't get snippy."

"Also, that word, *snippy*..."

"Someone's got a bit of anxiety around Little Richard. I'm just saying, do you have any experience with what you're suggesting?"

"Okay, maybe not a catheter. Maybe one of those astronaut diapers that woman wore when she drove across the States to kill her boyfriend's new girl," Richard says.

"That wasn't an astronaut diaper. She was an astronaut, but it was a regular adult diaper."

"Not sure about that, Tanya."

"Who was the stiff upstairs going to roll over on, again? This mess is so frigging complex."

"Way I understand it, there are these two groups of doctors. The one the stiff wasn't part of was running Oxy. And they were afraid he'd squeal on them to reduce his sentence for the kidnapping. So out came the pillow. But buddy who did it forgot about the security camera. Didn't even wear a mask. Got his red hair and freckles lit up clear as day."

"What an amateur."

Sounds like Shaughnessy all right.

A whoosh from opening doors rustles the leaves and the police glance over at the plant—Janwar's contorted form is now revealed behind it, with his hand cupped to his ear.

"What you doing there, bud?" Richard says.

"Moving along," Janwar says, realizing as he says it he's breaking the No. 1 rule of talking to cops, which is never to skip ahead in the conversation, because it threatens their sense of control. Janwar unfolds himself and heads toward the taxi stand.

"Hey, we're talking to you, and we're cops," Tanya says, but Janwar keeps walking and they don't follow him or shoot him, so all in all, his eavesdropping is a success.

It's all kind of poetic, in a way. Llew created a fake rivalry that turned into a real one. If not Pushers versus Mixers, maybe Pushers versus Llew, and at the very least Shaughnessy versus Llew. Perhaps now Shaughnessy will testify about the real-estate conspiracy to dial down his sentence and they'll all go to jail, Pushers and Mixers alike. Janwar just doesn't have the emotional energy left to evaluate how he feels about this new development. Two people are dead now, but all he wants is to go home. And, despite what he said to Llew, sleep.

His phone is blowing up with messages from Ajay and Garati. He decides he might as well face the music in person and doesn't respond.

Janwar waits by the curb outside Dr. Flecktarn's building. He wonders if Susan's been released. He checks his phone to see if she's texted him. She hasn't. He needs to stop thinking about her. There's no value in doing so. This encounter with Susan was a nice thing that happened, is how Dr. Brank would tell him to think about it, and to be thankful for that, not to mope about the fact that it wouldn't continue.

Good thing he's got lots of other things to have feelings about.

For starters, he feels foolish for being played. Maybe he's a genius with a syringe and a ventilator, and maybe he did gather some key information and escape from Llew due to a handful of objectively clever actions, but that doesn't mean he's a smart person by any other metric. He was manipulated into killing Diego and he didn't put together the various conspiracies until Llew spilled the whole story.

He also feels generic for being so predictable that Llew was able to call his number in potentia, without even having met him. Connect the dots on the med-student page in a draw-by-numbers book of occupations and you get a picture that could be Janwar or any of the other 286 students in his graduating class.

And he feels cheated by absurd circumstance out of a great reference for a placement in which he technically excelled. All things considered, he did induce like a motherfucker. If he'd gone to Toronto Western, or Vancouver General, or Foothills Medical Centre in Calgary, or Royal University Hospital in Saskatoon, or even Whitehorse General, he'd have done just as good a job and none of this would have happened. Well, that's not true. None of this would have happened to *him*. But regardless of what the police investigation turns up, if he'd gone somewhere else, there'd be no question at all of how he performed when it came to the crunch. His positive reviews from the classroom would have extended to his placement, and his life would have gone on as it should have… Instead, he killed a man, his supervisor, a criminal mastermind, was murdered, and everyone else in the department was at the very least an accessory to murder. This whole placement is a wash. He'll probably have to graduate a semester late now.

He can feel a chthonic breakthrough rising in his chest like fetid grey water in a backed-up sink. He's been living minute by minute until now, but returning to his usual environment and thinking about the future is making him lose control. It was so stupid to imagine, even for a second, that his traumatic experience had somehow cured him—

The taxi that pulls up is a navy-blue Crown Victoria. Janwar walks around to the back of the vehicle. The driver cracks his door.

"—charged under the Security of Information Act, relating to the possession of classified information about the Canadian Rangers. And now on to weather with Andromeda Lau—" the radio anchor says, before the driver turns the sound off. Must be whoever those military policemen were going to the holding cells to see, Janwar figures, distracted for the moment.

"Sorry, sir, the trunk latch is broken," the driver says with a heavy Caribbean-French accent. "Are you okay to sit in the front? Put your bags in the back?"

"Sure, no problem." Having to communicate with another human being slices the top off Janwar's anxiety. It's still there, filling his lungs and twisting his guts, but he has enough control to fake normalcy.

"Where to, sir?" The driver's ID badge, hanging from the rear-view, says "Manville," and Janwar, who, like most people, has trouble reading and speaking at the same time, almost says "Manville," but manages to catch himself and instead says, "The airport."

"*Domestique* or *internationale*?"

"Domestic. WestJet."

The name Manville reminds Janwar of Boystown, the gay area in Chicago, a neighbourhood Janwar liked when he visited family in the city, with its low-rise indie businesses and chilled-out vibe, so different from the skyscrapers of—

Janwar sits up straight. "Actually? Manville?"

"Yes, sir?"

"Can we make a stop first?"

"Yes, sir."

For a moment, as long as Janwar doesn't look at the red numbers counting up on the dashboard of the Crown Vic, Manville and Janwar could be detective partners investigating a crime scene. One black, one brown, one French, one English, one short and stocky, one tall and thin, one with a memory honed by driving the streets, one with the analytical skills of a doctor. His reverie is interrupted by a thump as they run over a rat.

"What's with all the rats?" Janwar asks.

"*Les égouts pluvials* backed up from the rain," Manville says. "Lots of creatures living down there."

"Like what?"

"*Les rats*. And *le choléra*."

"Cholera?"

"One of the other drivers got it after his sewer pipes burst and *merde* spilled into his basement. His skin turned *gris* and *sec* but *les medecins* fixed him."

"Wow, cholera," Janwar says. "In Ottawa. In the twenty-first century." He looks at his hands. No, that was stress. He doesn't have cholera. And, you know what, the return of his anxiety is not that bad. The fact that he hadn't panicked much during the most stressful moments of the last couple of weeks shows that it's possible for him to go through life with less panic. It'll just take work.

The condo development at Bronson and Lisgar isn't too far of a departure from their planned route. Orange-clad workers swarm the site. Janwar wonders how quickly construction will stop once Susan breaks the story. Will the building linger half-constructed for months until inspectors complete a report, itinerant construction workers camped out in its shell over the winter, warming their hands around fire barrels full of fibreglass shards, waiting for work to start again? And then what? The tenants will file a class-action lawsuit. Despite his boasting, the developer will declare bankruptcy and jump out a window. Someone else will purchase the property, and the work so far will be dynamited, collapsing in on itself just the way Janwar imagined his bone fragments blowing out as he hit the rocks at Thetis Lake...

The site looks to Janwar like any other condominium in the early stages of construction: yellow sheeting, towering crane, and pounding generators, "Hard Hats Must Be Worn" signs, rented fencing, rebar pointing out of poured concrete at weird angles—which always made Janwar imagine that the workers were sloppy until he realized that the awkward ends would be snipped like sutures with what was, in essence, a very strong pair of scissors. A giant version of the Leatherman Raptor paramedic shears he never got to use against Llew.

Diego had spotted something that differed from the original plans and decided, rather than informing the proper bodies and spending years in court to recover his investment, to use a quick and dirty way to come out on top. And who knows, maybe he didn't care so much about the environmentally friendly LEED status and did want the building to be completed so he could make his dirty money and still live there. Perhaps not being an avid reader of detective fiction or watcher of crime television, Diego didn't know, like the condo developer, that every blackmailer always gets killed. Nobody ever lives peacefully in a blackmailer-blackmailed relationship. Sooner or later, something has to break; death is the only way to ensure silence.

"Okay," Janwar says. "I might be asking too much, but can you do a Rockford turn?"

"Yes, sir."

"Really? Like in the TV show?"

"I was *un policier* back in Haiti."

Manville stomps on the gas while reversing out of the dirt parking lot, then steps on the e-brake and cranks the wheel around, spinning the car until it points forward, then shifts into drive and darts out into traffic.

Both of them with the biggest fucking grins on their faces.

NOTABLE INSPIRATIONS & THEFTS

CHAPTER 2 The documentary about the persecution of Roma during the Holocaust that Peter Wongsarat talks about at D'Arcy McGee's is Aaron Yeger's 2011 film *A People Uncounted.*

The hospital dead pool was inspired by Chester Himes's 1959 novel *The Big Gold Dream.*

CHAPTER 3 I ripped off the scene with the coffee filter from Jack Smight's 1966 movie *Harper*, starring Paul Newman. Harper is based on a novel by Ontario-raised noir writer Ross Macdonald, said by some to be the successor to Raymond Chandler.

RECORDING D The article about Venolia Parker is adapted from Laura Armstrong's story "Mississauga Doctor Sees Male-only Patients after Sexual Abuse Discipline," which appears in the 18 September 2014 *Toronto Star.*

CHAPTER 5 Janwar and Fang watch Juan José Campanella's 2009 film *El secreto de sus ojos* (The Secret in Their Eyes).

CHAPTER 6 SHROUD is a humanoid robot in Thomas Pynchon's 1963 novel *V* that was built by researchers to see how much radiation exposure a human being could take (SHROUD stands for "Synthetic Human, Radiation Output Determined").

The article about Ellis Flecktarn is adapted from Rosie DiManno's "DiManno: Resilient Witnesses Give Graphic Details of Doctor's Alleged Sex Assaults," which appears in the 18 January 2013 *Toronto Star*, and which also has the worst lede in the history of newspapers.

CHAPTER 7 Go see a Dan Deacon concert if he comes to your town. He's great. So's David Foster Wallace, whose first-ever story "The Planet Trillaphon as It Stands in Relation to the Bad Thing," published in *The Amherst Review* in 1984, lends its name to the band in the novel.

CHAPTER 11 The murderous astronaut who the two police officers discuss is Captain Lisa Marie Nowak.

ACKNOWLEDGEMENTS

After Navraj Chima, who deserves another mention, I want to thank my editor, Leigh Nash; the designer, Megan Fildes; the proofreader, Stuart Ross; my parents, Gerald Finger and Anne Hanson-Finger; my writing circle mates, Brooke Lockyer, Catriona Wright, Ian Sullivan-Cant, Shari Kasman, Ben Ladouceur, Laura Trethewey, and Ashleigh Gaul; and everyone else who's ever read and provided feedback on any sections, including Andrew Battershill, Zani Showler, Jer Lucyk, John Nixon, Lauren Mitchell, Terence Young, Rob Mousseau, Julia Chanter, Pauline Ricablanca, Gary Barwin, Andrew Forbes, Andrew F. Sullivan, Mike Sauve, Jeff Blackman, Peter Gibbon, Heather McCarthy, Bardia Sinaee, Ryan Hilborn, Sam Hiyate, Don Loney, Stephanie Coffey, Illya Klymkiw, and Andrew Faulkner. Thanks also to Tara Cremin for acting as an Irish English consultant and Marisha Tardif for doing the same for Welsh English. Thanks also to the Toronto Arts Council for the funding. And to anyone I've forgotten, my apologies!

INVISIBLE PUBLISHING is a not-for-profit publishing company that produces contemporary works of fiction, creative non-fiction, and poetry. We're small in scale, but we take our work, and our mission, seriously: we publish material that's engaging, literary, current, and uniquely Canadian.

We are committed to publishing diverse voices and experiences. In acknowledging historical and systemic barriers, and the limits of our existing catalogue, we strongly encourage writers of colour to submit their work.

Invisible Publishing continues to produce high-quality literary works, and we're also home to the Bibliophonic series, Snare, and Throwback imprints.

If you'd like to know more please get in touch:
info@invisiblepublishing.com

Invisible Publishing
Halifax & Picton